THE
COVERING

Dana Pratola

THE COVERING

Cover Art by *Nicola Martinez*

White Rose Publishing, a division of Pelican Ventures, LLC
www.whiterosepublishing.com
PO Box 1738 *Aztec, NM * 87410

White Rose Publishing Circle and Rosebud logo is a trademark of Pelican Ventures, LLC

Publishing History
First White Rose Edition, 2011
Print Edition ISBN 978-1-61116-101-4
Electronic Edition ISBN 978-1-61116-102-1
Published in the United States of America

Dedication

Dedicated to my Heavenly Father (Dad) Who loves me beyond all reason, and to my husband, Robert, and my kids, Rob, Danielle and Angelo, for believing this would happen.
Thanks also to Mary Grace for all the support and computer help ;-).

1

Tessa kept her eyes closed. Physically, she stood at the bathroom sink, her hands curled around the sides of the basin. In her spirit, she occupied that place where utterance slipped through the thin veil separating this world from the other. Where speech fell on holy and unholy ears alike. Where words were transformed into power. She was in prayer.

Head bowed, Tessa prayed first for her brother, Dominic, then her father and mother. After several minutes she paused, but the urgency intensified.

Her skin care routine abandoned, she went into her room and fell on her face at the side of her bed and with great distress, prayed in the spirit as she had nearly every day for the past two months. As though a life depended on it. She didn't yet know whose, only that it was a man and that whatever his need, time was running short.

When at last she felt the burden easing she took her Bible and notebook and sat cross-legged on the bed. She perused familiar passages and listed any verses that came to mind. There was nothing mystical in the process itself, but it helped her focus, hopefully revealing what God might want to show her.

"Can't You tell me who I'm praying for, Lord?" she asked. "Is it someone I know?"

Some moments later Tessa felt directed to turn to a

specific though unfamiliar verse in the twenty-seventh chapter of Job. She ran a finger down the fine paper of the page, stopping at verse nine. "Will God hear his cry when trouble cometh upon him?" she read aloud. From there she turned to a verse she'd read the day prior in Psalm thirty-four. "This poor man cried, and the Lord heard him, and saved him out of all his troubles."

She knew before asking, "He won't cry out for himself, will he?"

So it fell to her to be his voice. But try as she might, she couldn't think of what to say.

It didn't take long to see the problem. She was trying to use her reasoning to grasp the situation and as a result grew more confused. Confusion was not of God.

She commanded the devil to stop messing with her thoughts, then began to pray in earnest for blessings, health, and protection on the man's behalf.

Strength to withstand.

The words came unexpectedly, an urgent impression on her mind. At last she had a bearing.

ತ∽ಀ

An hour later Tessa flipped her chestnut braid over her shoulder and wiped an already spotless countertop. The task was intended less for cleanliness and more to help drive away some of the lingering consternation from her prayers. Like every other time God led her to pray for this certain individual, she knew the victory attained in the spirit realm was only advancement toward a goal and not the goal itself. More prayer would follow, and more victory.

Meanwhile she would make herself useful to Dominic. He kidded about her neatness, but cleaning was the way she'd relieved stress for most of her twenty five years. Besides, it was sweet of him to let her move back in until she found another apartment, so she would earn her keep with fresh laundry and scrubbed floors.

It also helped fill her time. The routine of practicing law twelve hours a day hadn't allowed for sudden stops, and relearning the art of relaxation was proving harder than expected. She'd never excelled at it to begin with.

When the wall phone rang she wiped her hands on a dishtowel before answering. "Silano residence."

"You can just say hello," Dominic said.

"It's more formal my way."

"Just say hello," he repeated. "Listen, I have a friend coming by. He'll be staying a few days. That OK with you?"

Tessa switched the phone to the other ear. "It's your house."

"It's yours, too."

She smiled, knowing he meant it, but wishing he didn't always sound so apologetic when he spoke of his ownership. Yes, their parents had given it to both of them, but Tessa's heart wasn't in the place like Dominic's, so she'd signed her half over to him, and that was that. It shouldn't be so hard for him to accept.

"I don't want you to be uncomfortable," he finished.

"Why would I be uncomfortable? The more the merrier."

"You say that now."

She couldn't tell if he was joking but giggled

3

anyway. "He isn't a convict, is he?"

She could hear Dominic tapping something. Probably the end of his pencil on the steering wheel of his police cruiser.

"Gunnar's not very social," Dominic said. "Set him up in Mom and Dad's room and leave him be. I'll try to get off early."

Tessa hung up, more baffled than concerned by her brother's ambiguous description of the houseguest. He had a lot of friends, but she'd never heard mention of Gunnar. Must be a new guy on the force.

She smirked when the phone rang a moment later. It was just like Dominic to see if she would answer her way or his.

"Hello."

"This Dominic's place?"

The voice was male and impatient, and she deliberated whether to tell him.

"Can I—?"

"Who are you?" he asked.

"I'm—who are you?" she returned.

"What's the address there?"

"Excuse me?"

"The address, the address. Dom's expecting me. He forgot to give me the house number, and his cell is off."

Dismayed that this churlish man was Dominic's expected friend, Tessa reluctantly gave him the address.

"Great. I'm—what the—"

Tessa's eyes widened as she listened to the man yelling at someone on his end. Something to do with a bike, breaking body parts, and a hospital. It was a little hard to piece together since his profanity was quite fluent. She'd never considered some words could be used in that particular order.

"Be right there," he said in a slightly calmer tone.

Only after hearing a click in her ear did Tessa realize those last words were directed to her.

Dominic could have expanded about his friend. Not very social? He was positively hostile!

Twenty minutes later the ground began to tremble. It started as a low vibration, building steadily until Dominic's Sports Legends Bobblehead collection threatened to leap from the shelves of the cherry wood cabinet in the living room. Tessa ran to the front window.

Turning into the drive was the loudest motorcycle she'd ever heard. At least she assumed it was a motorcycle, it looked like none she had seen before. The entire contraption, from the end of the lashing, curved tail to the tip of the spitting, forked tongue was matte black with barely a hint of green. Beneath legs poised to lunge, the tires appeared to devour the pavement. It was hideous, and at the same time, mesmerizing.

Stunned, she watched it stop inches from the front steps. The rider, a virtual extension of the machine in matching black, mercifully shut off the motor and let down the kickstand with a clever movement of his foot.

Gunnar, no doubt.

She had been practically immobilized by that dreadful sound, but now she could move again, Tessa didn't want to. Even as she watched the man dismount, letting the machine crouch onto the metal stand, she knew she should go to the foyer to welcome him properly, but a bewildering rush of panic kept her feet planted.

As he raised his hands to take off the helmet, she closed her eyes and sucked in a deep calming breath. When she opened them, he was gone. Though she didn't see his face, she had a hunch it wouldn't be friendly.

She heard the front door swing open, then shut with a bang. Solid boot heels struck the hardwood of the foyer in perfect sync with the thick thudding of her heart.

He was walking in her direction, and if she didn't move soon, would discover her frozen there like a rabbit in crosshairs.

Finding that idea worse than her fear, Tessa strode toward the foyer. Why should she be afraid of a man just because he'd been a little short with her on the phone and rode a motorcycle that looked like a demon? Just because he was ill mannered and didn't knock before entering someone's house didn't make him a savage. He was a friend of her brother.

Of course, her mind countered, he hadn't known the address, so how good a friend could he be?

Tessa pushed away her misgivings and swung around the doorway and into a human wall. She teetered for a second before landing hard on her butt.

From her seated position, her gaze moved up from scuffed biker boots and black pants. A matte black helmet dangled in front of her face and drew her gaze up the arm of a scarred leather jacket. She couldn't help noticing that shoulders filled the doorway.

She guessed right about his face. Definitely unfriendly. Eyes dark as a night sea glared down at her from beneath slashing brows, and an unsmiling mouth offered neither apology nor ease. What she didn't expect was his hair. There wasn't any, only the suggestion of it on a well-shaped head.

He made no attempt to help her, which surprisingly did more to bolster her courage than undercut it. He was a startling sight, but she would not be unsettled in her own home.

Tessa got to her feet and held out a hand, wishing she'd inherited her mother's ability to fabricate a smile on cue.

"Hello. I'm Tessa," she said in a voice belying her nerves.

The man didn't take her proffered hand, though in an impatient gesture, elevated the helmet a little in minor acknowledgement. She put her hand down and skirted past him.

"This way," she said.

He followed her to the front of the house, heels drumming close behind, his eyes hot on her back.

She fought an inexplicable urge to run straight out the front door.

"Where do I put my bike?" he asked, when Tessa turned to lead him up the stairs.

His voice, rich and authoritative in person, sent an odd tingle along her spine.

Tessa moistened her dry lips before she spoke. "You can bring it around back," she said, her gaze alighting on him momentarily before looking away. "On the side of the house by the shrubbery is fine." She managed to point in the general direction.

He shifted his weight, but didn't speak, waiting it seemed, for her to look at him.

She did. She could all but feel his penetrating eyes and was struck with the foolish notion he could absorb her thoughts. In that case, she needn't worry since she couldn't reasonably form any. Had he asked another question? Had she answered the first one?

When he turned from her and walked out, Tessa released the breath she'd been holding. "Stop it," she chided herself. "He's only a man."

It was true, but this time when the horrific noise began, Dominic's Bobblehead collection wasn't all that quaked.

As he rode to the side of the house Tessa hurried to the dining room windows. The machine was fascinating, but the man held her eye. As intimidating and strange as he was, she couldn't deny she found him unusually attractive.

Gunnar set the bike on the stand then swung his leg over and stood beside it. When he removed his jacket, revealing the form fitting gray shirt beneath, Tessa's hand automatically went to her throat. Muscles bunched in his back and arms as he unhooked the elastic cords securing a black duffel bag to the seat.

He set the bag on the ground before lifting a flap on a saddlebag, and removing a length of shiny silver material. With a deft motion, he snapped it out into the air and covered the bike before crouching to fasten it near the back tire, then the front.

Tessa ducked away from the window as he made his way to the front of the house, and at the sound of the door opening and closing, she tried to look busy, making a task of aligning the tablecloth.

"Where's my room?" he asked from the doorway.

Tessa gave the tablecloth a last tug. "That was quick."

Gunnar shifted his jacket and duffel bag to the opposite arm.

"That's some motorcycle," she said.

"It's...unique."

He returned an impassive stare.

Tessa considered herself an even-tempered person, one who went to great lengths to avoid confrontation, but this man was trying her patience. Best to show him his room and be done with him.

"Excuse me," she said and nudged past him to walk to the stairs. She didn't hear him behind her and looked back to find him in the same spot. "Are you coming?" she asked, this time without consideration to courtesy.

Her room and Dominic's were upstairs on the right, and between them the door leading to the attic. Passing it, Tessa wished she could isolate Gunnar up there, but Dominic said to put him in their parents' old room at the end of the hall. It made sense, taking into account his size and the fact that the attic held a single bed. But the thought of him sleeping so close to her brought no solace.

She entered ahead of him, her gaze shooting around the room. Although she hadn't been in here in years, everything looked pretty much the way she remembered. A solid blue quilt draped the queen size bed, with hand stitched throw pillows marching single file across the top. The lead crystal lamps and silver alarm clocks stood on their bedside tables, all polished and gleaming. Everything as it should be.

"This room gets great light." Tessa doubted Gunnar cared, but something needed to be said. "Make yourself at home. There's a sun porch downstairs and a library if you want to read," she continued, as he flung the duffel onto the chair-and-a-half that stood between two east facing windows. "If you need anything—"

"I won't."

"If you need anything," she began again, "ask Dominic. I'm sure he'd love to help you." She could almost feel the heat when his gaze whipped to hers.

"I said I won't need anything."

Her lips bowed in what hopefully would pass for a smile. "It must be wonderful to be so autonomous."

She thought the corner of his mouth tugged in response, but those near black eyes narrowed a fraction, long enough to distract her. When she lowered her gaze again his lips were fixed in an unyielding line. She must have imagined it.

"I hope you enjoy your stay," she said, wiping an undetectable speck of dust from the dresser top. "Dinner is at six. You're welcome to join us."

In the hall with the door closed behind her, Tessa clenched her fists. *Oooh!* How could she let him provoke her? He was obviously in the habit of intimidating people, but she shouldn't have let her control slip. She'd dealt with worse than him—attorneys no less—and held her own. If he wanted to take her on…

Dominic's friend, she reminded herself. There was no need to score a point or stand her ground. She would take Dom's advice and leave Gunnar be until he left in a few days. She made a conscious effort to relax her hands.

 махаровична

Gunnar retrieved the bottle he kept in his duffel bag and lowered himself to the edge of the bed. How did he end up here? Not just in this room with matching mahogany furniture, plump pillows and frilly wallpaper, but in this frame of mind. He was a fool to believe he had a grip on things, however briefly.

He opened the bottle and drained the amber liquid in two long pulls before tossing the bottle and cap back in the bag. Dragging a pillow into position, he fell back on it. Each corner was adorned with a gold silk tassel. He could appreciate craftsmanship, but everything in this room screamed look-but-don't-touch.

Dominic didn't mention his parents were pretentious snobs. He didn't mention Tessa either. Now that was a look-but-don't-touch woman if ever he'd seen one. How could it be possible she and Dominic were related? Maybe he was adopted.

Gunnar gave the tassel a brush with his finger and closed his eyes, hoping to sleep. Better, to never wake up.

2

After vowing never to return to this town, Tessa found herself standing in line once more at the small Italian grocery store. Funny how things didn't always work out as expected. Her career was a perfect example, she thought, glancing at the Law Coffee poster hanging below the deli counter glass.

Rather than grow to love her job as her father had assured her she would, she had only become stressed and disillusioned. She recalled with disturbing clarity the day she finally accepted that the law had less to do with right versus wrong than with shifting blame for profit.

Almost as sad was the day she realized law had never been her passion but her father's. That should have been incentive enough to quit more than a year ago. Sometimes tenacity was a bad thing. She might be there now if not for other circumstances.

As if the job wasn't disappointment enough, she'd lost her perfect apartment—3G, with the view of Laurence Park—when Mrs. Rayburn in 4G fell asleep with her tub running. What items escaped water damage were now in storage.

Then Scott, the man she'd envisioned marrying, made it clear that the only time he would appear in a church in a black suit would be at his wake.

It seemed to be a good time to leave North

Carolina and return to Jersey.

Here she could step back and figure out what *she* wanted to do with her life. She had savings put aside, a small inheritance from Grandmother Isabella, and thanks to some wise investments at her father's urging, there was no hurry.

But Tessa did feel hurried. She'd wasted so much time trying to please others only to end up no happier than she'd been in a courtroom. It was time to change all that, to use her natural abilities in a practical way that pleased her. And she knew just the thing.

At first the idea of opening an inn seemed crazy, no more than a fantasy, but the more she considered it, the more possibilities bloomed. It was in her makeup to be a nurturer but short of motherhood or returning to school for a nursing degree, she could think of no better way to use her intrinsic aptitude. It would be so fulfilling to create an environment where people would feel welcomed and accepted. More a home away from home than an inn. The type of home she'd always wished for.

Of course being a nurturer didn't guarantee success. Strategy was essential to achievement which meant researching suppliers, studying the lay of the land, zoning ordinances, etc. She already had a list and at the top: find an apartment. She didn't wish to be under Dominic's feet until she stood on her own. Tomorrow she'd call a realtor.

She came in through the back door to find her best friend, Connie, at the table sipping coffee and nibbling a donut. It made no difference that the house was no longer Tessa's, Connie was as close as a sister to Dominic as well, and felt entitled to do as she pleased.

"Making chicken parm I see," Connie said, as

Tessa pulled the array of ingredients from the paper bag. "I'll help." She gasped and held up a jar of red tomato sauce. "You're using jar gravy? That's outright sacrilege."

Tessa hung her head in mock shame. "I don't have time for the real thing. Can you forgive me?"

"As long as I can have some."

Connie nipped a cord of pale blonde hair from in front of her eyes, twisted, and fastened it to rejoin the others on top of her head. Though she intended to look carelessly sexy, Tessa thought the style ultimately made her look like a sea urchin. Connie felt around her scalp for any loose spirals before pouring breadcrumbs into a large bowl.

"I've rethought that dress; the one with the pearl edging," Connie said.

Tessa shook her head. Connie had torn through every bridal shop in the tri-state area looking for the perfect dress, and her boyfriend hadn't even proposed yet.

"Why don't you open a magazine, close your eyes, and pick one?" Not that Tessa would do such a thing herself.

Connie's eyes flew open. "You don't trust this kind of thing to a blind finger point! It's all about the dress."

"I thought it was all about the man, but I could be wrong. I don't have much experience with weddings."

Connie chuckled, dimples winking. "Neither do I, unfortunately. Mike better get moving or *I'm* going to ask *him*."

"You would do that?" Tessa cracked eggs into a bowl.

"Yes." Connie handed Tessa a fork. "He

contemplates things to death. Our timetables are completely out of sync. By the time he gets around to popping the question according to his timetable, we might be on our second kid according to mine."

"How many kids do you want?" Tessa asked.

"Three or four."

Connie moved around the room, ordering the table, fixing the place settings. She was a lawyer too, but loved it. She met the rigorous demands of the job, and was still always ready to help with advice, time, or a surprisingly strong back.

Yes, Tessa could picture Connie with a brood of children, hefting diaper bags, and kissing boo-boos. "You'll be a great mother."

Connie paused in the middle of pouring olive oil into a frying pan. "That's the nicest thing anyone's ever said to me."

"It's true, you're great with kids, and when I have mine they'll spend most of their days at Aunt Connie's."

"Don't get carried away."

"Anyway, you're getting antsy for nothing," Tessa said, bringing the chicken to the stove. "At least you found the right guy. I don't even have any prospects on the horizon."

"You could if you didn't keep to yourself so much."

"I don't," Tessa answered halfheartedly.

Connie plunked her hands on her slightly rounded hips. "You're already back two weeks and we haven't gone out. All you do is hole-up here and clean the house. It's not healthy."

The truth stung a bit. "Where are we supposed to go, to a bar? You know the types of people you meet in those places, and you're practically engaged."

"So we'll do dinner," Connie said. "Tomorrow night we'll go to a nice restaurant and let some attractive man send over a bottle of wine."

Tessa laughed. "Why don't I post an ad in the personals?"

"You shouldn't knock it. My friend Ilene's sister met her husband through an online dating service." Connie turned the frying pan on to heat. "There's someone for everyone. You just have to fish around. Put your bait out there and dangle it a bit."

Tessa's mind drifted to Gunnar as it had throughout the day. She couldn't picture a man like that in love. That didn't mean he couldn't be married for all she knew, but if his earlier behavior was any indicator, he was alone and would probably remain so. Maybe he was divorced. Did he have children?

Well, it wasn't her business in any case. No matter that she had never seen a man so well put together, or that she'd noticed his excellent bone structure beneath the bald head and scowling brows, it didn't concern her.

Tessa blinked when a hand passed in front of her face. "I'm sorry, what?"

"I asked if Carter called you. My cousin?"

Tessa flipped through her memory index. Carter, right. Connie's mother tried to fix them up. "Yes, he called the other day."

Connie leaned on the refrigerator. "You look distracted. Something on your mind? Or should I say someone?"

"All I have on my mind is getting dinner ready." Tessa positioned cutlets in the pan, but Connie continued to scan her face with curious eyes.

"Is it someone from North Carolina?" Connie's eyes reduced to blue slits. "You aren't back with Scott?"

Tessa snorted. "Don't be ridiculous."

"Then who?"

"There's no one."

"I'm a lawyer, I have ways to make you talk," Connie threatened.

"So am I, and I refuse to testify."

The phone at Connie's hip rang giving Tessa a reprieve. It was Mike, which meant by the time Connie hung up she would have forgotten the topic of conversation.

∂∽∾

An hour later Tessa put down the book she had been reading while Mike diverted Connie's thoughts to wedding bells and domestic bliss. She heard Dominic pull into the drive. Now he could act as buffer to prevent further inquiry.

He came in as Tessa pulled the chicken from the oven.

Dominic went to the stove and took a good long sniff. "Remind me to give you a raise."

"I helped," Connie said, snapping her phone back into its case.

"Hey, doll. Didn't see your car." He gave her a friendly peck on the cheek.

"I parked across the street. So much for your powers of observation."

"This has to settle a little," Tessa said, nudging him aside and sliding the pan to the back of the stovetop.

"That's OK, so do I." Dominic dropped into the chair formerly their father's, not exactly the head since the table was round, but it took in the entire room.

He strongly resembled their father with the wavy mahogany hair, intractable chin and moody hazel eyes. So handsome, so steady. Unlike their father, however, Dominic understood the importance of family.

John Silano loved his, but he had always paid more attention to providing for the family than to the family itself.

As the son, Dominic no doubt felt their father's neglect more directly than she, yet still retained most of his easygoing nature. He was a good man.

A sympathetic smile touched Tessa's lips. The split from Pauline had hurt Dominic bad and still he didn't vilify her, like some men might. As far as Tessa knew neither could be fully blamed. He'd said simply that in order for them to work it out, both he and his wife would've had to be different people.

What was the point of being together, Tessa wondered, if a person had to change so drastically? She ignored the twist of regret and poured him some spring water.

"Take your shoes off and relax."

"No point, I'm going back to work soon," Dominic said.

"What? Why?"

"Sorry, dear," he teased. "But I have to bring home the bacon."

"Not funny." Tessa poured herself a glass.

Dominic ran a hand through his already messed hair. "I'm taking Kevin's shift. As we speak he's in the hospital having his face stitched."

"What happened?" Tessa asked.

"He had a minor skirmish with a drunk and disorderly. Wasn't serious but he hit his head on the curb when he went down."

"How's the curb?" Connie asked.

Dominic chuckled. "It'll be fine but they're keeping Kevin till they're convinced his mental illness has nothing to do with the fall."

"He always did have a head like a rock," Connie said.

Tessa laughed with them but she didn't like the way Dominic looked, drained.

"Where's Gunnar?" he asked suddenly.

Tessa's stomach plummeted to the floor. What were the odds Connie wasn't paying attention?

"Who's Gunnar?" Connie asked.

"Upstairs, I guess. I haven't heard him all day." Tessa sipped her water.

"I hope he's getting some sleep," Dominic said.

"Who's Gunnar?" Connie repeated.

"A friend of mine," Dominic said.

"Is he a cop?"

"No."

Tessa cut into the chicken and heaped a serving onto Dom's plate. "You could have warned me."

Dominic looked at her, bemused. "You mean you don't find him an interesting conversationalist?"

Tessa couldn't help responding to the grin pulling at his mouth. "Interesting yes, though I did find his communication skills lacking."

"Did you pick up that he's aggressive and unfriendly?"

"Oh, that came across loud and clear."

"See? He has no problem communicating."

She looked at him with reluctant amusement. "I

stand corrected."

Connie set a spinach salad in the center of the table. "He's here the whole time and you didn't tell me?"

Opening the refrigerator to grab the dressing, Tessa left Dominic to answer.

"He's staying a few days while his house is being worked on. Maybe a week."

A week under the same roof, with that? Tessa thought. "I assumed I knew all your friends."

"I met him last year at a bike show," Dominic said, spearing a chunk of chicken. "We kind of clicked."

Tessa shot him a look. She would bet anything the story went farther than that, but the look he returned told her now wasn't the time to ask.

"Trust me, he's a good guy," Dominic assured her. "He wouldn't be here otherwise."

Well, maybe Gunnar would stay in his room most of the time, Tessa hoped, or go out. She would be looking for an apartment, anyway.

Dominic left as soon as his plate was clean.

Connie began her interrogation before the door fully closed. "Is that the guy you have on your mind?" she asked, pointing toward the ceiling.

"I don't have him on my mind. Like that." Tessa couldn't deny she thought of him, but how could she not?

The man was an experience.

"What does he look like?"

Connie would dog her until she dug up some information to chew on, so Tessa relented. "He's taller than Dom, maybe six feet, this big," she said, expanding her arms. "He's bald and very unfriendly."

Connie held silent a moment, piecing the

information together. "So he's, what...overweight?"

"No."

The light of dawning overtook Connie's pixie-like features, and she emitted a soft gasp. "He's gorgeous, isn't he?"

Tessa's brows drew together. Would she call him gorgeous? "You really have to see him for yourself."

"What does— Oh." Connie reached for the phone beeping at her hip. "I have to run. I'm meeting Mike at Dugan's Pub, and we're going to the movies. Why don't you come?"

"Thanks, but three's a crowd. I'm going to soak in a hot tub and go to bed."

"Party animal." Connie grabbed her purse. "Are you OK with...?" She pumped a thumb to the ceiling.

Tessa waved her off. "He's more bark than bite." She hoped.

After setting the kitchen to rights, Tessa checked the door locks, shut off all the lights but the one on the range hood, and went upstairs to run a bath. She paused for a second in the hall, inclining an ear but all was quiet in Gunnar's room.

Outside the wind grew wild, rattling windows and flinging bits of debris against the house with little snapping sounds. A storm was coming.

3

Vaulting from the bed, Gunnar slapped at his body, desperate to quench the consuming flames that caused his flesh to bubble and his skin to pucker and shrink away.

He tried to scream, but the nauseating stench of sulfur robbed his breath.

If he could just pass out from the pain it would be over. But he'd been asleep and that hadn't prevented this. Sleep prompted the nightmares.

His heart pounded so fast and hard, he expected it to explode in his chest, but he wouldn't be so lucky. Then, as quickly as the flames ignited, they vanished, and he collapsed to the floor, shuddering and wheezing. He sucked in as much air as he could with his face pressed into the carpet fiber.

As usual, the images of hell and its demons slowly dissipated, as did the pain. Though he would recall being racked with unspeakable agony, the only lasting physical effects would be strained muscles acquired from his ineffectual fight. Even now, his entire body throbbed.

When he was able to release his white-knuckle grip on the carpet, Gunnar pulled himself up to sit on the edge of the bed and dropped his head into his hands. He wouldn't survive another night of this.

Since losing his brother eight months ago, sleep

was an infrequent visitor. When it did come, it was fitful and merciless. When he woke, he thought of little else but the night to come. If not for the occasional bottle of Jack coupled with utter exhaustion, he wouldn't sleep at all. And then these…nightmares…

The latter brought him here. His body was deteriorating, his nerves shot. He'd lost ten pounds in the last month, and his temper, short to begin with, was now just bare wire exposed and waiting for someone to set him off.

Exploiting the kindness of a friend became necessary so he used the house renovation as a handy excuse, reasoning that if he got out of there the nightmares would stay behind. So much for that theory. He pressed his fingers to his eyes.

Evan would have attached some supernatural meaning to the terrifying dreams. His brother had believed all that hokey spiritual stuff—demons and angels, good triumphing over evil and all that crap. And since that arena religion thing a few years back, where people flocked to alternately cheer and sob and stuff some guy's pockets with cash, it was worse.

Jesus became part of every conversation. "Praise the Lord" for this, "Hallelujah" for that.

Even though Evan's gullibility was part of his charm, Gunnar had done all he could to discourage him from sharing the "good news." At least with him.

Icy despair spread through Gunnar's body. How could he have known the last phone call from his brother would be *the* last?

He'd been more than a little drunk and feeling nasty when Evan called, but it was an unforeseen spurt of guilt that factored most into his confession. In his inebriated state, it made sense to tell Evan of his sin.

Who else on this earth could claim to be as close to God? And what better way to persuade Evan to stop wasting time trying to save his brother's soul than to lay bare the blackness of it?

And just like that, he'd told him.

"I killed someone."

That should have been the end of it.

It should have, but rather than quit, Evan was adamant about speaking in person. Gunnar refused. Evan persisted.

Gunnar's heart gave a condemning thump, and he tilted his face to the ceiling. "He died trying to help me," he said, defying the lump in his throat.

"You should have died," answered a voice that seemed to come from within. *"If you die now it will make things right."*

Gunnar straightened, considering. *It will make things right.* In a twisted way, it made sense. If his life wasn't such a disaster Evan would be here, and though giving his life wouldn't bring his brother back, it might in some small way recompense. Maybe not for Evan alone, maybe for other things, too.

A crack of thunder shook the house, an affirmation as far as Gunnar was concerned.

Well, he would never be accused of procrastination.

He removed the .45 from its nesting place in his duffel bag and tossed it in his hand. He liked the weight of it, the easy fit of the checkered wood grips, the power contained in the cold, blue-black steel. It was an accurate weapon. Precise.

Gunnar thumbed off the safety.

"Do it."

Gunnar heard the words. Unreal, to be hearing

voices, but at that moment, rationality was an enemy to be vanquished.

"I can do this," he said, fighting the inborn will to live.

Perspiration beaded on his forehead, trickled down the side of his face and neck. His hands shook, his chest constricted, his breath came hard and fast. He was ready. He believed it with everything in him. Ready to silence the pain, the past, all of it. He lifted the gun, touched the trigger.

A picture of his sister, Samantha, flashed into his mind. She was wading through knee deep snow, wearing one of his sweaters, the green one she'd bought him, borrowed, and then kept. She was smiling as she stooped to loosely ball a handful of snow.

What a stupid time for that to come up. The mind truly was a mystery. But his had tortured him long enough. He forced the image out.

It popped in a second time. How could he do this to her again?

"I'm sorry, Sam," he whispered .

Gunnar sat on the edge of the bed, literally torn between life and death. Hours could have passed. So many thoughts and questions whirled through his mind, random, disjointed, but one kept resurfacing.

"Will Samantha be OK?" he asked aloud.

"She'll be OK. Just do it."

He couldn't remember ever hearing his own thoughts before tonight but in light of recent happenings, he accepted it. Yet, the voice didn't sound like his. It sounded urgent. And…impatient?

He was crazy anyway, right?

"Please understand," he whispered into the still air. "I can't take any more." Closing his eyes, Gunnar opened his mouth and clamped his teeth on the indifferent barrel, careful not to touch it with his tongue. He'd heard somewhere that the taste of metal put people off finishing the act and he meant to finish. He angled the barrel upward.

"She'll understand."

His grip faltered.

Yes, she would understand because she loved him. A misguided love. Her life's direction had been programmed by him, her past memories chiseled in stone as if by his own hand. And what memories had he given her? Pain, violence, and death. Betrayal and disappointment.

Gunnar repositioned his hand on the gun so his thumb was on the trigger. He could feel the steel resisting against the pad of his finger, pressing, tighter, tighter.

This time when Samantha's image intruded, she balled up the snow and threw it at him. He felt the blast of it on his face as shockingly icy as the moment she'd hit him with it three years ago at her house in New York.

An invisible mist evaporated from Gunnar's mind, suddenly allowing him to comprehend what had happened. What *could* have happened. The gun fell from his limp hand with a thud.

"This isn't me," he said in a voice laden with panic. "It isn't." Despite the fifth of Jack in him, rage was unimpaired and fired through him quickly to replace the alarm. He reached for the nearest thing handy and hurled it with all his strength.

4

Tessa woke to boisterous thunder, lashing wind, and driving rain. She hadn't heard anything of an approaching storm on the news, but it arrived nonetheless. When it left just as unexpectedly, she opened the window a little, letting in the unsullied air that a violent tempest invariably left in its wake.

She lay still, listening to her own steady breathing and the soft flap of the butter yellow curtains and tried to will herself back to sleep. She would blame the sporadic wailing of Mrs. Wilson's basset hound across the street, but there was something else, a tangible restlessness. The air was charged, ionized, and the energy coursed through her body with no outlet.

She should get up and do some sit-ups.

She glanced at her prayer journal. This would be a good time to spend with God. But she was a little hungry and relieving the gnawing in her stomach might help in relieving the gnawing in the rest of her body. Tessa pulled back the light blanket and moved toward the door.

Thunk!

The sound came from the next room. Her hand froze on the knob.

Gunnar Mason was in the next room.

She dared not budge. What if he heard her and came in?

The stillness returned, louder than she recalled. She tilted her head, eyes wide, alert to any noise. Tires from a passing car made a slurping sound on the wet blacktop. Her heart tripped and pounded.

It was then she remembered *Slaughter in Color*, the book she was reading before falling asleep. It lay on the nightstand, face down and opened to a grisly murder scene in the Tennessee backwoods. Fodder for an overactive imagination. Silly, she told herself.

Gunnar would have no reason to come in here.

After a few deep breaths, Tessa regained control of her breathing and opened the door. There was nothing to be afraid of.

Gunnar had probably knocked something off the table in his sleep. Or he might have rolled, thrown an arm out and—

The unmistakable shattering of glass reverberated through the house, closely followed by a steady stream of curses. Then nothing.

Perhaps the wind had picked up again and sent one of the branches from the old oak into Gunnar's window.

Tessa hoped he wasn't injured.

Fear, sharp and bright, cut through her, but she inched forward toward the light seeping under his door. Fighting back the adrenaline to keep from beating on the door, she knocked softly and braced for whatever lay inside.

The door swung open and the light leapt forward only to be dammed when Gunnar's form filled the gap. He was bare to the waist and adorned with a startling tattoo across his abdomen—a word, inscribed in indigo ink—but she averted her gaze before she could decipher it.

A deep breath was in order but the constriction of her chest wouldn't allow one.

He swept her with a cursory glance and stepped back. His way of inviting her in, she assumed.

With a hand over her speeding heart, Tessa hesitated before taking the step that would allow him to shut the door, effectively blocking her escape route. She should have woken Dominic. But now that she thought of it, she didn't know if he was home. To her relief, Gunnar left the door open.

"I'm sorry to bother you, Mr. Mason," Tessa said when she'd worked out the kinks in her vocal chords. "I heard a noise."

Gunnar flung a hand in the general direction of the source, but she was already taking in the room. She noted the absence of the small table, normally to the right of the bed, then, the lamp on the floor. Its base was chipped, but the shade looked to be in good shape. She picked it up and held it to her.

"What happened? Were you hurt?"

"Must have been the wind," Gunnar replied dryly, pulling his shirt on.

She followed his gaze across the room where shards of glass littered the floor beneath the window. Closer scrutiny revealed the glass and screen were both broken from the inside. She clasped a hand to her mouth when she saw her grandmother's Italian lace curtain pushed through the hole and hanging outside.

"The wind isn't responsible for this, Mr. Mason. What happened?" Then an odor invaded her nose. "And why does it smell like you've been lighting fireworks in here?"

"I'll pay for the damages," Gunnar said.

"Yes, you will. But I want you to tell me why

you—" Tessa froze when she spotted the gun on the floor.

She had seen Dominic's gun, but this one looked bigger, more menacing. Already sensitized, her mind tore off at high speed. Why did Gunnar have a weapon? He wasn't a cop. Was he a killer? Had he conned Dominic to gain entrance to this house? Did he plan to use the gun on Dominic? What would he do to her?

She returned her attention to him. He was watching her, a troubled expression on his hard face.

"Take it easy." He raised his hand in a calming gesture. "Dom knows I carry it." Keeping one hand elevated, he bent to pick up the pistol with two fingers.

Though she tried, she couldn't prevent the small strangled noise that sprang from her throat when he took a step toward her.

Gunnar rolled his eyes and reaching back, jammed the .45 into the duffel bag. "Better?"

She swallowed and nodded. She could actually feel her heart restarting.

"Don't ask," he growled.

She might have kept quiet if not for that tone in his voice, the sarcasm, as though she was an intruder. He wasn't going to explain what prompted such an outburst, and she didn't intend to provoke him, but neither did she intend to let him dismiss her. This was her brother's home, her home for the time being, and he would honor that.

She took a piece of glass from the floor and tossed it in the wastebasket before stomping to the window and pulling the curtain panel back inside. The delicate material was torn and ragged. "What reason could you have for this?"

"I said I'd pay for it, just give me a total."

Sensing he was keeping his anger restrained, her back stiffened. *His* anger! "Money isn't the issue, Mr. Mason. This lamp is a reproduction," she said, shaking it at him before setting it on the floor. "But many of the things in this house are original and can't be replaced." She mourned inwardly for Nana's curtains.

Gunnar sat on the bed and rubbed at his eyes with the heels of his hands. "I'm sorry," he said. "I'll go."

When he looked at her, the challenge in his eyes was in direct variance with his apology.

Tessa couldn't tell what to make of it. He had no right to give her attitude. But he looked exhausted and sounded penitent, if begrudgingly so. Maybe he hadn't gotten any sleep, or had a bad dream. She let the ruined curtain fall from her hand. It wasn't in her nature to condemn the repentant.

"You don't have to leave, Mr. Mason." She saw a shift in him, imperceptible unless one looked directly into those foreboding eyes. "It's not my place to ask you to." She went to the door. "I'll have someone here first thing in the morning to fix the window. In the meantime, clean up the rest of that glass. And I don't want to see that gun anymore."

She walked directly to Dominic's room and finding it empty realized he must still be covering Kevin's shift. *For the best*, she assured herself. He had enough strain on him.

It wasn't until she closed her room door tight and wedged her desk chair under the knob that the trembling began. She needed a lock on her door.

დოთ

Gunnar sat in the huge chair by the broken window watching the sun lighten the sky. He toyed with a jagged edge of wood on the window frame. He couldn't help comparing it to his life, fractured and splintered, mostly at his own hand.

He glanced at the bed and tried to picture himself sitting there with a gun in his mouth. The gun was real, this room was real, but the whole experience, the daze that had engulfed him during the time he contemplated pulling the trigger...could it have been his imagination? Another sick dream?

He rubbed the bridge of his nose then let his fist drop to his lap. No, he refused to slip into denial. He couldn't get that close to blowing his head off and then calmly tuck it away as though it never happened. He needed help. He would never sit in a shrink's office and get it, but he knew he needed it.

Gunnar gripped the arms of the chair, the one masculine piece of furniture in the room. Most of the other stuff looked feminine. Delicate. He fingered the lace of the torn curtain. Yet some things were stronger than they looked.

Like Dom's sister. Tessa.

Initially, he'd thought her the nervous type, a woman who would bolt in the blink of an eye. But she came to his room after hearing a noise. To check on him. He shook his head. She'd confronted him, and after seeing the gun, still hadn't run in spite of her obvious fear. Who wouldn't respect that?

She appeared timid on the surface, but there were glimpses of strength that hinted at how magnificent she would be when furious.

While he was definitely intrigued enough to want to delve into the prim and proper Tessa Silano, an undeniable part of him would just like to provoke her and watch her cut loose.

But she was the sister of one of his best friends. Off limits.

That reminded him, he would have to find Dom and apologize before he left. Later.

Gunnar took the two steps from the chair to the bed and fell on the soft quilt. He doubted sleep would come—might be better if it didn't. But he closed his eyes, anyway.

5

Sleep eluded Tessa. She prayed, read her Bible, and prayed some more. It wasn't fear of Gunnar keeping her awake, but the realization that she'd been terrified, despite believing she had such dynamic faith.

She was still pondering this at around six a.m. when she heard Dominic come in and go to his room. She concluded from the ensuing silence that he passed out, exhausted. Her conclusion was confirmed when she peeked in on her way downstairs and found him across his bed fully dressed, snoring. At least he'd taken off his gun.

After calling a handyman, she sat at the table and scanned the morning paper. Somewhere in this town there must be an apartment for rent. She didn't require much space, but...

Inspiration struck. Why rent an apartment only to relocate when she was ready to start the inn? She would look for a house. *The* house. Yes, with a manicured lawn and a nice sunny spot to plant flowers. Maybe a little section near the kitchen door for herbs, and a big yard where a dog could run. Not a show dog, either, a goofy mutt with floppy ears and scraggly fur.

She closed the paper with a snap and rose to make the coffee. Her parents had forbidden pets, but she hadn't realized how much she wanted a dog. She wondered what other things she might truly want if she indulged herself enough to consider them. A mature woman should know what she wanted. She should be able to make life choices.

As she filled the coffee pot with water, a blue jay arrowed past the window. No one told a bird what to do, and from now on no one would tell her. For the first time in her life, she didn't deem it rebellious or defiant to think so. There was guilt just the same.

"Hey, Tess!"

Tessa fumbled the pot in the sink when Connie bounced into the kitchen via the front hall.

"You scared me!" Tessa pressed a hand to her chest. "What are you doing here?"

"Some greeting."

"Sorry." Tessa held the pot up to check for cracks.

"You said whenever I want to borrow that Dave Matthews CD to come by. Here I am."

Connie looked much more attorney-like this morning in her plum-colored linen pantsuit and heels.

"You're working? It's Saturday," Tessa said.

"Yeah, well, you know how it is."

Yes, she did—working weekends, falling asleep on files and law books. No more.

"Here, give me that. You make it too weak." Connie bumped Tessa aside and tipped an extra scoop of grounds into the filter. "Are you OK?" she asked. "You look beat."

More tired than she'd believed, Tessa took a moment to clear her head. "I didn't get much sleep."

Connie's bow lips curved in a slow smile, and she hoisted her small frame onto the counter. "So what did you and Gunnar do all night?"

Tessa opened her mouth. A small sound escaped,

something between a squeak and a gasp. "Gunnar?"

Connie propped her elbows on her knees and leaned in. "Come on, Tess, yesterday you were keeping him a secret—"

"He just didn't come up."

"Your brother worked a double shift last night," she continued as though Tessa hadn't spoken. "I come in and catch you daydreaming...you didn't get any sleep...two and two."

"Well in this case it doesn't add up." Tessa stopped, bothered that she sounded...bothered.

"Well, I know you wouldn't sleep with him or anything."

"Of course not."

"It just looks incriminating," Connie answered. "You know as well as I that circumstantial evidence—"

"—sends some innocent people to prison, yes, I know." Tessa knew Connie was teasing but it didn't stop her ears from turning red.

To force the subject closed would only sharpen Connie's prey drive—it was what made her a good lawyer—so Tessa gave her something to nibble at and hoped she would be satisfied.

Connie "ah-ed" and "mm hmm-ed" between sips of coffee as Tessa gave her a synopsis of Gunnar's initial phone call, the motorcycle, the bad attitude. But watching Connie's eyes, Tessa could almost see the wheels revolving in that pretty blonde head, further underlining the negative aspect of chatting with this particular girlfriend.

Should have figured all the angles, Tessa scolded herself.

Connie would undoubtedly blab to her mother. Vivian was a nice woman but unfortunately, friends with Tessa's mother.

Since it was too late to stop the gossip train, Tessa was careful which details she let slip. To omit further physical description altogether would draw more attention, so rather than mention Gunnar's eyes were magnetic, she said they were dark brown. Rather than divulging he owned the best body she'd ever seen up close, she called him well built.

Naturally, Tessa didn't mention what happened in Gunnar's room. That went into his personal business and would be going too far. She told Connie his snoring in the next room had kept her up.

A glimpse at the clock had Tessa gulping her coffee. She expected the repairman any minute, and the last thing she needed was to explain his appearance to Connie.

"Oh, the CD," Tessa said with a snap of her fingers and opened one of the cabinets where the radio and CDs were discreetly concealed.

"Are you trying to get rid of me?" Connie hopped off the counter.

"I don't want you to be late."

Connie checked her watch. "Yeah, I'd better go." She swallowed the rest of her coffee and put the cup in the dishwasher. "But we're not finished. I want more details. Tonight, dinner, right?" Without waiting for an answer, she kissed Tessa on the cheek and strode out.

The synchronization was perfect. No sooner had Connie driven around the corner than Tom, the handyman, turned into the drive in his battered red van.

When Tessa went to the back door to meet him, Gunnar exited through the front. She didn't see him, but heard his motorcycle start and fade into the distance as she led Tom to the damage. She didn't know what she would have done if Gunnar had still been in his room.

As for Dominic, he'd always slept like the dead. The roar of Gunnar's bike didn't wake him, and Tessa hoped Tom's repairs wouldn't either.

∂∾⋘

"Hey," Dominic said from the top of the steps several hours later.

Tessa sprayed a dust rag with polish and smiled at him. "Well, look who is back among the living."

The wrinkles were firmly established in his uniform, his face was stippled with a night's growth of whiskers, his hair spiked in all directions. He rubbed his eyes, reminding her of Christmas mornings as children, of her bouncing excitedly in front of the tree while he fumbled around, barely conscious.

When he came into the living room, she gave him a hug.

"What's this for?"

"You're cute as a button," she said, releasing him with a squeeze.

"Hey, did you hear banging this morning?"

Tessa's heart lurched. "Banging?"

He nodded.

"Well actu—"

"I'm starved. Did you have breakfast?"

Tessa blinked. "It's one o'clock."

"I'm in the mood for eggs. Let's go to the diner."

"I could make eggs here," Tessa said, but he was already heading back upstairs.

"Just let me get changed. Oh, I'll see if Gunnar

wants to come."

"He left hours ago."

"Oh." Dominic shrugged as he reached the landing. "OK. Well, I'll just be a few minutes."

࿐

The Bell Diner had a four-foot illuminated hotdog on the roof. Pink and black vinyl coated every surface not covered in tan and white speckled Formica. Beveled mirrors surrounded customers making it easy to see where the staff was at any given moment.

Tessa could see the waitress leaning against a long counter popping her chewing gum and flirting with a man half her age. When she saw Dominic, the woman shifted her affections and pranced toward him.

"Officer Silano," she cooed.

"Hey, Lorelei."

"Are you here to arrest me?" she asked, stroking a painted nail down his sleeve.

"Have you committed a crime?"

She tucked a length of bottle enhanced auburn hair behind her ear. "Considering it."

Dominic smiled at her then slid into a booth. "I'll have coffee. You want coffee?" he asked Tessa.

"Yes, please." She sat opposite him.

Lorelei's eyes enlarged, finally spotting Tessa. "You two, a..." she began, swinging her pencil back and forth between them.

"My sister," Dominic told her.

Lorelei looked unconvinced. When she walked away, Dominic leaned closer. "Are you ordering anything with hash browns?"

Tessa opened her laminated single fold menu. "I

don't know. Why?"

"Because what I want comes with pancakes but I want hash browns, too."

"What if I want mine?"

"They're no good for you."

The second Lorelei set their coffee on the table the steaming liquid began to tremble in the cups. There was no mistaking the source.

"What in the world is that?" asked Lorelei, staring out the window.

Before the mechanical beast maneuvered into the lot, every head in the diner was turned to the window. Some gawked silently, others murmured.

There was a shout of "Awesome!" from a boy in the next booth. Everyone except the boy looked away when Gunnar pushed through the door.

"Saw your car," Gunnar said, coming to stand next to Dominic.

Dominic dragged his coffee over with him as he made room for Gunnar to sit. "We didn't order yet." He handed Gunnar a menu and looked around. "You'd think these people never saw anyone riding a demon before."

"You'd think," Tessa muttered into her coffee.

Gunnar's eyes locked in a brief conflict with hers until she looked away, unwilling to engage him here. Anywhere, for that matter.

"If you want to be inconspicuous you should drive a Volvo," Dominic suggested.

Gunnar's reply was less than civil and had the boy gaping before his mother demanded he face forward and "let the man alone."

Without preamble, Gunnar reached into his jacket and dropped a sizeable roll of bills in front of Dominic.

"I don't know what I owe you, so here."

Dominic looked at the cash, pushed it in front of Gunnar. "Don't start that again. I already told you you're not paying to stay in my house."

Tessa met Gunnar's gaze again, but looked up as the waitress approached.

All of Lorelei's good-natured flirting was on hold while she scribbled their orders, keeping her attention on the pad. When she walked away, her hips swaying to alternate sides of the aisle as she went, Gunnar faced Tessa.

"You didn't tell him?" he asked.

Dominic's gaze ricocheted between Tessa and Gunnar. "Tell me what?"

"No big deal," Tessa answered. "A minor incident."

"The money's for damages," Gunnar told Dominic. "I broke some things last night."

"This morning, actually, but there was no real harm done," she interjected, though Nana's curtains were a complete loss.

Dominic turned to face them together. "Whoa, back up. You broke some things...what does that mean?"

"I had a bad night."

There was deep regret in Gunnar's voice, and when Tessa looked at her brother's face, she recognized the emotions she saw there: patience and understanding. The same emotions he showed when dealing with her. She'd had no idea he and Gunnar were so close.

"So, what'd you break?" Dominic asked.

When Gunnar's shoulders relaxed, so did Tessa's, relieved they weren't going to discuss his problems in front of her. Gunnar turned questioning eyes to her.

"Oh, um, an alarm clock," she told Dominic.

Tom found most of it outside in the rose bushes.

"And one of the lamps is chipped here and there."

Dominic took a hundred off the roll of bills. The lamp was worth at least twice that much and all parties knew it.

When Gunnar lifted a suspicious brow, Dominic took fifty more.

"And the window and screen had to be replaced," Tessa said.

"The window and screen?" Dominic pursed his lips. "Impressive."

Tessa fidgeted, nervous for reasons she couldn't identify. "Yes, well, the table went through them."

"You had a busy night, pal," Dominic said to Gunnar. "That table's gonna cost you. It's one of a pair." He took another four hundred and looked at Tessa. "And how did I miss all this?"

She scraped her teeth across her bottom lip. "It happened before you got home."

"So the banging I heard this morning..."

She nodded.

"What'd the window come to?" Dominic asked.

"Tom gave us a break and did the whole job for two hundred."

Dominic shot her a reproving look. "Why'd you call Tom? Mom and Dad use him."

"I don't know any other handymen, and I needed someone quick." Tessa smiled sheepishly.

"If he mentions it to them they'll have questions, believe me."

"I know." Tessa stirred sugar into her coffee. "But by the next time they have him do anything around there he'll have forgotten. Anyway, you can tell them it was storm damage. From the storm last night," she added when he looked puzzled. "I'm surprised the power didn't go out."

"I spent most of the night outside," Dominic said. "The sky was clear."

"Maybe where you were but not here," Gunnar put in.

Dominic shrugged. "What else?" he asked, getting back to the original topic.

"That's it," Tessa answered.

"The curtains," Gunnar told him with an accusatory glare at Tessa that she didn't care for at all.

"They can't be replaced, there's no point mentioning them," she said.

He spoke to her directly. "I won't owe you. Name a price."

Did everything have to be a conflict with this guy? "OK, fine, a hundred dollars."

As the food was served, Dominic handed Gunnar the remainder of the money.

Tessa no longer had an appetite but scraped her hash browns onto her brother's plate and ate her scrambled eggs.

When they returned to the house, Gunnar went upstairs and Dominic pulled Tessa aside in the sun porch across from the living room. "Why didn't you tell me?"

"I started to when you asked about the banging. Anyway, he said he'd take care of it and he did. No big deal."

"I don't want you to get tangled with him."

"Tangled?"

"I mean it. I respect him, and I'd trust him with

my life—and I don't say that flippantly." Dominic tossed his keys on the white wicker table. "But with you I don't know."

"We had a few words, most of them unpleasant, that's it," she said.

He laid his hands on her shoulders. "I'm just saying watch yourself. He's not a man to get emotionally involved with."

Tessa backed away, folding her arms. "I can make that determination on my own, thank you."

"You don't have the kind of experience he has, Tess."

"No, and I didn't just fall from the sky, either."

"I'm not saying—"

"It doesn't seem you respect him as much as you claim."

"This isn't about respecting him; it's about you being naïve. You're my sister."

Tessa jabbed him in the chest with an index finger. "I'm a grown woman." If she weren't so outraged, she might have laughed as the initial denial on his face faded to reluctant acceptance.

"Just be careful."

∂∽⟋

Gunnar expected the knock at the door. "Come in."

He followed Dominic's gaze as he scanned the room, taking in the new bare window.

"A bad night, huh?" Dominic sat on the bed. "I'm trying to keep out of your business, but what's going on?"

"Don't worry, I came back to pick up my stuff."

"Don't be an idiot," Dominic said. "I'm not asking you to leave."

Gunnar took the big chair, settled in. "I don't sleep."

"So you said."

Gunnar didn't know how much to tell Dominic. People had a way of deserting you when they knew you were crazy. He rubbed a hand over the top of his skull, rough and stubbly since he'd decided to let his hair grow back.

"I told you I'm going through a rough time."

Dominic leaned back, propping himself on his elbows. "I have to say I was a little surprised when you asked if you could stay."

"I never asked you for anything before," Gunnar said, probably sounding a little more defensive than he meant to.

"No, it's OK. I guessed you had a reason other than your house being worked on."

Gunnar clasped his hands and let them hang between his knees. "I have these nightmares."

"Nightmares."

"For a while. They're getting worse." To his relief, he saw neither pity nor scorn on Dominic's face, only evidence that he was searching for words. "I figured if I got away from my house they would stop."

"Why here?"

"You were the first person I thought of. I should have gone to a hotel." Gunnar pushed to his feet.

Dominic joined him. "No, you did the right thing. I wouldn't turn you away." Dominic shoved his hands in his pockets.

Gunnar felt the awkwardness mounting. He had no business bringing his trouble into this house, yet standing here taking in the assurance his friend offered, he couldn't be sorry.

"I didn't mean to trash your place. I don't know what happened."

Dominic chuckled. "I take it your change of atmosphere didn't work."

"I think it did. Afterward I slept better than I have in a long time."

Dominic tilted his head. "Out of curiosity, how did my sister take it?"

Gunnar and Dominic shared a smile. "Not well. She was really mad. A little scared too, but...she's something else." When Dominic's smile faded, Gunnar sat back down in the chair. "I know, off limits."

Dominic went to the door.

"Can I ask you a question?" Gunnar asked.

Dominic lifted his chin.

"Is it because she's your sister or because I'm me?"

A grin split Dominic's face. "Both. Do I have to remind you of the episode with the dancer from Iowa?"

Gunnar grinned back with the recollection. "I see your point."

"Hey, I'm running up to see Pauline before I start my shift. I'll see you later."

"Reconciling?" Gunnar asked.

"Nah, she's having car trouble. But it's a chance to see her."

Gunnar could hear Dominic's heartache but didn't understand how a man could let a woman get to him that way.

6

For the next two hours Gunnar sketched and refined ideas for several projects. It was gratifying work, but his eyes were getting bleary, his concentration slipping. A mega dose of caffeine in the form of diner coffee could be just the thing, so he threw the pencil and sketchpad on the bed and walked to the door, pulling on his jacket.

He was tempted to overlook the slight hesitation as his hand touched the doorknob. However, when he realized he kept to the outer edge of the stairs where they were less likely to creak, he couldn't deny the truth—he was avoiding Tessa. It didn't sit well with him. She didn't sit well with him.

But he refused to be driven off by a hundred and ten pounds of female flesh.

At the bottom of the stairs, he paused long enough to decide which way he wanted to leave. Turning right he let out a breath...and sucked it in again the instant he saw Tessa standing on a stool in front of the kitchen window. The lowering sun shimmered around her, exposing soft brown and red highlights in her hair as she stretched to hang a planter. She looked ethereal, unattainable. Incredible.

Spying him she twisted, shifted her feet. And wobbled. Side to side, back and forth.

Gunnar's heart wedged in his throat, and he

sprinted towards her.

She'd already regained her balance by the time he reached her, but he snatched her by the waist and set her feet on the tile floor.

He frowned down into eyes wide and brimming with confusion, but also something else. Instead of slowing to its natural rhythm now that she was safe, his heart continued to hammer.

"You must spend a lot of time picking yourself up off the floor," he said. Finding the need for distance, he thrust her away. "Give me that." Gunnar seized the plant and hung it on the hook above the sink.

Tessa clasped her hands together at her waist and swallowed as if in preparation to speak, but only looked at him with those huge green eyes.

Coffee wasn't worth this. He lifted a hand in an annoyed gesture and moved past her.

"Wait."

Gunnar turned and found himself mere inches from her, the toes of his boots grazing her canvas slip-ons.

"Thank you," Tessa said, her voice a husky whisper that shot unexpected arrows of heat to his gut.

It gave him an odd pleasure to discern that she was nervous, and this time it had nothing to do with fear and everything to do with his being a man and her being a woman.

There was no pleasure, however, in discovering that he was nervous, or to admit his heart had been in his throat even before she'd started to fall.

He was suddenly aware of her hand on his, of the welcome sensation of simple contact. Then, as if he had become a poisonous snake, she dropped her hand and stepped back.

"Um, would you care for some coffee, Mr. Mason?" Tessa asked, busying her hands taking out mugs. "It's fresh."

"No." A few minutes ago, he'd wanted nothing more.

"Are you hungry?"

His stomach grumbled, but he needed to get away from her and regroup. "No."

"Gunnar."

The pleading tone in her voice held him, and he realized she'd used his first name.

"Please, I want to talk to you if you don't mind."

He did. Very much. He took another step toward the hall. "I'm on my way out."

"It won't take a minute."

He stopped but didn't face her.

"I'm trying to be polite, Mr. Mason. The least you can do is listen to me."

There was that spark again, that hint of irritation. Maybe it would be worth his time to have a cup of coffee.

When he turned she was twisting a silver ring around her finger, but stopped when she saw him looking.

"OK. Talk."

He came back into the room and watched her pour the coffee. His pulse was leveling so he reached for one of a dozen cranberry muffins heaped on a plate and took a seat at the counter.

Tessa licked her lips and smoothed her hands on the front of her pants. This time he couldn't guess the cause for her unease. Did she find it difficult to confront people in general, or had she only now become aware, as he had, that they were alone in the house?

He sipped his black coffee and waited for her to speak.

"I have the receipt for the repairs," she said at last, and opened a drawer containing loose papers, pens and elastic bands.

He took the pink paper she held out. "I already paid for the damages."

"I just wanted you to see the receipt for the window and to give you this."

Tessa stood on tip toes to reach a cookie jar on top of the refrigerator. She removed the ceramic head of a spotted dog and reached inside, coming down with neatly folded bills.

"What's this for?" he asked looking at a hundred and seventy-five dollars cash.

"I ordered a new table online. It's cheaper than the one you broke."

Gunnar looked at her, disappointed when she looked away to toy with her hands once more.

"Shouldn't your brother pick the table?" he asked, stuffing the money in his front jeans pocket. He would give it back to Dom later.

"Yeah, like he knows anything about furniture." A small smile came and went. "I want you to tell me what really happened last night," she said in a quick burst.

"No, you don't," he returned.

Her brows drew together in consternation. "Yes, I do. And I would appreciate it if you were honest with me."

Gunnar bit into the muffin and propped an elbow on the counter. She sat beside him.

"Mr. —"

"If you call me Mr. Mason one more time we're going to have a problem."

"I think I have a right to an explanation. Why did you freak out and trash your room?" Tessa asked, faintly exasperated.

Gunnar swiveled on his stool and eyed her. "I didn't freak out. If I had, the bill would've been a lot higher."

Tessa bit her bottom lip and laid her palms on her knees. "OK, then, why the temper tantrum."

His lips twitched with amusement.

She was impressive.

"Trust me, you don't want to know, and I'm not going to tell you."

When she opened her mouth, he extended a finger to silence her.

"It doesn't matter. I'm leaving, so there won't be any more trouble."

"Leaving? Why?"

"That's not your business." He'd only just made up his mind.

"I wish you would stay."

The instant the words hit the air he knew she regretted speaking them. He found it fascinating; the downward flutter of her eyes, the sullen pout of those gorgeous lips, the twin creases in the center of her forehead. How could a face express so much in a split second?

"Dominic wants you to stay. If you're leaving because of me—because we don't get along—"

"I won't lie; you're part of the reason," he told her. "But it's not because we don't get along."

Her eyes grew wide, a sea of green bidding him to come in and test the water, stirring things he absolutely did not want stirred. Things that could get him in trouble if he didn't leave now.

He broke eye contact first, stood and moved to the doorway. "I'll be back for my stuff."

7

Wednesday morning brought the kind of rain that tempted a run to the basement to see if priceless keepsakes were floating away in marked boxes. Outside, the gutter under the oak tree was overflowing. It clogged every year. But today it was releasing a steady cascade of water onto some object below.

Tessa needed to find the object beneath it and silence that infernal noise before it drove her crazy.

A door slammed above her. Another sound that was wearing on her nerves. The last few days most of Dominic's conversations with Pauline ended with a slammed door. From what Tessa could overhear, part of the problem stemmed from their communication being limited mostly to phone calls.

That marriage needed help, and while Tessa couldn't provide it, she did have a connection and continued to take it to Him in prayer. So far nothing visible.

Maybe Dominic wanted to talk. Not long ago, he would have pickled himself in alcohol in lieu of verbalizing his feelings—a contributing factor in his current predicament.

She was happy the only bars he took interest in these days had weights on them.

Halfway up the stairs the phone rang, and she

walked back to answer it.

"He did it!" Connie's animated voice charged through the phone lines.

Tessa didn't have to be told who or what. "Oh! Did he get on one knee?"

"Yes." Connie's voice hitched. She sniffed. "Right in the mud outside my house."

"You mean today? In the rain?"

"This morning on his way to work. He said he couldn't wait another minute. It was so romantic. Dad doesn't know if he should cry or pitch a fit, and Mom is so happy."

Tessa's joy spilled into her laughter. Maybe one day it would happen to her. Then again, why rush it, she thought, as Dominic descended the steps looking angry and dejected.

"Hold on." Tessa put the phone to her shoulder. "Can I get you anything, Dominic?"

"Nah." He yanked his jacket off the hook by the door and set out in the rain.

"Tell me everything from the beginning. Did you set a date?" she asked as Dominic drove away.

By the time Tessa hung up some forty minutes later, the maddening rat-a-tat-tat of water was waning but her resolve to find the source was not. She took her yellow slicker from the hook near the back door, slipping it on as she stepped outside.

The buffeting rain had become a soft shower but far to the west, jagged stripes of baby blue streaked the sky. She drew in a long, satisfying breath before going around to the right side of the house until she came to the gutter where rainwater dripped onto a shiny object.

She stooped to recover a piece of alarm clock and rolled it in her hand, a smile lighting her face as she walked toward the front of the house to check the mail.

Then she looked up and her heart stuttered.

A black '67 Pontiac GTO was parked at the curb. Tessa recognized it from a poster Dominic used to have when they were kids. But that one hadn't had Gunnar leaning on the fender. This one did, looking ornery as usual.

He wore blue jeans and a white T-shirt under an open button-up shirt with no jacket.

She shivered when closer examination revealed he was soaked to the skin. Through the wet material she could make out part of the tattoo on his torso.

She would be lying to say he hadn't come to mind since his departure four days ago. Gunnar Mason was a tough man to erase from the memory banks, and only in part because of his lawless appearance and less than adequate social skills.

But also because even when his clothes weren't molded to his exceptional body as they were presently, he was frankly the most striking man she knew. She doubted many people would agree.

Society as a whole held somewhat inflexible concepts of beauty.

She had too, until she'd met him.

Still, what most affected her was the memory of his arms around her. Though brief, it had kindled an expectancy in her that she could summon with little effort. It was better ignored.

Staring at his body really wasn't helping so she focused on the way he looked standing there, reluctant but perturbed, like a rebellious school boy in front of the principal's desk.

Her amused chuckle earned her an irate glare.

"Something funny?"

It may have been Connie's joy rubbing off on her or the blue peeking through the dreary sky or just the pleasure of hearing his voice, however gruff, but her mood was the brightest it had been all week. She walked toward him, despite his staring in that guarded way that made her think he might tackle her to the sidewalk if she moved too fast.

"Aren't you cold?" Tessa stuffed the piece of clock into the pocket of her slicker.

"I'm hot blooded."

No doubt.

He wore the sleeves of his shirt rolled up, revealing powerful forearms shaded by dark hairs. A closer look at his face revealed the shadows under his eyes.

"What are you doing out here?" she asked.

"Wish I could tell you."

It was a strange answer even for him. When he didn't elaborate she kicked a small rock into the grass. "Do you want to come inside? It's a good day for tea."

When Gunnar pushed off the car and walked past her up the path, Tessa rolled her eyes at his back. She didn't know what to make of him. Or herself for that matter. The "bad boy" type didn't usually attract her, but she could hardly deny his allure.

Her mother would have a stroke if she knew; her father might raise a disapproving brow, and her brother...she already knew how Dominic felt.

Inside the foyer, Tessa pulled off the slicker and draped it on the newel post. "Would you rather have coffee?" she asked, leading the way to the kitchen.

"Yeah, whatever."

Gunnar sat at the end of the counter letting the muscular bulk of his back slouch onto the wall. He looked drained. As she made the coffee, the silence descended once again, and her nerves drew taut.

He wasn't much for socializing but if he didn't say something soon—

"I need a place to stay."

She managed to bank the zip of elation and keep it from her voice. "You know you could have called instead of standing in the rain. What if I hadn't come out?"

"I may need a week."

When she met his gaze he held it, waiting. "That's fine. I mean it's up to Dominic, but...yes, it'll be all right."

"I caught him on his way out before," Gunnar said. "He's OK with it if you are."

Tessa wondered how long Gunnar had been waiting in the rain. Dominic left nearly an hour ago, and he could have been out there even before that. Weird.

"Well of course," Tessa said.

Gunnar didn't answer, but pulled a roll of bills from his pocket and presented it to her.

"Put your money away," she said. "This isn't an inn."

She also wondered, since he seemed OK financially, why he didn't go to an inn or stay at a hotel until his house was finished. It would be rude to ask.

"I don't feel right staying here for nothing."

"Just don't break anything," she answered.

"I won't."

The tone in his voice stirred her compassion, and she sensed in her spirit that he was asking for more than a convenient place to stay. He was seeking refuge.

She didn't know from whom or what, and

although her mind warned her he could be unpredictable, possibly dangerous, she had peace about him staying.

Tessa pondered this new revelation as she poured the coffee.

He gave a sharp nod of thanks and sipped.

"I was going to make a sandwich, do you want one?" she asked after a lengthy silence.

"No, thanks."

More silence.

"You'll want to get out of those wet things," Tessa suggested, finally, reaching for the bread on the counter.

He tossed back the rest of the coffee. "Right. I'll go home and get some clothes."

She turned to him. "You came to ask if you could stay but didn't bring anything with you?"

Gunnar straightened away from the wall. "I wasn't sure you would take me back."

She regretted bringing her gaze back to his. All at once, she felt as though she was standing on a retaining wall on a stormy night while the ocean beat relentlessly against it. The fear and excitement were equally real, and the temptation to plunge in, both terrifying and persuasive. Her pulse mimicked the onslaught of the waves. Her lids fluttered in defense, before his eyes could pull her in and sweep her out to sea.

In a minute, she would remember what she was going to say. "Um." Any time, now. "Why wouldn't I?"

"Why wouldn't you what?"

Quite in opposition to the mayhem within her, he sounded at ease, slightly amused.

Forcing her eyes to remain open, she couldn't be sure if he was toying with her. Why would he? She attempted an extraction from the corner he had somehow boxed her in and collided into his chest as he got to his feet.

His hand was on her arm, hot, branding her flesh. Neither moved for some moments. Then his head bent fractionally toward her.

She should go, but her body simply dismissed the order to flee. A little woozy, she swung her free arm back in an attempt to steady herself, and sent Gunnar's empty mug crashing to the floor.

The haze of desire was broken along with the mug, its fragments sliding across the stone tiles.

Reflex had her pushing past him, and her fingers made contact with the hard slab of his stomach. She drew her hand back at once.

"Easy," Gunnar said softly. He took her hand and shoved aside a large piece of ceramic with his boot before she could step on it.

Tessa didn't answer as he steered her away from the mess. How could she when she was no longer in possession of the ability to speak or think?

It had to be the awkwardness of the situation that sensitized her so. As she opened the pantry for the broom, she could swear she felt him looking at her. When she glanced back, his gaze was wandering the length of her body.

Her lips parted. She skimmed the tip of her tongue over her top lip just as his gaze flashed to her mouth. She had the impression he wanted to say something.

He turned and walked out the front door, taking her breath with him.

❧❦

Tessa occupied her body with housework, cleaning the closet in the foyer and doing laundry. Occupying her mind was more difficult. She listened to music, preaching, and prayed, but each time she succeeded in clearing Gunnar from her head, it took mere minutes for him to refill it. She hoped it wasn't cause for concern.

He affected her like no one else—he made her wonder, and want. If he could do that in a week's time, during most of which he was absent, what could happen in two weeks? A month?

Oh, that was silly, she realized, arranging the chairs around the kitchen table. She would have her own place soon, or he would go away. Even if they had to coexist for a time, there was nothing to worry about. It wasn't as if he was trying to tempt her or anything. He probably hadn't given their encounter in the kitchen another thought. He probably didn't consider it an encounter at all.

With the house spotless and the rain once again suspended above the earth, Tessa decided to drive to the supermarket and pick up a few things for dinner. Along the way, it wouldn't hurt to scope out the area to see where she might want to set up shop.

Upper Montclair appealed to her with its stately homes, shade trees, and well-tended lawns, and though it might cost a small fortune to live there, she could manage if she handled her finances prudently. Prudent was practically her middle name.

The streets were wet and shiny when Tessa pulled into the grocery store lot. The air smelled of damp earth, and the aroma of onions drifted to her from the

Bell Diner next door. Looking through the huge plate glass window, she could see Lorelei leaning across a male customer to retrieve a half empty ketchup bottle, her breasts straining under the uniform blouse.

Why were some women so secure in their sexuality, Tessa marveled, with a little pang of wistful admiration? And others...weren't.

Her stomach rumbled, reminding her she hadn't eaten.

"Tessa!"

Her mother came out of the antique shop across the street. As always, the reaction was a fusion of suspense and annoyance, with a dash of hope sprinkled in. It would be nice to experience the type of pleasant mother/daughter exchange she'd seen demonstrated in other families. Instead, each time they met was a waiting game in which Tessa counted the minutes, often seconds, until the first criticism.

It was hard, but she accepted that their relationship would never be perfect. They loved each other, naturally, but Anna could relate to the women on the charity committee easier than her own daughter. Admittedly, hosting fashion shows or galas held no importance for Tessa.

Her grandmother had been a kind of mediator, bridging the gap whenever possible, but since she died, Tessa and her mother seemed to grow even further apart.

Anna didn't understand Tessa's desire to be a separate entity any more than Tessa understood her mother's aversion to the idea.

So each regarded the other as an alien presence, better left alone. Which might account for why Tessa called her mother, *Mom*, but thought of her as Anna.

No, it wasn't a perfect relationship, but it was all they had.

Her mother came to her with that effortless glide Tessa couldn't help admiring. At fifty-five years old, Anna kept in excellent shape. Four days at the gym saw to that. A skilled hand with a makeup brush and maintenance visits to Hugo Spa took care of the rest.

As a girl, Tessa yearned to look like her mother, but puberty had had different ideas. In her estimation she was a bit too tall, a bit too thin with eyes and mouth a bit too large for her face.

Anna by contrast, was dramatic and beautiful.

"Hi, Mom." Tessa kissed her flawless cheek.

"I haven't heard from you," Anna said. "Here you are, home a week and you haven't called. What are you doing around town?"

With the first dig out of the way, Tessa didn't bother to correct her mother and tell her she'd been back nearly three weeks and had called her when the plane landed. "I have to stop at the market. I'm making salmon for dinner—"

"I had salmon yesterday," Anna interrupted, digging in her designer bag for cigarettes and gold lighter.

The smell of tobacco stung the air, and Tessa watched the wind dash away the pale gray smoke stream. Anna lit only five cigarettes a day, so didn't consider herself a smoker.

"Oh, look at this. I just unearthed it at the cutest little shop. Can you believe the luck?" Anna took a small wooden box from her bag and opened the lid, revealing a silver figurine of a girl with a parasol. "Isn't this the most adorable salt cellar? They're holding one of a horse and rider on reserve, but I had to get this one before someone snapped it up."

"Great," Tessa said, uninterested. A knot of tension was already building at the back of her neck.

Anna put the box away. "You'll invite your father and me when you've found a place." It wasn't a question.

"Mom, you don't need an invitation, you're welcome any time."

"Call and tell me when it's good for you," Anna said. She took a drag of the cigarette and dropped it into the curb. "I'll be in touch. Now I'm going home to take a nap. A woman my age can't afford to miss any beauty rest." She took Tessa's chin in her hand and angled her face from side to side. "It couldn't hurt you either, you look dreadful. Why aren't you using the eye cream I sent you?"

In a self-conscious action, which she despised herself for, Tessa touched a fingertip to the fragile skin under her eye. Leave it to her mother to detect the puffy evidence of sleeplessness, and to mention it.

"Bye, darling."

Anna was gone, leaving in her wake the lingering trace of smoke and expensive perfume. And the headache that was steadily expanding to Tessa's temples.

ও—ৎ

Using the key Dominic gave him, Gunnar went into the house and locked the door behind him. He was glad not to see Tessa. She would feel obligated to greet him and make polite conversation. For some reason that irked him. She'd shown moments of promise, glimmers of life all her own instead of the required behavior of a woman raised to reflect someone else.

Dominic didn't go into detail on the subject of their upbringing; he didn't need to. It was obvious from the house, and reaffirmed with the shared looks and comments that Gunnar had picked up that day in the diner; the Silanos expected certain things of their children.

He found it both perverse and interesting that the children of parents with impossible expectations were often indistinguishable from those whose parents had no expectations at all. He and Dominic shared camaraderie in their efforts to be nothing like the people who'd reared them.

Tessa, however, was a people pleaser. Gunnar hated people pleasers.

Still, that took a special discipline, he considered, as he stepped into the master bedroom and threw his duffel bag and jacket on the bed. He respected discipline. Discipline and the strength of his will were what pushed him to be the best at whatever he did, that kept him fighting each day to fashion a life from the hell he'd endured. They were what had kept him from spraying his brains all over this room.

As for the nightmares…well, no strength of will could make them stop. They'd resumed when he returned to his bed. The night he spent at the motel had been no better, and cost him a hundred bucks extra for the hole he'd punched in the wall. For whatever reason, the only relief he could find was in this house, in this room, on this six by five foot blue rectangle.

He refused to view coming back here as a defeat, but rather a chance to prove his resolve in resisting the temptation that was Tessa. He could and would stay under the same roof without giving in to lust for a woman he didn't even like.

He'd flirted with her. Man! He never flirted, he took, he demanded. Yet, he could find no other word for the way he'd knowingly teased her, enjoyed causing her thoughts to scatter. Too late, he'd realized his mistake and the next instant was imagining all sorts of physical scenarios: Tessa in his arms. Tessa's hair tangled in his fingers...he had to escape before...well, *before*.

As he stretched on the bed, a fragrance drifted past his nose, sweet and mild, and he turned to the vase on the dresser, now filled with red flowers. They were yellow last time. Silly woman. Tessa should know men didn't notice those things.

8

Gunnar woke in the dark hours later to the same fragrance of flowers, but couldn't immediately recall his surroundings until his palm slid across the smooth fabric and his fingers met with silky braided tassels. He sat up and pulled the short chain on the lamp, bathing the room in soft yellow light. The word *home* barely formed in his mind before he stifled it. Those thoughts had to be subdued.

So did his appetite; his stomach rioted, demanding to be filled. The new clock next to the bed read five after twelve. It was the most he'd slept in some time. He took his jacket, felt in the pocket for his keys.

The aroma of food halted Gunnar at the bottom of the stairs. He tossed the jacket on the staircase rail and followed his appetite to the kitchen.

Tessa stood at the stove wearing a light blue satin robe and fuzzy orange slippers. A radio murmured softly from an unseen source. To her credit, she didn't scream when she saw him, though she did drop the spatula.

Gunnar stayed put, not wanting to frighten her further. He could see the pulse jumping in her throat from five feet away. "I didn't mean to scare you," he said.

"Well you do," Tessa snapped in reflex.

He frowned at the wording. Not he *had* scared her,

but he *did* scare her. It shouldn't have mattered, but it did.

She carried the spatula to the sink and rinsed it off. "Weren't you sleeping?" she asked, half turning toward him. When he looked quizzically at her she added, "I heard you around five or six, then it got quiet. Squeaky floor boards."

Keep it light, he told himself. "Where's Dom?"

"He stopped home to change and went to see Pauline. I expect he'll stay there tonight." She hesitated. "I guess he told you they're having problems."

"Yeah. Bad deal." He listened to the shuffle of her slippers on the floor, moving to the stove, "What're you making?"

"Eggs. Since Dom wasn't here, I didn't bother to cook dinner. Now, I'm hungry."

"Me too." He paused as she watched him. "Starving. I was heading to the diner, but I really don't want to go out."

She just stared.

"I'll pay you for some of those," he said with a nod toward the pan. As Gunnar watched, her face softened, her body relaxed.

"Is money your solution to everything?" She returned to the eggs.

Gunnar stared back at her. Growing up, money was always an issue because he hadn't had any. Now that he did, it tended to solve some problems.

"I don't want your money," she said, when he didn't answer. "Is an egg sandwich OK?"

When she turned, the look on her face awakened a heat low in his belly. Those fascinating, innocent eyes fixed for a second on his mouth; her tongue ran lightly across her full bottom lip. He wondered if she knew she was causing another kind of hunger to simmer inside him.

Oh, the idea of kissing her senseless was appealing—extremely—but the fact remained that she didn't simply *look* vulnerable, she was. It didn't matter that they were alone. There was a line. Drawing on his new resolve, he took a seat at the table.

"Fine," he answered at length. Though he kept his voice steady, his pulse throbbed erratically. The way she averted her gaze, more so than the way she looked at him, was making him nuts. He couldn't win. "Eggs," he mumbled so she couldn't hear. He was going to concentrate on eggs.

"I was going to have some warm milk. Can I get you some?"

"Warm milk?" Distracted by the way her robe parted slightly when she shifted, alternately revealing and concealing bits of shoulder and leg, he would have accepted a glass of snake venom.

"I try to avoid caffeine after nine," she said, depressing the toaster button.

"Sensible."

She bristled, but soon recovered. "My grandmother's advice. She was a very sensible woman."

He noted the past tense. "Can I have mine cold?"

Tessa slid the eggs onto toast and offered it to him. "You must be a lot hungrier than I am," she said. His sandwich disappeared in three bites. "The next one is yours, too."

Gunnar looked up at her in appreciation. "Thank you."

Tessa giggled. "It's just eggs."

"No, it isn't." He couldn't explain it had nothing to do with eggs or the cold milk she set in front of him. He couldn't recall the last time he'd shared a meal with a woman in her kitchen. Had he ever?

You'll never have this.

The words whispered past his brain and were gone.

He watched her break eggs. He liked watching her, as at ease in the home as he was in the shop. Different surroundings, but talent was talent wherever you found it. If she chose to use hers plumping pillows and picking up damp towels, that was her gig.

"What do you do?" he asked her, deciding he really wanted to know.

Her shoulders slumped. "I'm usually a lawyer, but I'm between jobs. You?"

The answer was short because she clearly didn't want to discuss it. His, for the same reason. "I build things."

She gave him another sandwich. "That sounds interesting."

He took his time eating so that she could join him with her own sandwich. It was out of character, but he didn't want to be alone, and although she evidently wasn't relaxed with him, he hung around after he finished.

He couldn't say they conversed because he wasn't big on words, but as she cleaned up she commented on grocery prices, chattered on about Connie's engagement, whoever Connie was, and asked him if he'd heard of Rosemont Stables, which it turned out, wasn't related to horses but with a swim team Dominic used to captain.

To his amazement, he didn't feel bored or

pressured to keep up, but actually started to unwind. Nursing his second glass of milk he wished she would go on talking but knew it wouldn't be long before she politely excused herself and went to bed. She probably hadn't been awake this long since the night he'd trashed his room. Which reminded him, he should speak to her about that.

When she rose from the table, he stood with her. In slippers, the top of her head came to his chin.

"I'm going up, too." He watched the wariness come into her eyes. "You don't have to worry. I promise I won't throw anything out the window. Or through it," he added when her lips parted. "But I have to tell you, while I'm here there could still be some… disturbances," he said, for lack of a better word.

Her brows knit together.

"I have dreams," he said flatly. "Nightmares." Her clear green eyes were wide with concern, but he pulled away when she would have touched his arm. "It's no big deal. I just wanted to tell you in case you hear anything unusual."

Before she formed a reply, he left her to her speculations and judgments. He went to his room ahead of her, knowing she would feel safer if they didn't climb the stairs together. Ignoring the little twist in his gut, he took his sketchpad and pencils out of his duffel bag and sat in the chair by the window with his long legs stretched in front of him.

He was who he was, and if he made her uncomfortable, he couldn't help it. He flipped to a clean sheet of paper and tapped the end of the pencil on his chin. He didn't know her well enough for her opinion to carry any weight—or anyone's for that matter.

But it bothered him anyway to think of her in her room, alone, with the blankets to her chin, anxiously awaiting his next explosion.

Gunnar gripped the pencil tighter. He didn't want to think of her at all, or dwell on the fact that she was getting under his skin. Not the irksome sort of under his skin, either, but the sort that made him think of her more frequently, in new and varied ways. If he didn't find a way to stop it, she would be in his blood before long.

Work was an excellent distraction. His hand moved across the smooth white plane of the pad, depositing ideas in the form of lines, thick and thin, curved and straight. He shadowed here, dashed there, until the abstract lines took shape under his adroit hand, and his basic sketch became a more definite outline he could visualize and work from. He drew the motorcycle from the side, front, rear, and top. It would be revised no less than ten times, adding and refining details, but he loved the process from concept to completion.

He paused to give the paper an objective review. The bike had decidedly feminine curves. Interesting. It wasn't a style he leaned toward, but it would be gorgeous.

As for styles that didn't fit—Tessa a lawyer? How had that happened? She was bright, incontestably, with great attention to detail, but it was hard to believe she possessed the killer instinct required to swim with the sharks. It might have figured into her being "between jobs."

With the rough draft finished and his pencil poised above a clean sheet of paper, the phone rang. Who would be calling at...he looked at the clock...two thirty-seven a.m.? It wasn't his house so he didn't answer, but when the ringing stopped, he guessed Tessa had. Must be Dominic.

Gunnar hiked his foot up across the opposite knee, his pencil trekking over the paper in quick, erratic movements. The ringing started again. Maybe Tessa was sound asleep and hadn't heard it after all. He should answer it. He let his foot fall back to the floor. Dominic wasn't home and it might be an emergency.

He walked to the table on the other side of the bed and answered the phone. "Hello."

Click.

It was crazy, especially knowing Tessa for so short a time, but in under three seconds his mind made the broad crossover from curiosity to suspicion. It was none of his business, but it rankled that it might be a man calling her.

To see if it was all clear to stop by.

He went back to the chair, back to work, but his gaze kept darting to the phone. It was realistic to presume there was a man in her life. She was a beautiful woman and sexy, no matter how she tried to underplay it beneath layers of modest clothing. More than that, she radiated warmth and kindness. It wasn't possible he was the only one who saw it or the only one who wanted to react to it.

His stomach knotted.

Gunnar glanced at the pad, not surprised to find her face looking back at him through trusting, luminous eyes. "Beautiful," he murmured, touching a finger to the page.

Beautiful women can't be trusted.

With a flick of his wrist, he tore off the paper, crumpled it, and threw it in the wastebasket.

Women are deceitful creatures.

A nasty thought, and Gunnar was tempted to say so aloud, but common sense came to the fore. Wrong numbers and prank phone calls happened all the time. He had no right to accuse Tessa of anything. She wasn't his property or his lover.

He ran a hand over his face. Man, his mind was getting the better of him.

Deceptive.

Or was *she* getting the better of him? Some women got their kicks from messing with a guy's head. Most women, in fact. Was Tessa so different? No. No one was that demure, that pristine. She was a lawyer. Lawyers were calculating and shrewd.

Deceptive.

He wasn't aware of snapping his pencil until he stuck his finger with a sharp edge. He cursed. So what if she was waiting for a man? It made no difference to him.

Yeah, sure it didn't.

❧

For the second time in five minutes, Tessa answered the phone to hear a dial tone. Half awake, her first concern was for Dominic. Perhaps he'd been injured on the job. He'd mentioned a rash of burglaries in the area, broadening steadily in their direction, the perpetrators increasing in their boldness and violence. But before fear could creep in, she remembered he was with Pauline tonight.

Maybe they'd argued and he'd come home, forgotten his house keys and was using the phone signal he'd used as a teenager when sneaking in after curfew. Ring once, hang up, call back. With her brain fuzzy from sleep she couldn't recall if it rang more than once.

She wouldn't rest unless she took a look outside, so Tessa pulled on her robe and set off downstairs.

The only light came from the small bulb in the range hood, but it illuminated enough of the hall that she could find her way. She went first to the front of the house, peering out the windows, but didn't see Dominic or his car. He wasn't at the back of the house either. Must be a wrong number.

As she started for the stairs, Gunnar was standing in the hall. The sight of him was enough to paralyze her vocal chords so she could no more than gasp. She slapped a hand to her chest to keep her heart from streaking off.

"Waiting for someone?" His words were sharp and laced with acid.

Perhaps she had startled him, too.

"No." She tried a slow, deep breath to return her pulse to its habitual pace. "The phone woke me. I thought it might be Dominic. You?"

"I was awake."

The words landed like an indictment. Tessa could guess no reason for it. A chill shot up her spine, but she ignored it.

He looked angry, his features hardened and severe, but he also looked burdened. He must have had another bad night.

Instinctively, she touched his arm. "Did you have a nightmare? Do you want—"

His iron fingers banded her upper arm. The rest of her words slid back down her throat.

"Don't ever touch me," he ground through

clenched teeth.

She wanted to scream, but fear squeezed her throat as firmly as his hand squeezed her arm. Demands for release, pleas for mercy boomed inside her brain but refused to become audible. What sound she could manage was a squeak in the back of her throat.

He continued to stare at her, eyes shuttered, revealing nothing.

"You'll touch me only if I want you to," Gunnar said, his tone velvet now, but still loaded with contempt. Standing toe to toe with her, he ran his hand possessively up her free arm, then down to grasp her hand in his. "And when I want you to," he said, laying her stiff, trembling fingers on his chest.

She couldn't fathom why Gunnar would deliberately want to hurt her when she had done nothing to him, but then, she didn't know much about him except that he could be aggressive and was tormented by nightmares. Such a man might be capable of anything.

Her mind raced through acres of senseless terrain. They were alone in the house. If he attacked her, she stood no chance to fight him off. Aside from his obvious size and strength, he carried a gun.

Seconds seemed like minutes before a beacon arose in the midst of the turbulent sea of thought. Forcing her vocal chords to cooperate, she murmured, "Jesus."

As unexpectedly as it ensnared her, Gunnar's hold loosened.

Tessa broke free and ran to her room, slamming the door behind her. She berated herself for forgetting to ask Tom to install a lock when he was here. Fear sprang on her, harsh and vivid, as she watched the door, expecting Gunnar to burst through any time. She grabbed the cordless phone, ready to punch in 911.

A few seconds later, she heard the drumming of heavy boots up the stairs and along the hall, followed by the slam of his bedroom door.

9

Gunnar had made her more afraid than she'd been in her life, but she didn't call the police station or try to contact Dominic. Instead, she dragged a dresser in front of her door, drew her knees up to her chest on the bed and shivered for nearly an hour. She felt as though she'd seen it in a movie, not experienced it firsthand.

She was far too frazzled to risk sleep. Neither would she go out that door until she knew he was out of the house.

Tessa took a shaky breath. She hated being wrong. She had begun to trust him. OK, trust might be too strong a word, but she hadn't been *as* afraid of him. Having once modified her first impressions of him from dangerous lunatic to antisocial outcast, that view needed further amendment.

Her mother's voice rang in her ears, telling her she was too trusting. The possibility her mother was right would add to her anxiety if she dwelled on it, so Tessa tried to distract her mind with Connie's bridal shower, house hunting—anything to crowd Gunnar out of her head. All useless. Her gaze kept returning to the blockade in front of the door, her mind to its necessity.

She couldn't understand it. Their time spent eating egg sandwiches had been pleasant. Though a bit tense, Gunnar was more approachable than she'd ever seen him. Then suddenly he transformed into Mr. Hyde.

How could Dominic befriend someone who behaved that way?

Tessa's lids were weighted, but when she closed her eyes, she felt the nudge inside her. Recognizing it instantly as the Holy Spirit, she began praising God for His protection and mercy. After delivering her safely from Gunnar's threat, she expected the words to feel more genuine but they felt stilted, repetitive. She continued on.

It didn't take long for God to bring her to the point.

Gunnar is hurting. Pray for him.

Tessa paused. So? He should be after what he did. She pulled down the collar of her robe far enough to find the marks on her upper arm where his fingers had dug in. He was an animal, living in captivity, but never really tamed. Never to be trusted.

She sprang from the bed and paced the carpet. Gunnar is hurting. Hah! She doubted he felt anything but rage. And why should she care? She hadn't heard of him before last week, and soon he would be gone from her home and her life. Thank God.

She stopped, crossed her arms and tapped her foot. It wasn't often she disregarded a direct order. She wouldn't now, but since God knew her thoughts anyway, she decided to air them.

"I don't want to pray for him," Tessa said aloud. "He's arrogant, nasty, abusive, and even though I believe You're always with me, he frightens me."

The enemy wants you to fear.

Tessa didn't want to hear, but she felt each syllable deep in her spirit. She nibbled her thumbnail. Even knowing it was the right thing to do, and being urged by the Holy Spirit to view the situation objectively through spiritual eyes, praying for Gunnar seemed next to impossible. She could chalk Gunnar's warning not to touch him up to his nature—he wasn't good with people. And looking back, she could even accept he hadn't meant to bruise her—he didn't know his strength. But how could she be expected to forget his suggestive words, and more than that, the demeaning intention behind them?

Tessa moved to the window, but not to view the gray on gray clouds stacking to the west or the swirl of leaves blowing across the sidewalk. She closed her eyes, and asked God for the grace to help her forgive Gunnar's barbaric behavior. She considered the shock and confusion in Gunnar's eyes when he released her, emotions mirroring her own, though at the time she was too engulfed in fear to care.

His aggression seemed to come out of nowhere, and reflecting, he'd appeared as shaken as she, as though he couldn't help himself. He was obviously in some kind of emotional crisis.

Tessa returned to the bed and stared at the ceiling. She recognized that in order to have a relationship, both parties needed to have a say, so she lay in silence listening for God's side. One by one, verses of Scripture came to mind. Some she knew off hand, others were vaguely familiar, but God was plainly speaking to her.

As she continued in prayer, three things became clear. First, and most astounding—Gunnar was the person she'd been praying for all this time. She had to chuckle at God's sense of humor and wisdom, having put her in the routine of praying for Gunnar before they'd even met. Knowing that once they had, she wouldn't want to.

The second revelation was that a major event was

happening in his life, and third, she was being charged to cover him in prayer so he could get through it.

After being gently chastened, Tessa repented of her stubbornness and fears. Gunnar's problems didn't excuse his behavior, but her heart was softened enough to pray for him. And herself while she was at it. The next time she saw him, she wouldn't cower. He wouldn't want to hear her, but she would have her say and clear the air. Closing her eyes, she prayed until sleep enfolded her.

☜∼☞

Tessa was horrified when she opened her eyes. The clock hands were in all the wrong places. She had overslept by five hours! Right before sheer panic set in at being unspeakably late for work, she remembered she was unemployed. She got up anyway, showered and dressed.

"Since when do you get up at eleven?" Dominic asked from the kitchen table the moment she entered.

"I don't."

Her curt reply caused him to glance up from the morning paper. "You OK?"

"Fine. Sorry."

Tessa picked up the coffee pot but rather than withstand Dominic's coffee, dumped the contents in the sink and started fresh.

"That's just wrong," he said.

"Sorry, I can't get used to drinking sludge," she replied, pushing down the tangle of nerves coiled in her stomach. She concluded it would do no good to disturb Dominic with an account of the confrontation with Gunnar. She could handle it.

But guilt niggled. "Why are you here?"

"I live here. It's where I keep my razor and my lousy coffee."

"When did you get in?" she asked.

"Missed my curfew, Mom. Sorry."

Her shoulders slumped. "I don't want to be nosy. I don't know when you're coming or going."

"I'm flexible. It works for me." He sipped from his cup, grimaced, and rose to pour his concoction in the sink. "Like your organization and timetable work for you."

Tessa paused with the coffee can in her hand and frowned a little. "You make me sound rigid and boring."

"Never boring."

She turned back to the task at hand. "I saw Mom yesterday."

Dominic tossed the paper aside and the sports section slid to the floor. "You're not her, Tessa. Just because you're organized doesn't make you a condescending pain."

She pushed the on button and retrieved the paper but stopped before she could reinsert the sports section in the proper order. She set the whole thing aside to prove she could.

"See?" Dominic said, grinning at her self-control. "She would have made me pick it up."

Tessa smiled. He was in a good mood today. "How'd it go with Pauline?" she asked hopefully.

"Slept on the couch. Bummer. But I'm meeting her for dinner tonight. We're going to talk some more." His roguish tone told her he hoped for more than talk.

"It'll all be OK, you'll see," she said, opening the refrigerator. "Do you want an omelet?"

"No thanks. I grabbed something on the way home. Oh, by the way," he said, leaning back against the counter and resting his palms on the edge. "There'll be a vacancy in the building down the block from the firehouse. The guy who lived there slipped in the tub and broke his neck. It isn't in the paper yet."

Tessa shivered delicately. "No, thanks." She started to reach for the eggs when the memory of sharing them with Gunnar changed her mind. Cereal would do.

"You're too sensitive. People die at home all the time; someone has to move in afterward. There's a place right on Bloomfield Avenue if you don't mind blood stains."

She took the milk from the fridge and jabbed him in the ribs with it. "Jerk."

"Hey, I'm a cop. Can I help it if I have an inside track?"

She took out a bowl, pulled a spoon from a drawer. "I talked with a realtor. I'm looking for a house."

"No kidding?" Dominic asked.

Tessa gave a half shrug. "Makes sense."

"I think that's a great idea."

Happiness flooded her and she felt foolish. "Yeah?"

"You get to shovel your own snow, rake your own leaves, weed your own garden—what's not to love?" Dominic poured the cereal into Tessa's bowl, added milk and helped himself to a spoonful of frosted wheat.

She lifted one brow. "You sure you don't want breakfast?"

"I don't want to fill up. I'm meeting Gunnar at the

gym."

"Oh." At the mention of his name, her heart fell to her knees. She paused, wondering if she should ask… "He left already?"

"Yeah." Dominic poured a cup of Tessa's fresh coffee. "He was leaving when I came in."

"Is he always so…surly?" she asked.

Dominic sipped and returned to his spot at the counter. "More so, lately. Are you having a problem with him?"

Tessa observed her brother's sudden alertness and forced a smile. "No, no problem. He makes me a little on edge, that's all."

Dominic laughed. "If he didn't, he wouldn't be Gunnar." He took a good swallow, hissing when the coffee burned his throat. "You want me to talk to him?"

"And tell him your little sister is scared of the big, bad man? No way." She thrust her chin at him. "And I'm not scared. Bad manners are annoying, but nothing to be afraid of."

"That proves you aren't Mom. She's terrified the social construct will collapse if you don't use the right fork at dinner." He gulped the rest of his coffee, put the mug in the sink and kissed her on the cheek. "I'm going right to work from the gym." He paused on his way to the back door and snapped his fingers. "Oh, Connie called."

"Shoot!" Tessa thumped her forehead with her fist. "I was supposed to get together with her."

"So she said."

10

Gunnar's knuckles whitened on the steering wheel as he whizzed past the other cars on the road, just blurs of color. He didn't really care if he arrived in one piece, but since he didn't want to kill anyone else, he eased off the accelerator.

He couldn't shake this unsettled, agitation. Since meeting Tessa, his life had taken a disturbing twist, and he was agitated ninety percent of the time. He punched the radio button off. Nah. His life had always been a twisted mess thanks to his bad choices. This time, however, he hadn't seen the bend in the road, and had been nailed head-on by a five-foot five, green-eyed compact.

Deciding at the last second to stop for gas, Gunnar hit the brakes and yanked the wheel hard.

The driver of the car behind him swerved just in time, then leaned on his horn, shouting his opinion of Gunnar's driving skills through the window.

Gunnar was too wrapped up in his review of the last few days to mind. He'd made a huge mistake going back to Dominic's house. After damaging property and upsetting Tessa, it should have been simple to stay gone.

Gunnar got out of the car and slammed the door, causing the guy at the next pump to flinch. He'd rather pump his own gas than wait. He had to be moving, doing something.

It was possible he was losing his mind. What had he done to Tessa? Whatever it was it must have been terrible. He recalled leaving his room, his mind filled with images of her meeting a man at the door, and being upset to find her smiling. It didn't make sense, but it was what he remembered.

She touched him and he'd wanted to be pleased, but then...he couldn't wrap his brain around it. There were chunks of his memory missing.

He'd touched her. Or she touched him. No, it had to be his doing because she looked scared. He could still picture her running blindly toward the stairs, her hair flying behind her.

Because of him.

He had a bad feeling the images he couldn't bring to mind were the very ones he needed.

He had to apologize, and that ate at him. On the rare occasion he apologized, it was to make himself feel better. But this time he would mean it.

He could see her face, the disorientation and horror, her cheeks drained of blood, her lips quivering, but forming no words. He wished he could change what happened, but she would never believe him.

What could he say to her, anyway? That jealousy had driven him downstairs to begin with? The idea was as crazy as expecting her to believe it.

Back on the road, he waited at a light, his foot itching to make the transition from brake to gas. The second it turned green the car behind him beeped. He glanced in the mirror to see who could possibly be more impatient than him, but the space behind him was clear. Weird.

He returned his attention to the road, was about to

touch foot to pedal when a dump truck raced through the red light, causing the front of his truck to shimmy in its wake.

Gunnar might not have even registered how close he had been to total annihilation if not for the horrified, open mouthed expressions of other drivers across the intersection. He spotted a woman on the sidewalk holding both hands firmly over her mouth, her eyes wide and disbelieving. It must have looked pretty bad to them, too.

His heart smacked his ribs as he drove away, grateful he wasn't part of a dump truck's front grill and remembering this wasn't the first time he could have been killed in recent weeks. The bike falling from the stand and missing his head by inches certainly would have crushed his skull, and the fall he'd almost taken down the basement steps...

He shivered, then shook the creepy feeling away. He had to be more careful.

Dominic's car wasn't in the gym lot, so Gunnar went inside to the nutrition center for a bottle of water. Some would call it a glorified juice bar where patrons could sample anything from kelp shakes to power bars with ground insects.

To him it was a thinly veiled singles' bar where Spandex-swathed women propped themselves in their most appealing arrangements, hoping to gain the attentions of vain, tanned men, most of whom were too engrossed in one another to notice. The one thing it had going for it was that from here he would be able to see Dom when he came in.

But when a curvy redhead sent him a smile and a wink, Gunnar left and walked into the main gym area. Right now he had enough on his mind. He straddled an empty preacher curl bench and twisted the top off the water.

Beside him, a man with four world bodybuilding titles to his credit made guttural sounds like a wounded animal as he curled dumbbells that weighed more than some adults.

On the other side a man wearing a muscle shirt, draped loosely on an inadequate frame, shouted encouragement to his girlfriend as she squeezed out reps on the fly machine.

The room smelled of sweaty vinyl and resonated with the sounds of hissing breath, grunting, and metal plates slamming back to their starting places. Someone called a greeting, and he lifted a hand in reply, but still he thought of Tessa.

Slender and sensuous, with eyes that inspired men to write love songs—and him to think that way—she had no clue how attractive she was, which only increased her appeal. And she was completely oblivious to the power—yes, *power*, he admitted reluctantly—she held him with. If he believed in such things, he would swear she'd cast a spell on him. How else could he explain that, when he should be running as far from her as he could, he sought refuge under the same roof? Brilliant.

Across the room, a woman with arms almost as large as Gunnar's checked her body for definition and symmetry in a floor-to-ceiling mirror. Gunnar sipped from the bottle and replaced the cap. If Tessa was built like that, he wouldn't look twice.

But Tessa was lean and graceful as a cat. She reminded him of a feline in disposition too; jumpy one minute, mildly annoyed by his presence the next. He had seen her angry and liked it, but never again wanted to see her afraid, especially of him.

Gunnar crossed his arms on top of the machine and looked through the tinted window to see Dominic's car pulling into the lot.

Tessa was a strange creature. She hadn't made him leave when he'd given her ample reason to do so, and going by the smile on Dominic's face as he stopped to exchange pleasantries with an acquaintance in the lot, she hadn't told him, either.

Gunnar adjusted the weight on the machine and exhaled as he pulled the weight, squeezed. She was special, but it could be only a matter of time before his friendship with Dominic was tested. No woman was worth risking the best friend he had.

❧

With a dust rag tucked into the belt loop of her trim khaki slacks, Tessa pushed and pulled the heavy vacuum across the living room rug. She'd called Connie to apologize, telling her she slept in because she was praying into the wee hours. True, but again, only partially. She couldn't tell Connie what happened with Gunnar. She'd rehashed it a dozen times, and it still made no sense.

The sooner she moved the better, but she wouldn't settle for any of the former crime scenes Dominic suggested, and the realtor who phoned earlier to tell her a new house had been listed, called back two hours later to say it was sold.

On the brighter side, Gunnar couldn't stick around indefinitely.

She turned. Startled to find him only steps away, she screamed and fumbled for the off switch.

It might be funny, she thought, as she wound the cord around her finger to keep her hands busy, how her resolve to face him had been so fierce when barricaded in her room, but melted away when he came into view. It might be, if it happened to someone else.

Tessa concluded it was due at least in part to his appearance. If he didn't go out of his way to look so threatening, to be so muscular and, and, tattooed, her heart wouldn't be bouncing off her ribcage.

She bit the inside of her cheek. He wore jeans and a gray T-shirt with a decal of a woman draped over the hood of a sports car. He smelled of clean laundry and soap. His hair was growing in, one black millimeter at a time and judging by the shadows under his eyes he hadn't slept. Somehow, he presented a less dangerous figure. And a more appealing one.

Shocked by the direction of her thinking, she pulled the cord tighter, and tried to concentrate on the blood rushing to her fingertip while she waited for him to speak.

"I had nowhere else to go last night," Gunnar told her. His voice was brusque, but edged with guilt.

Something in Tessa, purely female and having nothing whatsoever to do with spiritual matters, relished it. He met her gaze briefly, the muscle in his jaw clenching and unclenching.

"I waited for the cops but they didn't show," he said.

Tessa's finger began to throb, and she released the electrical cord. "I didn't call them." Her voice was steady despite the nerves.

"You didn't tell Dom, either. Why?"

Several answers came to mind but she settled on,

"I just didn't."

When he came forward, she backed away.

Gunnar froze, watching her carefully. The next time he moved it was to take a step backward. "Why, Tessa?"

"I didn't want to answer a bunch of questions," she answered with a half-truth.

Gunnar's eyes narrowed. "You're lying." When she opened her mouth to deny it, he raised an accusing finger. "Unless you're one of those chicks who likes to get pushed around by men."

Her temper rose, but then his gaze sharpened on hers, giving her reason to believe he was trying to make her angry enough to tell him the truth.

She decided to do just that. He wasn't going to like it. "I think at first I went in shock."

The prompting gleam in his eye vanished, replaced by marked discomfort.

"Then I started to get mad…"

His brows knit together.

"And then I prayed for you."

Gunnar looked as though she'd just told him he was on fire. "Why?" he demanded.

"Because you need it."

He hooked his thumbs in his front pockets and shifted from one foot to the other. Flabbergasted was one way to describe him. Nervous was another. Because both were so unusual for him, Tessa found it more than a little difficult to keep the mirth from her tone.

"I'm sorry if it bothers you," she said, unplugging the vacuum. "If it makes you feel any better, I didn't want to."

"You're nuts."

This time when he came closer, she didn't back away, but kept a close eye on his movements.

"You're a *Christian*." He pronounced it like one of his colorful expletives.

She lifted her chin. "Yes."

"Figures."

Gunnar stalked out and pounded up the stairs. She braced for the slamming of the door, but it didn't come.

In fact, no sound emanated from above for thirty minutes, during which time Tessa finished tidying, then decided to mop the kitchen floor, though it didn't need it.

She was hoisting a bucket filled with soapy water from the sink when she saw Gunnar in her peripheral vision. Stopping short, water sloshed onto the floor.

"Will you stop doing that?"

"What?" he asked, reaching behind her for the mop leaning against the door frame.

She froze long enough to see his intent before swiping the long handle from him. She'd had time to ruminate on their earlier exchange. Time enough to shore up her nerve should they have another clash, which wasn't as difficult as she might have guessed. An attack on her faith dispatched her anxiety faster than anything.

"Stop sneaking up on me. Every time I turn around—"

"You should pay more attention."

"And don't cut me off when I'm talking," she said.

Gunnar watched her blandly.

"Could you?" She gestured for him to move back so she could sop up the water.

He complied. "Do you have a minute?"

Tessa plunged the wet mop back into the bucket. She didn't want to be cornered, so she motioned him back further to allow access to the hallway. She may not be afraid of him at the moment, but there was no way of predicting what else could set him off.

More confident with multiple exits, she leaned on the mop handle. "What is it?"

His mouth thinned. He rolled his shoulders as an athlete might before an event. "I want to apologize. I seem to be overreacting to everything. It's no excuse, but I'm under a lot of stress."

He wasn't himself. Apologizing for his behavior definitely wasn't his style. It couldn't be easy for him. It shouldn't be.

"I don't know what happened. I wish I did," he said.

Her compassion awakened, but knowing it could be foolish to let him see how soft she really was, she fixed him with the most unaffected look she could manage.

She felt worse when he quietly walked away.

She was still wrestling with it when she heard his car start and speed down the block.

❧❧

Three cups of coffee persuaded Tessa to rearrange all the cookware in the pantry. It was a bigger job than anticipated but she hoped to be finished by dinner.

While her mother could barely find the kitchen with a GPS, Grandma Isabella had loved to cook and kept a full stock of cookware on hand for when she visited. There were pots and pans, some gadgets Tessa couldn't identify, much less use, and more dessert molds than she'd imagined existed. She found it hard to believe anyone would want an armadillo shaped dessert, but she was prepared in any event.

"Yoo-hoo!" Connie called as she flounced through the back door.

"Oh, hey. I wasn't expecting you."

"I can tell." Connie set her purse and briefcase on a chair and surveyed the mess.

"I'm trying to get a grip on things here," Tessa said.

Connie picked up a metal circle held together by a clamp. "Where does this go?"

"Inside that bigger circle there." Tessa squatted in the midst of a sea of plastic and metal. She'd modified her idea of grouping things by size to grouping by shape. It wasn't working any better.

"I'll give you half my savings to end this misery right now," Connie said.

Tessa laughed. "Half of nothing is nothing."

"Come on, I left the office a little early. It's warm, let's go out."

"Out where?"

"Who cares? Out is out. This stuff'll be here when you get back."

"That's what I'm afraid of." But the offer tempted.

"We'll take a drive, grab some dinner. My treat," Connie said, clasping her hands together under her chin. "Please."

"Dinner? It's only..." Tessa glanced at the clock. How could that be? She was losing track of time too often lately.

"It's going on five," Connie said.

Tessa stood and looked down at herself. Her pants were dusty, her shirt wrinkled and she smelled of cleaning solution. "You'll have to up the ante."

"We'll go someplace with real glasses," Connie said.

"No plastic forks?" Tessa asked, leery.

"I promise."

"Deal."

"Great, but I have to warn you I'm going to ask you to be my maid of honor, so maybe you should make yourself more presentable."

"Oh!" Tessa drew Connie into a tight squeeze. "Yes, I'll be your maid of honor!"

Connie's face shone with joy. "You can't accept until I ask you officially. I have it all planned."

"OK, I'll be quick."

Tessa changed in record time and stepped into the hall outside her room as the front door opened downstairs. She caught her breath. Dominic wouldn't be home yet. That left one person. Wonderful. If Gunnar walked into the kitchen...with Connie...

Tessa made a bee-line to intercept, but all hope was dashed when she heard the astonished, "Wow."

Tessa bit down on her bottom lip as she entered the room in time to see Connie approaching Gunnar with the boldness of an ill-behaved puppy.

"You have to be Gunnar." Connie's countenance was as bright as her voice and when he only stared at her, she drew closer.

Gunnar slid his gaze to Tessa then back to Connie, who was circling him like a rancher around a bull at auction.

"Is that a tattoo?" Connie asked, indicating the back of his neck. Gunnar didn't reply, and Connie picked up her things, unperturbed. "Well, it's nice to kinda meet you. Come on, Tess, I'm starved."

When he turned to watch Connie move toward the door, and his shirt stretched taut over his back, Tessa noted the portion of tattoo peeking from his collar. Funny she hadn't seen it until now.

She should have taken advantage of Connie's exit and left, but pride restrained her.

Gunnar's attitude in general was disgraceful, but Connie was her best friend.

"Connie, this is Mr. Mason." She saw the muscle in his jaw twitch. "Mr. Mason, this is Connie. She's a friend of the family. My best friend."

Gunnar responded with a negligible lift of his chin, more than Tessa hoped to get.

"I'll be right there," she said to Connie.

Connie reluctantly departed with a final backward look, her cell phone already open.

"You have no manners at all, do you?" Tessa snapped at Gunnar the moment they were alone.

"Very few," Gunnar answered. "My head is splitting. Do you have aspirin? Anything?"

She felt bad at once, but with his standard scowl in place, how was she to tell he was in pain? She sighed. "Yes, of course."

She went into the hall to the half bath on the left. Reaching toward the medicine cabinet, she gasped when she looked in the mirror to find him behind her. Since it was impossible to keep her distance in a room barely large enough for her alone, it was critical to keep her composure.

"I can get it myself," she said evenly.

His eyes darkened, and though he didn't shift, she felt more crowded.

"What is it about you?" he asked.

"What?" she squeaked, then cleared her throat.

"Something makes me want you," he replied bluntly. "And at the same time be rid of you."

"What a thing to say," she said, her voice dropping to a whisper. As she watched in the mirror, his hand came slowly to her throat. She would have prepared to fight, but the sensation of his rough palm on her skin was so tantalizing she simply couldn't ready a proper defense.

His hand was wide and calloused, his fingers strong and sure as he rubbed them along her throat and jaw, seeming to experiment with the texture of her skin, transforming the contact from that of warning to wanting. No less threatening.

She had more to lose this way.

He slid his hand to the back of her neck and into the yard of thick hair hanging loose there. His other hand traveled to her waist, his thumb drawing small circles on her ribs.

"I have no idea how you get to me this way, but it's all I can do to keep from finding out."

His voice, thick as honey, seeped into her ear and multiplied heat throughout her body.

She wanted to close her eyes and let the sound of it wash her away, but she had stood here before, at this precipice where he could either ground her, or let her fall, and it would be unwise to disregard the danger.

He turned her slightly toward him, and her gaze came to rest on his firm, unsmiling mouth. He drew closer, so close she could feel the heat of his lips on hers. She didn't want to look into his eyes. Too dangerous. He left her no choice when his fingers constricted in her hair and coaxed her face up.

"Maybe it's the contradictions." His voice was cooled enough to sharpen the edges already rough with repressed need. "The way you're coy and distant with me until I'm this close to you." He watched her so intently.

Her eyes grew heavy, her mind clouded.

"Then I see the change in you. I see that you want me, too."

"I don't want you," she said, but her voice was weak, unconvincing. "Let me go."

He held her a few more seconds before stepping back. "Whatever you say."

Tessa fought to control her breathing. And her embarrassment, when it slowly dawned on her that she wasn't distressed because he'd almost kissed her again, but because he hadn't, again.

He was definitely toying with her.

Well, she wouldn't allow it to continue. She needed to draw a boundary even he would understand.

As she skirted past him and back into the kitchen she silently asked God for help. God was the One Who prevented her from calling the police or telling Dominic, so He was responsible, right?

"Yeah, you're full of contradictions," Gunnar said from the bathroom. "Or should we call it what it really is?"

"What are you talking about?"

Tessa heard the medicine cabinet open, close, and the rattle of pills as he emerged with the small plastic bottle of aspirin in his hand.

"The role you play. The one where you come off all concerned, but underneath you're just a snob. Doesn't your religion call that hypocrisy?"

Prompted by adrenaline, Tessa took a glass, filled it with tap water and thrust it at him. She wouldn't give him the satisfaction of answering.

"Hmm."

Something in the one syllable put her back up. "'Hmm', what?"

Gunnar swallowed the pills, set down the glass, then picked an apple out of a large silver bowl and bit in. "Contradictions again. I don't get how you can be so pious, but not defend yourself. Oh, unless it's the martyr thing."

"Why are you doing this?"

He took his time answering, eating the apple, and in the meantime fixing her with that uninterested look she was beginning to loathe.

"What's the matter, princess? Don't appreciate being the one examined for a change?"

Tessa planted her fists on her hips and met his insolent eyes with sparks of her own. "You're being a jerk."

Gunnar arched a mocking brow. He took another bite. "There's also that condescending tone."

"I don't have a tone."

"Come to think of it, I don't know if you think you're above me...or everyone," he said, half to himself.

"You're out of line."

"Am I?" He started to leave.

Tessa grabbed his arm.

He tensed, but when she feared he would lose control he took his time in turning to her. She took several cautionary steps away and glanced toward the window. Knowing that Connie waited outside gave her a small measure of reassurance.

He watched her eyes. "Careful, highness. If your friend hears us argue she might stop believing you're perfect."

Tessa felt her face shading red, her ears burning with heat. "I have no intention of arguing with you."

"But you'd love to. I bet she'd be shocked to learn what thoughts are going through that gorgeous head of yours. The things you'd say to me if you could bear to bring yourself down to my level."

Gunnar brought his hand up but froze when she flinched. He let out a frustrated throaty sound. "I'm not going to hit you. Is that what you think of me?"

She didn't answer. After their earlier episode and having only moments ago expressed a latent wish to have her out of his life, what was she to say?

"OK." Gunnar nodded. "I deserve that." He tossed her the half eaten apple and walked away.

11

Tessa tried to enjoy a meal with her best friend, but the words Gunnar had hurled at her, left an ache deep inside. Her sulky, petulant reaction made it easy to identify—wounded pride.

Through the long-sleeved shirt, she rubbed her arms where his fingers dug in that morning. His words hurt more. She didn't think she was condescending, but was she? She'd certainly never intended to judge him.

Yet she had since first setting eyes on him.

Gunnar was right. And barring her pride, no matter how crude or angry he'd been, one minute threatening to seduce her, the next throwing her faults in her face, she felt awful. It gave her much to ruminate, but this wasn't the time.

She looked at Connie, patiently sipping diet cola from a tall glass. Waiting for Tessa to spill her guts.

"I'm sorry, Connie. My mind took a vacation."

"Start at the beginning," Connie said, swirling ice around with her straw.

"The man is impossible," Tessa blurted.

"I saw."

Tessa waved the comment away while the waiter cleared their salads. "Never mind."

"Forget it. You're already in too deep."

"Do you realize on a list that includes my mother,

you're the nosiest person I know?"

"Yes," Connie agreed. "Why don't you get it off your chest? You're dying to."

Yes she was, if for the sole purpose of hearing aloud how crazy it sounded. Still, some things went beyond gossip and the need to defend herself. Personal things she wouldn't discuss for Gunnar's sake. Or her own.

"There isn't much," Tessa said.

"Uh, uh." Connie snatched another piece of bread from the straw basket. "You told me enough to divert me once and I fell for it, but now I want the goods, the real stuff."

"Let's wait until we get our food."

Like a magician's bunny, the waiter appeared at the table and laid down their plates. Well, no point evading.

Gunnar had already made an impression on Connie. One not likely to be erased from her mind.

"Maybe discussing it isn't a good idea," Tessa said honestly.

Intrigued, Connie leaned conspiratorially closer. "Why, is it juicy? Are you two...getting close?"

A good question, Tessa conceded. She supposed they were, in some befuddled way.

"No, you'd tell me, right, Tess?" Connie asked.

Tessa looked around to see the other diners occupied with their food. "No, I'm not involved with him, Connie. He's a guest, my brother's friend. It's just...nothing."

Connie grabbed Tessa's wrist as she reached for her water glass. "I saw the way you looked at him," she said. "You're tied in knots."

Tessa started to deny it, but Connie plowed on.

"I know how it is. Mike does the same thing to me. Half the time I can't think of anyone or anything else. He can make me happy or drive me insane in a snap. I want to talk to him about anything just to hear him talk, and when he laughs it's…a gift."

Connie's eyes sparkled when she spoke of the man she would spend the rest of her life with.

"Well it isn't that way with me and Gunnar," Tessa said thoughtfully, before reason hit her. "There is no me and Gunnar. We have Dominic in common, that's all. He's staying until his house is finished and he's leaving."

Connie grinned. "Whatever."

Tessa bit into her grilled chicken, hoping to keep her mouth full and leave no room for her foot.

"Why didn't you tell me how hot he is?"

Tessa almost choked. "What?"

"I'm engaged, not blind. I mean, you said he was well built, but I didn't picture that. He's built like a heavyweight boxer."

"Connie." She had no retort. "You're right, he is hot."

Connie slapped the wood table and gave a hoot that caused most heads to spin in their direction. "You're bad, Tess, living with that—I always hated the word *hunk*, but it fits."

"I don't live with him."

"Sorry, cohabitate. Come on, give me a scrap," Connie said around a mouth full of *penne*. "I'd have to be blind not to see the sparks. Just tell me how much they've ignited." She winked. "Did you kiss him?" she eyed Tessa hopefully.

Tessa rolled her eyes. "Almost."

Connie dropped her fork and hurriedly took a sip

of her soda. "Now you have to give me details. Please," she added when Tessa withdrew.

"You can't tell your mother," Tessa told her. She saw the light of victory in Connie's eyes and giggled. "Seriously, not a syllable to your mother."

"Not a syllable." Connie crossed her heart, not daring to look away.

"We were in the bathroom, before we left…" Tessa said, omitting mention of the first missed kiss, which would only add evidence to Connie's case that more was going on than Tessa admitted.

"What were you both doing in the—"

"Connie."

"And…?" Connie made a forward motion with her hands.

"I went to get him some aspirin," she answered. "He followed me in and the next thing I know he's this close," she said, bringing her hand to within inches of her nose.

"Oh," Connie placed a hand on her abdomen. "What happened?"

Tessa unfolded and refolded the napkin next to her plate. "We got in a fight."

"A fight?"

Tessa's brows drew together over Connie's enthusiasm. "A disagreement."

"How did you go from practically kissing to fighting? You were only alone with him for a couple minutes."

Tessa looked around the room.

People were eating, talking, one reading alone, and here she sat, at an inquisition.

"Believe me, with Gunnar, a couple minutes is all it takes. The man is…difficult. It's for the best." She reached for her fork, but was intercepted when Connie grabbed her hand once more.

"Are you crazy?" Connie asked, incredulous. "A man like him doesn't come around every day. And you could use a little shaking up, Tess."

Irritated, Tessa took back control of her hand and her fork. "The truth is we don't like each other. We can't be in the same room—any room—without sniping at each other." It made her a little sad.

Connie laughed. "Ever hear of sexual tension?"

"That's crazy," Tessa assured her. "We just have different lives, different views."

"OK, have it your way."

"Well, did you and Mike fight all the time or was it love at first sight?"

As Connie launched into the dynamics of her romance with Mike, Tessa gave herself points for the art of the dodge. She also gave Connie's notion some consideration. Could that really be the source of the conflict between her and Gunnar?

He wasn't the first man to attract her. But by comparison, they were childhood crushes. None of them had caused a power failure in her brain or her throat to go sand dry simply by walking into a room. And they'd never caused her to anticipate a kiss so much.

On the other hand, none of those boys had made her mad enough to want them evicted from her home, or intimidated her enough to make her build a blockade.

No, she argued inwardly, any friction was due to a personality clash and a touch of insanity on his part. If he made her feel new things, it was because he manipulated her. A man like him had plenty of experience with women and how to make them...

Maybe Gunnar had a point, she thought, sipping her soda while Connie exalted Mike. She was judgmental.

৵৽৽

Standing in her driveway several hours later watching Connie drive off, Tessa was sure there could be no better friend then Connie, and that God sent her to earth to point out the humor in the things Tessa took so seriously. Spending time with Connie, recalling favorite movie scenes, window-shopping, or singing off key to the car radio, always made Tessa feel better.

So much so that at some point between calculating the waiter's tip and walking to the car, she decided she wasn't going to blame Gunnar because her hormones did a dance whenever he was near.

He didn't manipulate, he just happened to be one of those potent males that stirred women up.

Avoidance was the key to preventing any further complication in their current living arrangements. She could steer clear of him; it was merely a matter of planning.

Besides, she didn't have time to dwell on Gunnar and their strange relationship. She was going to be the maid of honor at her best friend's wedding! Planning the bridal shower, the bachelorette party, and dress fittings, would occupy a great deal of her time. She wasn't positive how or where to begin, but was happy to do it.

Her own mother was well acquainted with the ins and outs of organizing such an event, but the idea of consulting her would slash Tessa's happiness by at least a third, so she rejected it.

She fished in her bag for her keys.

Connie and Mike were so young and idealistic, so much in love. When they looked at each other no one else mattered.

The romantic in Tessa hoped it would always be so.

Despite her parents' marriage, which she viewed as one more of convenience than love, and Dominic and Pauline's, filled with drama and emotional clashes right from the start, there was no reason to lose faith in the institution.

If God ordained it, it was good enough for her. When she married, it would be forever.

The idea of marriage widened Tessa's smile. She knew she would marry one day, and that her husband would be a man of strength and character, a great father, and good provider. Handsome, naturally. She would leave the details to God.

Though some would call her a late bloomer, she was in no hurry. She couldn't give herself to someone before she knew what she could offer, and was only beginning to discover herself, to unearth her strengths and weaknesses.

The smell of pepperoni tickled her nose the second she walked through the back door. It didn't matter that she'd already eaten; she loved pepperoni. Following her nose to the front of the house, Gunnar stepped in from the sun porch holding a pizza box.

"Hello," Tessa said.

Gunnar transferred the box to his other hand. "I was hungry."

She put her purse on the stairs. "So I see."

"I was going to get rid of this before you came

back."

Tessa looked at the box, disappointed. "It's empty?"

When he nodded, her mouth moved into a transitory pout.

"Here, give it to me. The garbage has to go out anyway... What?" she asked, when he glowered at her.

"You're not taking out the garbage."

"I'm not?"

Gunnar took the box and moved along the corridor.

She shrugged. She may be a modern woman, but if a man wanted to take out the trash, more power to him.

When he returned a few minutes later, Tessa was sitting on the floor in the midst of the mess she'd left earlier. She pushed her hair behind her ear and glanced up to find him watching her. His scent drifted toward her, making her think fleetingly of the sea and a brightly painted lighthouse.

The chore forgotten, Tessa rested her palms on her thighs and stared back at him.

He had changed into faded jeans and a white ribbed shirt that performed double duty, serving to emphasize his build, while also proving that ignoring him as planned wasn't an option.

The weight of his stare was almost tangible on her skin, making her feel exposed and vulnerable.

She moistened her lips. "How are you?" she asked.

He looked at her oddly.

"The headache."

"Almost gone." His voice was deep, a little rough, and she suddenly had trouble remembering what she'd asked him.

Silence crept in, bringing with it that intangible shift in the air, the shift that had the potential to shoot them from stilted conversation to explosive contact in a heartbeat.

She could sense the energy, extending seductive fingers, drawing, evoking. It was best sidestepped, but before she could contemplate evasive action, he presented her with the closest thing to an actual smile she'd ever seen from him. Just the slightest curve of lips, which took him several steps away from the dark, brooding savage and made him appear almost friendly. He might be out of his mind, but wow, he was beautiful.

⌀∾⌀

Thirty seconds of silence had Gunnar worried that Tessa might be pondering what had happened before she'd left with Connie.

No sooner were they gone than he'd felt a stab of remorse. It happened so seldom that he analyzed it closely and concluded that he'd been angry at himself and taken it out on her.

He'd done more than his share to solidify her belief that he was a lunatic, but it made him angry that she feared him. And it made him angry that he could be so affected by her while she could remain so…well, he couldn't say unaffected. He felt her response. But she wasn't troubled by it like he was.

Still, that was his own disappointment to shoulder, and he shouldn't have foisted it on her. He gave an inward sigh as he watched her, sitting among the pans and whatever those things were.

The fact remained, it wasn't her fault he wanted

her so much or that he thought of her almost constantly. With his life in turmoil lately, his lust was running amok. That never happened. He knew dozens of beautiful women and didn't think of them at all when he didn't want to.

Assessing her, Tessa's was a different beauty, an odd, 'the-pieces-are-unusual-but-make-an-irresistible-whole', kind of thing. Her mouth was wide and full under a narrow nose that could be too small for her face if not balanced by that tapered, stubborn chin.

A chin, he mused, that could thrust forward in determination or annoyance with little provocation. Her eyes, a translucent sea green, snapped to life when she was annoyed. Or excited.

A part of him knew the instant he looked down into them, that she would be trouble.

Even the simple way she dressed was beginning to get to him. There was no reason for it. She wore loose fitting pants and blouses most of the time, probably not to entice the male of the species. Well, she didn't comprehend how a man's mind worked, but he did — at least this man's mind. He could ignore the outer wrapping altogether to visualize the form underneath whether she wore a bikini or a rain barrel. There was a great body under there.

Aside from her physical appeal, the fact that she'd spoken to him after the way he'd treated her — again — proved Tessa owned a generous supply of courage, and forgiveness.

Things usually soured whenever they were together, however.

He needed to make an effort to be friendly. It stood to reason, if they got along he wouldn't have this prickling guilt, and if he didn't have that, he would have less cause to think of her. A logical conclusion, and one he'd reached when she was absent.

But the way she was looking at him now made his mouth water. He knew all the signs of a woman's interest, no matter how subtle, and she was definitely sending signals. Although possibly, she didn't realize it. It would be best to vacate.

Against his better judgment he stayed. He found himself smiling as he entertained a daydream of burying his face in all that silky hair.

When she smiled back it brought him up short, and he groped for something to say. "Don't you stop? Cleaning, I mean."

The look she returned told him the idea hadn't occurred to her. "I like order."

"So I see."

"I can't see letting a job go undone once you know it needs doing," she answered.

Gunnar straightened.

She had pride and work ethic, but what else was there in her life?

"You have any hobbies? Vices?"

"Excuse me?" Her eyes were wide and ingenuous, yet at the same time held some primitive knowledge.

Maybe trying to be nice wasn't the way to handle this.

"Never mind."

When he moved to leave, Tessa hopped to her feet.

"Thanks for taking out the trash."

Gunnar stopped. "Thanks for the aspirin."

"If you need anything else, ask."

At that moment, with her hands unconsciously winding together and her teeth nibbling gently on her bottom lip, he needed nothing more than to take hold of her and complete the kiss he'd only hinted at before. Her lips held a mysterious temptation for him, and he wondered if kissing her now would break the spell. It could be exactly what he needed to purge her out of his system.

Having touched her, he knew how soft her skin was. He'd felt her sweet breath on his face, and her pulse beating under his fingertips. He'd smelled the delicate scent of her and knew how her eyes glazed with desire. It would be too easy to close the distance between them and rediscover it all.

Tessa continued to look at him with guileless eyes while her whole being called to him.

He knew then, beyond doubt, that a kiss would not be a simple thing with her. Rather than being purged of her, he might be possessed by her.

This time when his common sense told him to back off, he did, right out the front door.

12

In the morning, Tessa and Dominic welcomed their aunt Elaine.

It wasn't her habit to announce her arrival or commit to a scheduled length of stay, and though her lack of structure drove Tessa mildly crazy, Elaine was one of the few family members she enjoyed spending time with.

Even thinking it made her feel somehow disloyal. Perhaps she would have less guilt if Elaine were her father's sister instead of her mother's. At least it would make more sense, for never were two sisters less similar.

Elaine was animated, cracked her knuckles, and smoked long, thin cigarettes that smelled of cinnamon apples. She was also clever at poker, which Tessa knew both fascinated and goaded her brother.

Before he dropped her bags to the foyer floor, he'd already challenged her to a game of five-card stud.

Elaine cupped his face in her hands to kiss both of his cheeks. "You don't learn, do you?"

"I'm a gambler, what can I say?" Dominic replied.

"No, sweetie, you're not." She laughed, gathering him and Tessa in a collective hug. "I've missed you!"

"How's the book coming?" Tessa asked.

There was always a book. A prolific science fiction author under the pseudonym Paul Harper, whenever

Elaine visited, the clack of typewriter keys from the attic guest room was almost constant, interrupted sporadically by foul language.

It seemed like a lot of work to Tessa, but Elaine loved it.

"Terrific!" Elaine answered. "A bit of a departure though. The subject is death and taxes, I'm calling it *Inevitable*. Careful with that," she told Dominic as he lifted a black case. "My baby's in there."

"Hungry?" Dominic asked. "Tessa's going to make pancakes."

Tessa lifted a brow. That was news to her.

But she soon warmed to the idea and a few minutes later was dumping blueberries into batter and shaking her head at Elaine and Dominic's good-natured argument over a proposed bear hunt to squelch overpopulation. It was a longstanding quarrel, both for the state and the two of them.

"You're only saying that because you don't live here and never had to dodge one on your way to the garage," Dominic told his aunt.

"Sweetie, you live in the city. When was the last time you saw a bear?" She smiled back at him. "A real one."

"I have friends who live less than ten miles from here and bears raid their trash all the time," he said.

"Oh, pooh. If they'd keep their trash locked—"

"Why should they have to lock up their trash?"

"So bears don't get in it, naturally."

Dominic's voice resonated with humor. "You'd sing another tune if a bear raided your trash."

"Indeed I would, since I live on the nineteenth floor."

Tessa chuckled and dropped batter onto the

sizzling skillet. "We're almost ready here."

"Tessa, will you be sitting at the table or are you going to zip around the way you always do?" Elaine asked.

"I don't zip around."

"Yeah you do," Dominic said, adding sugar to his coffee. "You're in perpetual motion."

Tessa pouted.

Gunnar said pretty much the same thing yesterday. Hmm, he'd asked if she had hobbies...

She loved to study the Bible and pray, but neither of those could be called a hobby. Well, she exercised four days a week to stay fit. No, that didn't qualify. Hobbies...hobbies...she'd think of one if it took her the rest of the day.

He'd mentioned vices too. Would mocha lattes fall into that category?

As for Gunnar, she imagined he had a few vices. Women, most likely. Maybe gambling or alcohol, too. He left after their conversation last night, and she hadn't heard him come in. He likely spent the night attending to one such vice—not that it was any of her business what he did or with whom.

Ignoring the twinge of disappointment, Tessa stacked the pancakes on a plate and began unloading the dishwasher.

What type of woman would Gunnar be attracted to? Easy. She would be tall, drop dead gorgeous, with long blonde hair and a liberal helping of curves. She would have a voice like a sultry summer night and a way of seduction to make him forget, at least temporarily, all the anger he seemed determined to carry with him. She would smell like sin and—

The rattle of silver in the drawer brought Tessa

back to reality. She'd closed the drawer harder than intended and jammed it off track. "Shoot." She jiggled it back in line.

"You OK?" Dominic asked.

"Fine."

Pastor Caswell liked to say where jealousy was, anger followed, and Tessa had to agree. She was angry with herself for being jealous.

Gunnar may be attracted to her, but for a woman to keep his attention she would have to be beautiful, exciting, sexy. None of those words described her.

It was a simple matter of chromosomes she decided. Tessa didn't need a man in her life. She had other things to make her feel fulfilled.

Since Elaine hadn't rented a car, she talked Dominic into accompanying her to find a hostess gift. She would be dining with friends this evening and wanted to find "just the right thing."

Tessa understood this meant long hours of shopping, a fact no one need share with Dominic.

His countenance revealed he knew what he was up against, but how could he refuse his favorite aunt?

Tessa declined the invitation to tag along. Disgrace though she might be to her gender, she didn't enjoy power shopping. She preferred strolling through shops, enjoying the displays, and talking with people. Besides, uncovering her capacity for jealousy had put her in a sulky mood. It was a beautiful day. Maybe she would drive up to Highpoint and take in the view.

Just then, she heard a car pull in and Gunnar's voice growing louder and then fading as he drove by the window. The car door closed followed by the crunch of his boots in the gravel outside.

"I don't care how much work it takes, get it done,"

he barked into a cell phone as he came through the door. "I'll be there soon, and if Alexandra calls tell her I'll get back to her later."

So she has a name, Tessa thought, dismally. *Alexandra.* How glamorous. Tessa hated her already.

"Forgive me, Lord," she mumbled under her breath.

She rinsed the sponge in the sink and gave the front of the stove a good wipe. When she looked up, Gunnar stood in the doorway, arms crossed and keys dangling from his finger.

"Something wrong?" he asked.

"No, why?" She gave him a smile, but he narrowed his eyes.

"You look mad."

Tessa stretched her back. "I just don't feel like cleaning today. Actually, I may go for a ride," she said. "It's a nice day and Dominic and Aunt Elaine are out."

"Aunt Elaine?"

"Oh, our aunt—obviously. She's staying in the room above ours—yours and mine—your room and my room," she amended awkwardly. "She's staying a few days."

His brows elevated fractionally. "Really."

"Mm-hmm, in the attic. She's a writer, Elaine Martine—well, Paul Harper." Her throat felt like it might close. "She writes mostly fiction."

"I know who Paul Harper is," Gunnar said.

"You do? I mean, of course you do," she faltered. "I didn't mean—"

"I saw a few of her books in your library. I like sci-fi. You may think I'm a barbarian, but I can read." When her eyes grew wide, he actually laughed.

It was a rich, satisfying sound, and Connie's words

came floating back. Tessa did feel as though she'd received a gift. "I didn't know you'd been in the library."

He took a few steps closer. "There's a lot you don't know."

Tessa swallowed. This wasn't right, this attraction. She hardly knew the man. Aside from that, she couldn't in good conscience, pursue a man who was attached to someone else. "I apologize if I came across as condescending," she told him, lobbing the sponge into the sink and patting her hands dry on the thighs of her jeans.

"All you have to do is ask," he said, brushing her apology aside.

"What do you mean?" She reached for the bottle of hand lotion she kept next to the sink. "Ask what?"

"Whatever you want to—" He stopped dead, apparently surprised by his own words. But he didn't take them back.

As baffled by his mood as his offer, Tessa squirted lotion onto her palm and began massaging it into her hands. She gave a nervous snort. What would she ask him? How he could cause such uproar in her system from several feet away? Why he made her want things she didn't understand? There were a thousand other things she could ask.

"What does the tattoo on your stomach say?" she blurted, coloring instantly, embarrassed to divulge that particular picture was still fresh in her mind from the first night he stayed here.

For an answer, Gunnar started to lift his shirt.

"I don't want to see it!" Tessa moved as far back as the counter would allow. "I was just curious—I didn't get to read—"

Eyes steady on hers, Gunnar pulled up his shirt far enough for her to see the tattoo.

Tessa put a hand over her eyes, but not before taking note of the definition of his abdominal muscles.

"Now's your chance," he said, reaching across and taking her hand from her face.

POWER. The solid blue letters, written in calligraphy, formed a slight arch over his navel. She looked away, uncertain how to act, what to say. She felt like a fool shying away from a little peek at male flesh. Did she really just hide her eyes? It wasn't as though she'd never seen a man's torso before.

"Hmm. Nice."

Gunnar let go of his shirt and her hand. "You asked."

Well, that was simple. Uncomfortable and humiliating, but simple. Tessa wondered if he would indeed answer other questions as openly as he implied, like what the word meant to him, that he would bear the mark permanently.

"And the other one?"

"Which?" he asked.

She only knew of one other. "The one on your back."

"Don't hide your eyes."

Tessa was determined to stop fluttering, but when Gunnar turned around to lay his keys on the counter and peel his shirt completely off, she thanked the heavens he wasn't looking at her.

Not only did she have an unobstructed view of his upper body, but he couldn't see her jaw drop to the floor.

Outstanding. This was clearly what God had in mind when He made man.

Muscles, thick and corded under taut, olive skin, were the canvas for a tattoo beginning in the center of his back, spreading up between his shoulder blades and continuing to the nape of his neck. It was the figure's hands, raised in worship that Connie had spotted above the collar of his shirt. But more captivating were the wings of creamy white that unfurled from the figure across the wide expanse of Gunnar's back. She'd never seen white tattoo ink.

"It's an angel," she whispered. He was such a serious, threatening entity...yes, the angel fit him as nothing else could have.

"You expected the devil." He faced her.

She was careful to keep her gaze on his face. "No, no. I thought you'd have a dagger with a snake wrapped around it."

When he grinned, she did the same. It was a presumptuous thing to say, but he didn't seem offended.

He lifted his chin in a nod, put a foot on the seat of a chair and worked his right pant leg up, over the solid calf muscle to reveal a dagger with a snake wrapped around it.

She giggled, slapping a hand on her mouth. "I'm sorry."

"Stereotypical right of passage. It was either this or a dragon."

"You're kidding?"

He smiled and tilted his chin in a lighthearted gesture. "I was fourteen." He shrugged. "Just the kind of people I hung with."

Tessa experienced mixed emotions—part relief, part disappointment—when he pulled on his shirt.

"You're in a good mood today," she remarked,

and immediately wanted to bite her tongue.

"Yeah. I had a good night."

"So you slept well?"

"I haven't slept yet," he said.

The knot reformed in her belly. "That's too bad."

"This time it isn't. It was a very satisfying night."

She twisted the ring on her finger. She was glad he felt so good today, but the last thing she needed was to start thinking of him and his girlfriend. Together. She could feel the stains of scarlet creeping up her cheeks as Gunnar shifted his feet and watched her.

His expression was indecipherable, and Tessa expected his mood might swing again.

"Are you blushing?"

"It's a little stuffy in here, that's all," she said, struggling to hide the distress in her voice. "Of course I'm not blushing. Why would I blush?" She cleared her throat. Her hair hung loose and heavy on her neck. She picked it up, let it fall and waved a hand in front of her face.

A moment of silent scrutiny passed. "Would you take a ride with me?"

Tessa stared at him, disoriented. He could sure turn the course of a conversation. "A ride?"

"Yeah."

"Why?"

"I have to check on a delivery at work, and I want to show you something. You said you might go out, anyway." He picked up his keys and bounced them on his palm. "You might find it interesting since you're part of the reason my night was so successful."

She didn't know what he meant, but didn't think it was a good idea. "I don't know," she answered with an apologetic smile.

Though his expression didn't change, she sensed his disappointment.

"I'm going to take a quick shower," he said. "Think about it."

She watched him walk away. Certainly, he didn't mean for her to think of him in the shower…When she started doing just that she stopped, exhaled.

He meant for her to consider taking a drive. With him. Alone.

He was two or three inches taller than Dominic and a half size broader. He could take her Only-God-knew-where and do Only-God-knew-what with her. He seemed to be in a good mood, but having witnessed first-hand his capacity to snap without warning, it would be unwise.

On the other hand, he had never hurt her—intentionally—despite plenty of opportunity, with Dominic gone most of the time. And his tone, so expectant, told Tessa it was important to him.

So she would trust God and go. Who was she trying to fool, anyway? She wanted to be with him.

When he came down several minutes later, she met him at the bottom of the stairs, and without a word, followed him outside. He opened the car door for her, and before she could sit, he reached in to take a blue folder off the seat and chuck it in the back.

When he got in next to her, he paused with his hand on the ignition key and sighed. "I won't hurt you."

The look he gave her told her he was asking for her trust and that to refuse him could do damage she couldn't foresee.

Tessa gave him a tenuous smile. "I know." But her muscles were stretched tight as bowstrings.

13

During the silent ten minute drive, Gunnar barely glanced at her and took a hand off the wheel only twice: once to switch on the radio, a minute later to switch it off.

Tessa wasn't great with directions, but knew they traveled west and tried to commit the street names to memory. She told herself it wasn't in case she should need to escape, but it was just reasonable to want to know where she was.

As if reading her mind, Gunnar shot her a look. A guilty flush heated her face and she stared out the window. When he slowed and changed direction off the main highway onto a long, gravel road, panic chomped at the bit, but she strove to rein it in. They were still within plain sight of passing motorists, albeit at some distance. No cause for alarm. She sent up a silent prayer.

Two buildings came into view. Coated in peeling paint and surrounded by dirt and tire tracks, they appeared little more than shacks with large plastic garbage cans lined up like soldiers in the alley between. A small sign hung above one corrugated metal garage door, but was impossible to read from this distance.

The buildings could have housed anything from a clothing outlet to a slaughterhouse. She remembered him saying he built things. Entirely too vague for her piece of mind. Was it kitchen cabinets? Swing sets? Why hadn't she just asked him directly?

Gunnar pulled behind one of three cars parked in the dirt, then reached onto the back seat to retrieve the folder. Tessa shook the grisly image of a shop of horrors from her mind as he came around to open her door.

Following Gunnar, she heard the high-pitched sound of what could have been a dentist drill. It was sporadic and mingled with the sound of something banging against metal. Although the volume ebbed and flowed, the noise remained fairly constant. Next to the building on the left, crates the size of couches were lined up. The words Mason Custom were stenciled on them with smaller stamps of a stylized MC. Maybe he made furniture.

She could read the sign over the roll up garage door now. It also read Mason Custom, but put forward no clue as to what lay inside. There was a regular door cut into the larger one, and Gunnar stopped before pulling it open.

"I should warn you," he began, his jaw tightening when her face paled. "There are men in here who don't always know how to behave in front of a woman."

"Men?"

"So you may hear some rough language. If anything's too out of line, say so."

With that he held the door open and stood behind her, leaving her no choice but to step through.

The chaos she'd heard from outside now made sense. There were pieces of metal everywhere, some large, some larger. Electrical cords ran in every direction, work benches with complicated-looking machines were situated along the far wall, and steel tables bore the weight of numerous boxes containing more metal pieces. It looked like a giant had haphazardly tipped over his toolbox. She had no doubt Gunnar knew where to locate each screw, washer, and bolt.

The building was bigger than it looked from outside. There was an office to the right and parked at its door was Gunnar's motorcycle. In fact there were motorcycles all around, most unfinished, but well on their way to becoming spectacular.

"You build motorcycles," she said with great relief.

In a far corner, a man with a torch watched his progress through a flip down welding helmet as blue sparks flew into the air.

In the opposite corner, one man held a long, curved piece of metal, which she guessed to be a fender, while another man banged on it with a rubber mallet.

The place smelled of grease and new rubber combined with the lingering aroma of coffee.

Layered above it all was the pungent fragrance of aftershave emitting from the man nearest her. He wore jeans and a black leather vest with no shirt, and when he let loose a whistle, four pairs of eyes fastened on her.

Gunnar took her by the elbow and steered her toward them. A man as tall as Gunnar but thick in the gut, lumbered over.

"This is Max Tully," Gunnar said. "He runs things most of the time. And Alan, David, and Randy." He motioned to them in order, and Tessa gave each a diffident smile.

Gunnar tugged her lightly, discouraging conversation and causing her to realize he'd only introduced her because she would expect it.

"The seat in?" Gunnar asked Max.

"In your office."

Tessa didn't know when she'd felt so self-conscious.

The men eyed her, none troubling to conceal their appreciation for the female form, but when Randy mumbled to David, Gunnar's gaze shot to them. They stopped talking instantly.

"So you're what's keeping the boss away," Max said. He scratched the stubble on his chin. "I knew it was broads or booze."

Gunnar ignored Max's comment and opened the office door for Tessa to step inside. "It's a mess in here," he said, sliding a stack of parts catalogues off the torn suede chair so she could sit.

She remained standing. "You own this business," she said as he closed the door.

"Stunned?"

She was. "Not that you couldn't have your own—it's—you're obviously intelligent." Great, she'd offended him.

"Forget it." He tossed the blue folder onto the desk causing papers to spill across the scarred veneer top.

The sounds from the shop resumed, muted through the door, as was the radio filtering classic rock.

Tessa looked around while Gunnar stared at the box on his desk as though it contained some deep mystery.

"Is anything wrong?" she asked.

"I'm deliberating what method of torture to use on Baron if this seat has to go back. They sent me two already, both wrong." Gunnar reached in the top drawer.

When Tessa saw the glint of a jagged blade, she almost gasped. Gunnar looked exasperated, but said nothing.

"Sorry, I'm a little jumpy. I'm out of my element."

He gave a grumble of assent and sliced the packing tape. In seconds, the seat was in his hands and he was turning it sideways and upside down, running his fingers over the seams, examining each detail.

"About time," he said at last.

She was glad for Baron—whoever he was—that Gunnar found it acceptable. Since this was the first time she'd seen him pleased by anything, she stepped in for a closer look at the custom stitching. "It's very pretty."

Gunnar replaced the seat and let out a sound close to a groan. "Only a woman would call a cycle seat pretty."

Her brow lifted in mock derision. "And only a man would contemplate torture over a cycle seat."

He gave a soft snort.

"Is it for one of those?" she asked, pointing toward the shop.

In answer, he idly picked up a sketch from his desk, handed it to her. "It's a retro cycle. The customer's particular. But so am I."

Tessa regarded the intricate detail. She found it hard to believe the parts she'd seen scattered around would eventually come together to form this. "Is this your work? The drawing?"

"Stunned again?"

Her gaze locked with his. "No." Following impulse, she laid a gentle hand on one cheek and rose on tiptoes to kiss the other one. "But you are full of surprises."

Gunnar reached up to touch his cheek as she moved away to take in the rest of the room.

"Oh, may I?" she asked, itching to inspect one of the drawings peeking out of the folder.

Gunnar nodded.

These were bolder, more colorful, and larger in scale.

"You didn't do these." She smiled, when he looked at her quizzically. "The style is completely different. Not better," she added. "Just different."

He handed her a sketch of an armored horse, drawn to morph animal and machine into one.

"Can you do this? I mean build it to look like this?" She knew the answer. She'd seen the way his gargoyle looked alive when it moved.

"That's what I get paid for," he answered.

"And you design them yourself?"

He picked up the folder and handed it to her. "Mostly." His face was unreadable when he came to sit on the edge of the desk, their thighs brushing.

"Alexandra Clark," Tessa read the name on the tab of the folder.

"She does some of my graphics." Gunnar rolled his shoulders. "I get the whole idea down but she decides where the lines should be painted, etching, all that. We were at her place all night finishing those."

He worked with Alexandra.

Tessa wanted to be relieved. But that didn't mean they didn't have a deeper relationship of some kind. A feeling like a hot knife jabbed her just under the ribs.

"This is a chess set," she said, after leafing through the sketches. She studied one of a parapet that appeared to be made of stone. She couldn't imagine how he would make it work as a motorcycle, but she thought he could.

"It's for a client who wants to play with his friends." Gunnar put his hand on the desk, inadvertently brushing hers. "When he called, I thought he was a nut and blew it off, but when he showed up in person and paid up front I had to take him seriously."

She felt the light touch of his fingers but didn't move her hand. "Isn't that going to be some job? It could take...well I don't know, but it's huge, right?"

Gunnar scratched the back of his neck, drawing her attention to the thick rope of muscle that ran up the side. "Well, it can take up to eight weeks for each bike. We're talking thirty two bikes...maybe up to three years."

"Three years? That's quite a time investment."

Gunnar shrugged. "More or less. Once the designs are done, the rest is just fabrication."

"What if this client doesn't like them?"

"He will."

"You're pretty confident."

"I can't afford not to be. I'll be moving the shop and changing out all the equipment. It's going to take money and time, and I can't let the transition slow us down. We'll have to bust our—" he paused, gritted his teeth. "—work really hard till this is done. But I won't let the opportunity pass. It's the difference between being one of the best or dominating the bike world."

"And you want to dominate." She smiled.

He didn't.

"And the men you have can handle it?" She realized immediately how stupid the question sounded, but Gunnar seemed to be weighing it.

"They better." He stretched back to reach the desk drawer. "This is what I wanted to show you."

The motorcycle in the sketch was sleek, graceful even though motionless, and undeniably feminine in design. "It's a woman," she said, delighted.

"It's you."

His eyes were sharp and intense, and the desire she saw there startled her. Her heart gave a yank.

"Me?"

"I had this mental block, and wasn't getting much work done. But the other night when I picked up my pencil...you came out. The ideas have been flowing since."

She tore her attention away and back to the page. "I'm flattered. Sincerely flattered."

"I want you to have it when it's done," he told her.

She looked at him, alarmed. "You mean the motorcycle? I couldn't."

"It's female, you said it yourself. I can't ride it."

"I'm sure you'd rather sell it."

"No." His reply was swift.

"But I can't ride."

"I'll teach you."

The notion should have terrified her. She found it tremendously exhilarating. Why shouldn't she learn to ride a motorcycle? The old Tessa, the boring one who followed the rules and did the expected might be afraid to try a new, dangerous venture, but this Tessa was different. The more consideration she gave it, the more pleased she became. A smile burst forth on her face.

Gunnar watched her keenly for several seconds, then hurriedly got up and flung the door open.

Perplexed, Tessa laid the drawing on the desk and followed him into the main shop. A short time ago, the somber cloud he lived under had started to lift. Now it threatened to return. Maybe she could distract him a little longer.

Gunnar's long legs devoured the ground with effortless strides but she caught up to him, dismissing the press of curious eyes. She grabbed his hand.

"Let's get a sandwich," she said, not ignorant of Max's jaw falling open, or that all work abruptly ceased.

Gunnar looked down at her, tightened his hand around hers and pulled her outside.

Before the door was closed, Gunnar used his body to maneuver her against the wall, pinning her hands at her sides. His touch was gentle, but his mouth came down on hers with a hunger so fierce and fervent that she fought for breath. He broke free for only an instant, long enough to scan her eyes, requesting her permission.

She gave it freely and dragged in a lungful of air before he recaptured her lips.

Tessa's mind seized. She should be pushing him away. Instead, she tried to recall why she should want to. She knew in her heart that this was what she'd been waiting for since the first time he had brought her to this precipice of sensation in the kitchen. Now she finally knew what it was like to be guided beyond.

She shouldn't want this, but went with him willingly, setting off on a journey of discovery.

His arms came around her waist and lifted her off her feet, and she took pleasure in the feeling of the ground simply dropping away beneath her and the only safety, Gunnar.

But just as swiftly, her feet touched the ground, and she rocked to maintain her footing. It took a few seconds to comprehend he had released her.

The haze of want dissipated slowly, but when she could see clearly, Gunnar's disconcertion was as apparent as her own, his breathing as ragged, his eyes hot as they searched her face.

After a moment, he took her hand and led her to his car, keeping quiet until they were both inside.

With a groan, Gunnar tipped back his head on the seat and closed his eyes. "We have a problem," he said, his voice laced with repressed need.

She wasn't as sophisticated as some women who enjoyed playing games with men, and didn't pretend to misunderstand him. "I don't see why it should be a problem."

"I want you. And I know you want me." He turned to face her, daring her to deny it. "But you're not—I can't—" He growled one of the words she'd heard him use on the phone that first day. "It can't happen."

A hot ball of emotion rolled in her stomach, but she wasn't certain what to call it. Rejection? Relief?

"Why?" she asked. A logical question. "Because of Dominic?"

His look plainly stated Dominic hadn't crossed his mind.

"You need someone who comes from the same place, wants the same things," he said. "You said you're out of your element here."

"I meant around power tools."

He shook his head firmly. "You're not the fling type, Tessa, and I'm not looking for more than that."

Outrage was the one solid emotion she did

recognize. What made him think he could tell her what kind of woman she was? Men, she was learning, could trigger any variety of feelings. Determined to remain calm, Tessa folded her hands in her lap.

He was looking for a way out before he even got involved. Or was he already more involved than he wanted to let on?

"Of course I'm not looking for a fling, it never entered my mind. I let you kiss me, that's all," she said dryly. "But I don't think you want a fling, either."

Gunnar started the car and grabbed the wheel with both hands. "I don't want to hurt you."

She met his look evenly and clicked her seatbelt into place. "You don't want to hurt me, fine. One excuse is as good as the next."

"Excuse?"

"Whatever."

His eyebrows rose, challenging her.

Having no answer, Tessa stared out the window.

The drive home was silent.

14

While Tessa entered the back of the house, Gunnar snarled at his reflection in the rearview mirror.

"Idiot."

He'd warned himself to be careful. Since their first meeting, when she'd managed to chink the armor around him without even trying. He hadn't been careful. Today, seeing her reaction to his work, how she regarded what was important to him as something special and worthy of notice, the armor had cracked further. And when she'd kissed his cheek, it was as though she had effectively poured herself into him through that widening fissure.

And become part of him.

Taking her to work was bad enough, but why did he take her into his office and close the door? Him, plus Tessa, plus a confined space, equaled bad idea. And to see her come alive at the mention of learning to ride a cycle, the way she went from panicky to curious to thrilled in a few seconds...he'd been done in.

He shouldn't have kissed her, either. This inexplicable need for her was growing each day, and he'd compounded it. He'd suspected this outcome, and done it anyway.

"Idiot." Gunnar banged a fist on the dashboard.

He knew if he stuck around, he would do anything to be as much a part of her as she was of him.

He might succeed, but it would be to her detriment, and it was ripping his heart out. Funny way to learn he still had one.

He climbed out of the car, despite the sudden spinning of his head, and slammed the door with a force that rocked the car like a docked boat. No more procrastination. He had to abort this thing happening between them before it became unmanageable.

When he entered, Tessa was sitting on a stool with the phone receiver to her ear.

He didn't care who she was talking to. The conversation was over. He took the phone and hung it up.

"Hey!" she protested. "That's my mother."

"She'll call back." Better yet...he took the receiver and let it dip toward the floor, twirling first one way then the other at the end of its coiled cord.

"When she can't get me she'll come here, and, believe me, neither of us wants that."

"I don't care, I need to say this." He paused a beat. Best just to get on with it. "My life is screwed up, and I can't be around you." He threw his keys on the counter. The headache was coming back, and it required substantial effort to keep focus. "It has to stop."

"What has to stop?" Tessa slid from the stool to stand in front of him.

"This...whatever it is." He gestured vaguely with his hands. "Whatever we've got going here. It's best for you if I go."

In an explosion of temper he didn't expect, Tessa jabbed him in the chest. "First of all, you invited me to come with you, I didn't stow away in your trunk. Second, don't paint yourself as some martyr. You're running for your own good, because you're scared!"

Gunnar drew a deep breath as she huffed and moved around the kitchen.

She couldn't be more wrong. And right.

He raised his hands and let them drop. "OK, I'm selfish."

Tessa made a frustrated sound in her throat. "There's no talking to you," she said, and stormed from the room.

Perfect. He couldn't have planned it better. While she was having her fit, he would grab his stuff and leave.

No. No way was she having the last word.

He caught up with her in her room, grabbing her arm to reel her around so he could talk to her, but this time she didn't freeze or flinch.

She brought her free hand back as far as she could and slapped him across the face. Hard.

Time and motion stopped for the space of several heartbeats, but the echo of the slap rang in his ears.

He looked down at Tessa's face, set and angry. If he were the type to fall in love, this would have been the moment.

One by one, his fingers lifted off her skin, but he took another few seconds before he spoke. "You take some chances."

A bead of sweat ran down his back. The headache raged now, and his eyes felt like they might burst. The room tilted on its axis, and he reached out to keep from falling.

Then Tessa was at his side, anger disregarded in her alarm. "Gunnar, are you OK? Did I hurt you?"

He would have laughed, if he didn't feel like his brain would explode through his temples. With his arm slung around her shoulder, Gunnar helped her direct him to the bed.

"Oh no, oh no," Tessa repeated as she slipped out from under his arm. "I'm sorry. I shouldn't have hit you. I've never hit anybody, except Dominic when we were kids."

He found that if he sat motionless and didn't close his eyes, he could manage a chuckle. "Easy, bruiser. I'm just dizzy."

"Dizzy? Are you sick?"

"No. I just need to stay still a minute."

Tessa brought her hands to either side of his face, cool silk next to his skin. He wished that she would go on touching him.

"I don't think you have a fever." She disappeared into the bathroom to return in moments with a thermometer. "Here, put this under your tongue."

Gunnar turned his face away. "I don't need that."

"You might be coming down with something."

He tried to stand, but Tessa shoved him back before he could gain his footing.

"Careful," he warned, but the word was more plea than threat.

This time when she thrust the small glass tube at him he took her arm. "If I'm getting sick, a thermometer isn't going to help."

Tessa pulled her arm back and propped her hands on her hips. "Stop being a baby."

Gunnar didn't care for the way she bossed him around. It was enough to show weakness in front of her, but he wouldn't let her scold him like an uncooperative child. "I'll be fine, I'm going to go to my room and lay down for a few—" This time the attempt to stand was foiled by the spinning of the room.

"You'll have to stay here for the time being," Tessa said and pushed on his chest when he started to rise. "Lie down."

He must have because he was now staring at the ceiling, and she was sliding his boots off. "I can get to my room."

"I doubt it."

She might be right, but he didn't have to like it.

"You got hit with this thing fast," Tessa said, from the bathroom where she was running water.

"I've been feeling lousier than usual the last few days."

The side of the bed barely dipped when Tessa sat beside him, her green eyes filled with concern as she placed a cool cloth on his forehead.

The simple action moved him. Gingerly, he took her hand. "You don't have to nurse me."

"Yes I do," she answered with a gentle smile.

Yeah, she would consider it the right thing to do. The Christian thing.

An uncomfortable silence crept into the room.

Tessa flipped the cloth, laying the cooler side on his forehead. "I'll make tea," she said, standing.

He didn't want tea, but it would get her away from him so he could think.

She was gone a few seconds before she ran back in. "You kissed me."

"You catch on quick," he said from beneath closed lids. The room remained steady for the time being.

"You kissed me and you're sick," Tessa said, her voice edged with panic. "I'm going to be next."

Gunnar opened his eyes and pulled the cloth off so he could tip his head forward. When he did, the room became unstable again. "That isn't going to happen."

"What do you mean? That was some kiss, not just a peck. It's probably already starting." She hurried from the room.

Gunnar lay back, placed the washcloth over his eyes and smiled. *Some kiss.*

♥

An ounce of prevention is worth a pound of cure. It didn't help to repeat it over and over while she filled two cups with steaming tea and treated each with a generous helping of honey. She could feel her throat closing. She was slicing lemon when the doorbell rang.

"Great," she mumbled, wiping her hands on a rag. "Terrific," she said under her breath when she opened the door. "Hi, Mom."

"Are you all right? What happened?" Anna hiked the strap of her bag onto her shoulder. "I kept calling but busy, busy."

"I'm fine."

Anna walked past her daughter, peering into each open room. "You worried me the way you hung up, and I couldn't get you on the line. You know what's been going on with all those break-ins. It was all over the news last night, just ask your brother."

Tessa followed in her mother's perfume wake, as she made her way to the kitchen. "I'm fine, Mom. I was...the phone..."

"I swear, Tessa, sometimes I don't think your head is attached." Apparently content with Tessa's physical appearance, Anna set her bag on the floor near the stool and bent down to replace the receiver.

"I was making tea," Tessa said when her mother's eyes lit on the cups. "Would you like some?" She

138

wished she didn't sound as though she were making small talk with a stranger.

"Two cups?"

"That's OK, there's plenty. Lemon?" She hoped the casual evasion would be enough to sidetrack her mother from further examination.

"Who is the other cup for?" Anna asked. Her gaze focused on Tessa.

"It's a—"

Both women turned when the back door opened, and Elaine swept into the room.

"I hope I'm not interrupting," Elaine said in a voice that always put Tessa in mind of sugar poured over rocks.

"Elaine!" Anna swanned to her and took her hand in both of hers in a greeting reserved for old friends or special acquaintances.

"What kind of hello is that?" The bangles on Elaine's wrists jangled as she threw her arms around her sister. "That's better."

"Hey, Mom," Dominic said from behind her, carrying in a number of bags from various retailers. One look at him attested that Elaine had run him ragged.

Tessa took the bags from him and set them on the counter, her stomach clenching when she noticed Gunnar's keys. In a subtle move, she opened a drawer and swept them in unnoticed.

The tea forgotten, Anna grasped Dominic's hands and gave them a squeeze.

Tessa smiled serenely, though her thoughts raced at a frenetic speed to put together a solution to her predicament. Gunnar was in her room! If he called out, or worse, came down...well, it would look bad.

"When did you get here?" Anna asked Elaine, slipping from her designer coat to reveal slim fitting tweed slacks and a cocoa blouse.

"This morning," Elaine said. "I'm on a working holiday, so I decided to impose on my favorite nephew for the weekend." She cracked her knuckles to Anna's unspoken horror. "What a double pleasure to find Tessa here." She tipped her head toward Tessa. "Dominic told me you're back for good."

"Quit her job, packed her things and came home," Anna interrupted before Tessa could answer.

"Well—" Tessa started.

"She's staying here until she finds a place. A small house," Anna said.

"How goes the hunt?" Elaine asked Tessa.

"You know how it is," Anna answered again. "The market's rough. It could be months before she finds a suitable home."

"You don't say," Elaine replied dryly.

Tessa was too nervous to appreciate the sarcasm. Nervous and guarded. The only people she'd told about renting a house were Dominic and Connie. She ruled Dominic out instantly, which meant the information had filtered through Connie to Vivian to Anna. She couldn't help wondering what else had filtered through.

There was a muffled sound from above. No one seemed to hear, but Tessa.

"Tessa, are you sure you're all right?" Anna asked.

Tessa whipped around to find all eyes on her. "Yes, fine."

"You look a little pale. But you always look pale," said Anna. She turned to her sister. "I'm always telling her she needs plenty of fresh air, water and rest if she wants to keep that sallow look at bay."

"Indeed." Elaine gave Tessa a quizzical look.

Tessa swallowed. The sound of her heart must be audible, and it was all she could do to stay in her skin. She could imagine one of those cartoon bubble things above her and everyone reading, *"There's a man upstairs in my bed."*

The rational side of her brain told her that as a mature woman it was absurd to get in such a state. The irrational side argued that this was her mother, who discussed everything with her father and absurd or not, Tessa didn't want her parents to suspect her of having pre-marital sex.

"Weren't you serving tea?" Anna asked.

Relieved that her mother must have dismissed the mystery of the second cup or supposed it was for Elaine, Tessa smiled. "Dominic?"

"No, thanks. I have to go in a minute." He sent Tessa a meaningful look. The interrogation into his life would soon begin, and he didn't plan on sticking around for it.

"But I just arrived," Anna complained. "You can spend a few minutes with your mother."

When Anna went to a cabinet to get the sugar, Tessa jerked her head at Elaine, the one person she could trust to get her out of this mess.

Picking up the cue, Elaine edged toward the hall. "Tessa, come with me a minute. I want to show you the hand towels I found at the dollar store the other day."

Tessa's lips twitched.

Anna had no interest in anything found at a discount store.

They left Dominic to fend for himself, hoping his mother wouldn't ask how things were going with his estranged wife.

At the end of the hall Elaine turned to Tessa "What is it?" she asked, keeping her voice low.

"There's a man in my bed."

Elaine laid a hand on Tessa's cheek. "Is that all? You had me worried."

"Aunt Elaine—"

"I was young once," she said with a wink.

"It's nothing like that."

Elaine patted Tessa's arm. "Your mother won't hear it from me." With that, she returned to the kitchen.

Fabulous, Tessa thought miserably.

If her aunt jumped to conclusions, her mother certainly would, and what would Dominic say when he'd already made a point of telling her to stay away from Gunnar?

Well, if he saw Gunnar's car, he must've assumed he was asleep. At least she could count on him not to say anything.

When Tessa was able to sneak away with a cup of tea, she found Gunnar stretched across her bed on his back, one arm flung overhead, the other at his side. His eyes were closed, shielded by impenetrable lashes.

Tessa stood near the bed not wanting to disturb him, but finding it impossible to look away. This present chance might never be repeated, so she took the opportunity to view him thoroughly.

Her pulse thudded thickly as she noted the steady rise and fall of his chest, his stomach. She forced her gaze back to his face. Her senses sharpened, alert to the slightest change in his breathing. It continued its deep, easy rhythm.

He looked so out of place with his tanned skin in

such contrast against the stark white of the duvet, and his heavily muscled frame made the carved headboard seem delicate by comparison. He took up most of the bed.

When he moved Tessa rattled the china, and tea splashed over the cup rim onto the saucer.

She scrambled to manufacture an excuse for why she was standing here ogling him, but drew a blank. Fortunately, she didn't need one. He rolled to his side and pulled his arms into his chest, but didn't wake.

He looked vulnerable but no less dangerous. Perhaps more so, his stillness, so electric, even at rest.

She let her gaze traverse his face, to his mouth. A woman could be misled by this more passive looking beast. And be devoured in one bite.

And what of her? He was dangerous, not because she feared him but because she didn't. Being alone with him had revealed her own vulnerability. Yet God had put him here and she prayed for him daily.

Strength to withstand, the Holy Spirit had told her.

She still didn't know what Gunnar needed to withstand, but as for her, she prayed she could hold out against the physical and emotional sensations that assailed her whenever they were together.

Regretfully, Tessa left the room and pulled the door closed behind her.

15

Tessa woke with a kink in her neck and numbness in the fingers of her left hand. Since getting Gunnar out of her room was impossible, and sleeping on the couch would cause Dominic to ask questions, she had slept in the chair next to her bed. She was disappointed to learn it wasn't as comfortable as it looked.

She would have spent the night in her aunt's room, but soon after Elaine came in from her dinner engagement, the clicking of keyboard keys began, and Tessa hadn't wanted to disturb her progress.

But Tessa was worried. Not because her hand tingled with renewed circulation, but because Gunnar hadn't stirred all night. Once during the night, she'd thought he said her name, but when she looked over he'd been in exactly the same position he was in now. She walked to the side of the bed to check his breathing.

Satisfied he was alive, she went down to the kitchen to make a pot of coffee. It was seven thirty, which meant if Dominic came home last night he was likely out for a run. That gave her a half hour, more or less, to produce some answers.

He would be mad. This was his house, and Gunnar was his friend, and while she might be able to explain that Gunnar got sick and needed to lie down, how could she explain why he was in her room to begin with? She considered the truth, dismissed it. Would she believe it if someone told her? Doubtful.

Guilt wound around her. *Like a snake around a dagger.* She sighed inwardly.

But some things were personal, brother or not, and she wasn't willing to share the whole truth with him.

Dominic would have to get used to thinking of her in a different way—as an adult.

She filled a glass with cold, filtered water, brought it upstairs and set it on the bedside table. Gunnar needed to stay hydrated. She looked down at him. Boy, there was a lot of him to hydrate. But how to get him to drink?

Tessa was contemplating the dilemma when a sudden eruption from above gave her a jolt. She cupped the back of her neck, listening to her aunt's muffled voice through the ceiling, then went in the hall for a better listen.

It sounded like a one-sided argument comprised mainly of threats. Initially thinking Elaine was on the phone, Tessa understood that wasn't the case when the words, "I'll tell you what you can do with your spell check!" rose louder than the rest, followed by, "I did fine with a pad and pencil before you came along, and I'll do it again!"

Tessa never heard anyone threaten a computer before, but Aunt Elaine was one of a kind.

The buffer of carpet couldn't disguise the thump of angry feet as she strode to the door and down the narrow staircase leading from the attic.

When she emerged through the door, Tessa smiled. "Coffee?"

"You are a champion of all things good and just," Elaine said.

"You're exaggerating a bit."

Elaine slipped an arm around Tessa's waist and started down the stairs to the first floor. "To you it's only coffee. To me it's life's blood."

"Were you up all night?" Tessa asked.

"Most of it." Elaine looked her over. "You don't look like you slept too well."

"I slept in the chair in my room." Tessa shook her head when her aunt would have spoken. "About yesterday. Thank you for deflecting my mother, but it wasn't what you thought."

Elaine smiled.

"Seriously. Gunnar—Dominic's friend—wasn't feeling well and he sort of passed out in my room."

"Your brother's friend?"

"He could be really sick. Come see for yourself."

"He hasn't left?" she asked, surprised.

Elaine led the way back upstairs and continued to the side of the bed. "Well, would you look at that," she said, all female appreciation as she stared down at Gunnar.

"I didn't want to cover him, he looked pretty warm," Tessa said, recalling his *hot-blooded* remark. "He's been sleeping for..." She glanced at the clock. "Twenty-one hours!"

Elaine poked a finger in his ribcage. "Hey." There was no response. "Maybe he isn't sick," she told Tessa. "Could have overdosed on something."

"It must be the flu," Tessa said. "He had a headache the other night, and he might have a fever. I hope I don't get it."

"Well, that's how it is when two people are close." Elaine met Tessa's arched brow with one of her own. "I mean it's easy to spread a bug when two people are in the same house," she amended.

"What do I do with him?" Tessa asked, walking into the hall. Elaine followed, glancing back at Gunnar and tapping a stubby nail to her front teeth. "I don't know what's wrong with him. He hasn't had anything to eat or drink, and I can't leave him in my room."

Elaine's expression sobered. "Dominic doesn't know he's here?"

"He's staying here, so Dominic knows he's here, he just doesn't know he's there," Tessa said, pointing to her bed. "And he'll be back soon."

"Hmm. Well let me have another look at him, huh? You go get the coffee ready."

A few minutes later Elaine entered the kitchen with Gunnar's clothes.

"You undressed him?" Tessa asked. "How did you do that? *Why* did you do that?" Bad enough to have a man in her bed, now she had a naked man in her bed! Momentary panic set in, and Tessa's gaze flew to the windows for any sign of her brother.

"He was sweaty." Elaine planted her feet and sent back Tessa's disbelieving stare. "It isn't that I don't appreciate the male body, but I am old enough to be his mother. Wow, that's depressing," she added.

"So he's completely—"

"Naked as a newborn," Elaine said.

Tessa bit her lip.

"Have you seen his tattoos?"

Tessa fidgeted. Things had worsened in mere minutes. "Thanks for your help, but you shouldn't trouble yourself. You're a guest. You should be resting or working, not undressing strange men."

Elaine let out a spirited, room-filling laugh. "I can think of less entertaining things to do with my time," she said. "Stop standing on propriety, Tess. You'll make yourself a wreck trying to be perfect. I need to throw these in the laundry."

Tessa watched her aunt disappear through the cellar door. The comment wasn't meant as a barb, but pricked, nonetheless. She tried so hard to break out of the mold her mother stuffed her into and learning from a trusted source that her efforts were feeble at best, was discouraging.

If she could at least claim to be helping Gunnar out of sheer compassion, well that would be useful in redeeming this feeling of failure. But she didn't have that to fall back on, either. She wasn't sure of her feelings for Gunnar, but compassion was at least fourth on the list of motivating factors.

And here she was, climbing the stairs, trying to reason her way back to the perfect list. Most discouraging. Why couldn't she be more like Gunnar? It was evident he didn't care what people thought of him.

She remembered the first time he'd ridden to the house. She'd been so taken aback by his imposing glower and mysterious demeanor she actually trembled. Then she thought of the way he kissed her yesterday. She'd trembled then, too.

At the top of the stairs she heard a low groan and hurried to find Gunnar sitting up with her sheet pooled at his waist.

One large bicep flexed as he kneaded the back of his neck. He looked like a man stumbling out of a dream, and she watched his expressions change, knowing he was trying to piece together the past day's events. After a few seconds, he glanced down, peeked under the sheet. "Where are my clothes?"

"My aunt has them," Tessa said, stopping inside the door.

"Why?"

"You were sweating. She wanted to keep you— oh." Tessa quickly covered her eyes when Gunnar started to throw back the sheet.

He stopped. "Give me a break. I don't have anything you haven't seen before."

Tessa let her hands fall to her sides, but her cheeks warmed.

Gunnar cocked a brow. "You're kidding. You've never seen a naked man?"

Tessa tipped her chin. "Of course I have." *On TV.*

He snickered. "When?"

When she didn't answer right away she watched that magnificent face go through several more transformations before coming to the logical conclusion.

"Don't tell me you've never—"

"I don't sleep around." Intellectually she comprehended there was no reason to be embarrassed. Quite the opposite. Yet...

"Never?" He pulled the sheet tighter around him. "Ever?"

Tessa exhaled sharply. "Why does it matter?"

"Our patient is up?" Elaine asked, pushing past a grateful Tessa.

"Where are my clothes?" Gunnar asked her.

"In the wash. You'll have them back soon enough."

"I have other clothes in my room."

Ignoring him, Elaine sat on the edge of the bed and gave him a pat on the cheek. "You had some nap. Do you feel any better?"

Gunnar moved his face away. "I don't nap."

"I suppose not. I'd say it was closer to a coma, since it's Saturday," she countered.

"Saturday?" Gunnar watched Tessa move to the window. "Saturday," he repeated.

Elaine regarded him with cool eyes. "Tessa is convinced you have the flu, but I'm not. Are you into anything you shouldn't be?"

"What are you asking me?" he demanded.

Unruffled, Elaine smoothed the sheets under her hand. "You've been basically unconscious for almost a full day. Don't you find that odd?"

"It's exhaustion," he said.

"Tessa's very worried. She watched over you all night."

"You didn't have to do that," he told Tessa.

Elaine cocked a half smile at him. "Do you need anything?"

"Yeah, my clothes. I want to get up."

She nodded and pursed her lips. "Well it's a shame to hide all that, but suit yourself." With an appreciative lift of brows she walked out, with Tessa following close behind.

∽∾

Tessa was in the basement pulling clothes from the dryer when she heard Dominic come in from his run, whistling. She knew he would head directly upstairs to shower and prayed she'd remembered to close her bedroom door.

When he came back down, still whistling, and told her he was leaving early, she let her muscles relax.

Carrying Gunnar's freshly laundered clothes,

Tessa slipped quietly into her room to find it empty. She assumed he was back in his room and didn't want to disturb him so she laid the clothes at the foot of her bed, took a stack of papers from the desk and went down to the sun porch.

She pulled a wicker chair up to the matching table and began sorting through a mound of envelopes bound together with her checkbook in a rubber band. Checks and balances, facts and figures were what she needed to fill her mind, rather than images of a man she barely knew. A naked man. Numbers were constant, they weren't unpredictable or moody and under no circumstances did they make her blood run hot.

Ten minutes later Tessa threw down her pen and dropped her head into her hands. Her hair fell forward partially shielding her face. She was getting nothing done, and it was Gunnar's fault. It had to be his fault. Paying bills and justifying her checkbook had always been a simple task, but now she struggled to get through it.

She started to lean back in the chair when a knock behind her nearly toppled her. She righted herself just in time.

"Gunnar!"

"You told me to stop sneaking up on you, so I knocked."

She regarded him before she stood.

He was trying. And fully dressed.

"So, you're up and about." She placed a hand on his forehead. "No fever."

Gunnar remained very still.

At once aware of his proximity, Tessa stepped back. "Your color is much better, too. Are you hungry?"

"Starving."

"They say to eat light after a fever."

"I don't care what *they* say. And I didn't have a fever," he argued.

"So, why were you sweating?"

"Because it's hot in your room, and I'm hot-blooded."

His smile was so unexpected, it left her no option but to return it. To hide the flush stealing along her neck, she skirted around him and started for the kitchen.

"Do you want French toast?"

"Depends. Is it any good?"

Tessa gave a soft sniff. "I make excellent French toast."

"Count me in."

He swayed a bit, and she urged him into a kitchen chair. He might feel better, but he had a way to go. She took a glass down from the cabinet and half filled it with orange juice.

"Drink this."

"I don't like orange juice," he said.

Tessa stared at him until he took a sip.

"Happy?"

"I'll have this ready in a few minutes." Tessa slid a cutting board in front of her. She enjoyed the surprise on his face when she began slicing French bread into thick slabs instead of pulling white bread from a bag.

"You like to cook?" he asked.

"Yes. I'm dreadfully domestic," she said, inwardly flinching at the punch of self-consciousness she felt when declaring it aloud.

"Do you want some help?"

She knew he offered to be polite, but hated to turn it down. "Can you beat eggs?"

"Yes, I can beat eggs."

A cranky child, she thought, and smiled at him. When he didn't reciprocate, she opened the fridge. The air hinted of that subtle, indefinable something that caused things to change between them. She had to be careful.

She broke several eggs into a bowl, added half-and-half and set it in front of Gunnar. He wasn't much for conversation, but Tessa couldn't very well putter around in awkward silence, so while she prepared breakfast, assembling ingredients, frying sausage and brewing coffee, she commented on the weather, the price of groceries, and the importance of "going green."

If he minded the discussion, he didn't say anything and fifteen minutes later she took a cookie sheet from the oven, slid golden brown medallions onto a plate and dusted them with powdered sugar.

"Thank you," he said when she set a plate in front of him. "For everything."

She looked at him, but his eyes were on his plate. "Can I ask you a question?"

He moved his head in assent and dug into his breakfast.

"What's wrong with you?"

Gunnar swallowed before answering. "You'll have to be more specific."

"Are you sick? Is it the flu?"

"If you're worried you'll catch it—"

"I'm not worried for myself." True enough, she'd recovered from her initial fear. "But you may need a doctor."

He glanced at her. "It's exhaustion."

She raised one eyebrow. "With a fever?"

"I didn't have a fever."

"You might have, we didn't check."

Gunnar put down his fork. "Maybe it's the flu. Or maybe it's a new disease destined to kill off the planet."

Tessa sat across from him. "I'm sorry, I'm concerned."

When he looked at her, the irritation was gone. He sighed. "I told you I don't sleep much. It caught up with me."

She quirked her lips. "Hmm. You should be all caught up now."

"And dehydration. It's happened before."

When the phone rang, Gunnar plucked the receiver off the wall and handed it to her.

"Hello," she answered, watching him.

He focused on his food.

"Yes, this is she. Oh, hi! Yes, fine. Monday at eleven. Thank you." Tessa handed the phone back to Gunnar. "My realtor," she told him, refilling his empty plate.

"Going somewhere?"

"Well yes. I can't keep sitting around here doing nothing. I need my own place."

Gunnar chuckled. "Doing nothing? You're one of the busiest people I know."

She wasn't sure what he meant, so didn't reply.

"You're working all the time. You should open a bed and breakfast."

"What?" she asked, delighted.

His comment had come off the cuff with no real intent, but struck her like a whip crack. Starting a business posed tremendous risks, and she was riddled with misgivings about whether she really possessed the nerve to try, but his words soared through her, fanning a flame in her spirit.

"You relate to people," he said in that accusatory tone of his. "You're efficient, responsible; it should be easy for you." He looked at her then. "Are you OK?"

Tears stung her eyes. How was it that her parents missed in her what he could see so plainly? She tried to blink back the flood but in the end, spurted like a broken water pipe.

Gunnar jumped to his feet, though he didn't come closer.

Through the blur of tears, she saw his face, panicked, desperate and uncertain whether to run from the room or from the house.

She let out a watery laugh and got to her feet to pull a paper towel off the roll. "I needed to hear that," she said, dabbing her cheeks.

"Yeah…"

"Really, it's a confirmation of something I'm praying about." The mention of prayer appeared to distress him further, so she tried another smile, having more success this time. "I don't want to practice law anymore, and you helped me, right this moment to solidify my plans."

Gunnar put his hands up. "No, don't blame me, I just made an observation."

When Tessa stepped closer, he moved back. "What's the problem? I'm thanking you."

"Will you be thanking me if it doesn't work?"

"Don't be silly, you don't have that power. If my choices don't work, it isn't your fault. I'd already decided to do it, God just used you to confirm it."

Anger, quickly controlled, flashed in Gunnar's eyes. "No one used me."

With that, he sat back down and ate his meal. When he finished he murmured a "thanks," and left the room. Tessa didn't see him for the rest of the day.

৵৽৽

The week passed with barely a sighting. Whenever Gunnar came in, he marched right to his room, and when he departed it was without so much as a backward glance. He joined Dominic on a few of his morning runs, but yesterday, when Tessa met them at the back door with hot coffee and muffins, Gunnar made an excuse and left. In fact, he made it his habit to vacate a room whenever she entered.

She wondered what to make of the man as she leafed through the Sunday paper at the breakfast table. Perhaps she'd freaked him out with her display of tears the day they'd discussed opening a B & B, or maybe it was because God had come up again. She decided it must be a combination of the two, but she had news for Mr. Gunnar Mason. Just because he got prickly about his emotions didn't mean he could dampen her spirits.

His issues with God were his problem. As a Christian, she spoke of God in real and practical terms in her everyday life.

If it disturbed Gunnar, he may as well continue avoiding her.

When she flipped a page and it tore right out, she knew it was time to eject Gunnar from her mind. There were more important things to dwell on. She had a meeting with a new realtor tomorrow afternoon. The first one seemed more interested in making a sale than in meeting Tessa's requirements, but Fey Beaumont understood Tessa's needs.

A house with potential. She pictured it as she walked down the hall toward the front door. A Victorian, small enough to be homey, but large enough for guests to enjoy their privacy. There would be a library with ceiling high shelves and an English garden in back where guests could sit and talk on carved stone benches. A large porch was essential, to offer respite from the hot afternoon sun, or a calming place to wind down at the end of the day.

Excitement bubbled in Tessa. She looked forward to the work, the preparation.

Right now, however, she had a few minutes to pamper herself, so she went to her room and took her nail polish bag from the dresser top. She was feeling a little *Manhattan Red.* After finding the shade, she sat on the chair with one foot propped on the windowsill and began to dash on glossy polish. It was likely the most fun she would have all day.

She missed Aunt Elaine, who was on to bigger and brighter things with interesting companions.

Tessa could check the mail at any time and not be surprised to find a simple post card from Norway or an authentic fan from Hong Kong.

There was a woman who knew how to spoil herself. Elaine's freedom was one of the things Tessa admired most. Not that she herself possessed any great desire to travel the world, but just thinking she could was liberating.

Tessa was on the fourth toe, scraping off excess polish with the edge of her thumbnail, when the phone rang. She replaced the brush in the bottle, then half hopped, half hobbled to answer.

"Hello."

"Hello," came the female voice. "I was told I might reach Gunnar Mason there. Is he in?" The woman's tone was provocative, silky smooth.

Tessa felt a hot stab of jealousy. She cleared her throat. "No, he isn't. Can I take a message?"

"I'm sorry to trouble you, but I tried his cell and he doesn't answer. Would you tell him Samantha called?"

"Yes, of course."

"Thank you."

There was no reason to be incensed by a phone call from another woman. Tessa's mind conceded that. Her heart held a different view. Alexandra, Samantha, who else?

She finished her toenails and shuffled on her heels to bring the polish bag to the dresser with an indignant thump. Was it too much to ask that a few minutes of personal indulgence not be soured by thoughts of Gunnar and his throng of women? She had to find a way to keep her mind busy.

Tessa fanned her feet with a magazine. She would have sat back and read it while her toes air dried, but for the restlessness creeping in. She supposed she could go through her already faultless drawers and fluff some shirts and underwear, but how long could that distract her?

Sitting on her bed, Tessa opened her Bible to Proverbs. The words were comforting and powerful but not what she needed at the moment. She needed to get to the bottom of things. She closed the Bible.

"What's the deal, Lord?" she asked aloud. "I don't have the same burden to pray for Gunnar as when he first came, so why is he still here if the danger is passed?"

She didn't expect a voice from heaven, but it would be nice one of these times. "I don't want to complain, exactly," she said, winding a rope of hair around her finger. "But it's making things hard on me. I'm attracted to him. Why throw us together if there's going to be all this tension?"

She looked at the sky through her window. The clouds were choppy and white, like a gallon of vanilla ice cream after a scoop was dragged through it. Her mind was muddled when it came to Gunnar. She was all but positive he didn't believe in Christ, he was stubborn, aggressive, and unfriendly. Not her type at all.

Yet, occasionally she saw something more. The fact that he had the opportunity to take advantage of her and didn't, told her he possessed a strength of character many men lacked. At least the men she'd met so far. He was rugged, hard-working, creative...

Tessa sighed, annoyed with herself for weaving a romantic fantasy featuring Gunnar as hero.

"He doesn't believe in You, so what's the point?" she asked God.

The sound of a car pulling into the drive moved her to the window. She was appalled to find her palms already sweaty, her pulse accelerating. More appalled by the sinking disappointment when she realized it wasn't Gunnar's car, but Connie's mother's.

When she saw Anna emerge from the passenger seat of the silver Mercedes, Tessa exhaled noisily. "Just what I need."

Hurrying downstairs, she gritted her teeth, remembering that only a short time ago she was looking for a distraction. This ought to qualify.

16

Before Tessa could get to the kitchen door Connie charged through it, her words coming in a mad rush. "I'm sorry, Tess. I stopped at my mother's and your mother was there and before I could stop them we were here."

"Don't worry, I'll cope." Tessa was doubtful

"Cope with what?" Vivian asked, coming in. Her hair was blonde this month, a departure from her usual mousy brown. She was heavier than her daughter by a good forty pounds, but every bit as spunky and charming.

"The wedding," Connie supplied.

"Come here, kid." Vivian embraced Tessa in a bear hug, then kissed her cheek and stepped back to inspect her. "You're prettier than ever."

Tessa rolled her eyes, smiling. "You say that every time you see me."

Vivian set a bag on the table. "And it's always true."

"Good morning, Tessa."

Tessa hugged her mother. "Good morning," she said, trying to sound carefree and welcoming.

How Anna and Vivian had become friends was beyond Tessa. Vivian preferred garage sales to upscale boutiques, jeans to designer pantsuits, and never wore diamonds to the supermarket. An odd pairing.

"Sorry to stop by without calling," Anna said.

"You're setting some kind of record." It was meant as a dig, and Tessa regretted it instantly.

Her mother didn't seem to catch it.

Vivian draped an arm across Tessa's shoulder. "She said you were acting strange the last time she was here. We're more or less here to spy."

Tessa looked to Connie who shrugged, helpless. The good Lord only knew how much Connie revealed to Vivian about Gunnar and how much of it got back to Anna. Fortunately, Connie knew nothing of Gunnar's stay in her room.

In an uncharacteristic gesture, Anna took Tessa by the shoulders and skimmed her hands down her arms to clasp her wrists. "Nonsense. We're here to discuss wedding plans, not spy. It's not a bad time I hope."

"No. Just doing some primping." Tessa wiggled her bright red toes "Do you want coffee?"

"Iced tea will be fine for me if you have it," Vivian answered.

"Me too," Anna said.

Connie handed Tessa a business card. "It's Carter's number. I know you're not interested, but he made me promise to give it to you the next time I saw you."

Tessa took it reluctantly and read it. On the back he had written, *Thinking of you. Please call me, Carter.* She put it on the counter.

"My sister told me he's gaga for you," said Vivian.

Tessa nearly shivered before facing her. "What?"

"All he's done is rave about you since your date."

"It wasn't a date, it was a phone call," Tessa answered, taking a pitcher of iced tea from the fridge.

"Carter...he's Diane's middle boy?" Anna asked,

her tone casual enough to raise the hairs on the back of Tessa's neck. Her mother didn't do casual.

"Yes." Vivian said, moving into the living room. "Carter's the first in our family to finish college. He's currently with a computer software company, but he's designing his own programs."

Anna took one of the glasses Tessa offered. "I haven't met his father but he must favor him with the fair complexion."

"Oh, definitely his father. He's blond and six foot three."

"Oooh, sounds like a Viking."

"Mom!" Tessa laughed. She had never heard her mother describe any man with interest, much less Vikings. She wondered how long her mom and Vivian worked on this little skit.

"For you, dear. I'm thinking of you," Anna said.

"Hey, let's talk about Mike," Connie said, raising her glass in a toast.

Tessa mouthed a thank you to Connie as they all sat. The subject of Carter would be dropped in favor of something—anything—else.

By two o'clock the living room was littered with bridal magazines, photos, travel brochures, and samples of everything from ribbons to silk flowers.

Vivian and Anna were in charge of lists. Lists of caterers, gown designers, limo services, and printers.

Although Tessa had mentally planned her wedding from the age of seven, she was just learning all that it entailed. She couldn't complain; she was the maid of honor, after all, and would stand dutifully by while the bride sneered at, and second-guessed, every suggestion.

Tessa gave her opinions, but found she was most

helpful when she stayed out of the way as Connie and Vivian disputed practically everything. They squabbled over the guest list, the music and the centerpieces and heatedly deliberated the pros and cons of ice sculptures. They shuffled and reshuffled the seating for the reception no less than twelve times, and had moved on to debate the method of transport for the ring from the rear of the church to the front.

"A nice box speaks of romance and secrets of the heart," Connie said, admiring a photo of an antique mahogany box.

"And a silk pillow isn't romantic?" Vivian pointed to the pillow at the top of the next page. Connie groaned. "What if the ring bearer slips? He won't knock his teeth loose on a pillow," Vivian argued.

"Who is he?" Anna asked.

"Mike's cousin, Andy," Connie answered. "He's six. And he'll make it down the aisle fine."

"Not if he slips on a pile of rose petals," Vivian interjected.

Connie rolled her eyes. "Not again."

"You have too many," Vivian said, tapping her pencil on the list that called for the petals of one hundred white roses to be strewn down the center aisle of the church. "You might as well scatter banana peels."

"Mom, you're being a fusspot. No one's going to slip."

"My concern is for you in your heels."

Connie tossed the magazine on the coffee table and opened another. "Didn't I tell you? I'm going barefoot."

"Barefoot!"

Connie hooted and threw an arm around her

mother. "I'm kidding. Mike's too tall for me to go barefoot. But you need to relax."

"I couldn't agree more," Vivian said.

"Is there any more pizza?" Anna asked.

Tessa opened one of the three boxes and handed her a slice with mushrooms. The woman sitting on the couch with pizza in one hand and a notebook in the other resembled her mother, but had barely criticized her, and only half-lackadaisically tried to dominate the conversation in the three hours she'd been here. *System alert.*

"What do you think of this centerpiece?" Connie asked, holding up a photo.

Tessa took the picture of a circle made of small paper lanterns and votives. "It's nice. If you're not worried you'll set the hall on fire."

"You're right."

Vivian slapped her knee. "If I said that you'd argue till you were blue in your face," she told Connie.

"A mother's advice is never appreciated," Anna stated.

Ah, she's in there. She might be on her best behavior, but she's in there.

An hour later, Anna and Vivian occupied the sofa, each at an end with their legs extended beside the other as they continued to look through magazines.

"Diane tells me Carter's having a home built in Morristown," Anna said.

Subtlety not being Anna's strong suit, it became obvious as she heralded what few things she could assign as Carter's attributes, that the "mothers" planned to follow through with their match-making.

Vivian laid it on thick, certifying to the room that in this unsure world of divorce and abandonment,

Carter was a safe bet.

Tessa crossed her arms, watching the co-conspirators waste their time. Even if Carter's hands weren't smoother than her own, she wouldn't be interested in a man who could use the word *astonishingly* five times in a four minute conversation. He had the personality of a chew toy and half the charm.

Tessa sent Connie a pleading look, but Connie's eyes were riveted on the figure towering in the doorway. One pair at a time, all eyes followed.

Gunnar's sullen eyes took the room in at a glance before he started to walk away.

"Wait!" Tessa jumped to her feet, thinking it better to introduce him than to leave him open to speculation. In the process, she tripped on Connie's knee and would have smashed her face on the arm of a chair, but Gunnar was quick and yanked her upright. "I want to introduce you," Tessa said, without breaking rhythm.

Gunnar let her go, but Tessa held on hoping he would interpret the small squeeze on his arm as a plea not to make a scene. "You already met Connie."

"Hey," Connie raised her glass of iced tea to him.

"This is her mother, Vivian."

With a little tug from Tessa, Gunnar took Vivian's outstretched hand.

"This is Gunnar Mason," Tessa said.

Vivian leaned forward in her seat. "Nice to meet you." He gave a noncommittal grumble.

Tessa hesitated before turning to Anna, whose eyes were narrowed to slits. Maybe she should have let him leave. "This is my mother." She held her breath, expecting the worst.

Gunnar didn't smile, but neither did he growl. It

was progress. He stood with one hand clutching his jacket and the other forming a fist at his side. Tessa could tell by her mother's expression that she found his etiquette deficient.

"You're a friend of Tessa's?" Anna asked, with special emphasis on *friend*.

"Yeah," Gunnar answered.

"Dominic's, actually." Tessa shot her mother an admonishing look that went unobserved since Anna's eyes were fixed on Gunnar.

"Have you known each other long?"

"Mother."

"Just making conversation, sweetheart." Anna smiled at Gunnar. "I don't mean to pry. But how long have you been acquainted?"

"I hardly know her," he said. "But I plan on changing that." In a move both challenging and possessive, Gunnar's arm came around Tessa's waist and cinched her closer to his side.

She stiffened.

Anna's face paled, her eyes enlarged.

Tessa tried a hesitant smile, and Vivian and Connie laughed outright.

"How much better?" Anna asked.

"Better," Gunnar answered.

"For heaven's sake, Anna, stop giving him the third degree," Vivian said. "Tessa is a big girl."

"Of course she is," a defensive Anna countered. "I'm curious about what goes on in my only daughter's life, that's all. I don't see what's wrong with a few simple questions."

Tessa pushed away from Gunnar and stood between them. Anger quickly replaced her initial dread. "Stop it, both of you."

When Gunnar's brow lifted, Tessa parried it before addressing her mother. "I appreciate your concern, Mom, but I'm an adult and what goes on in my life is my business."

Gunnar smirked in a self-satisfied way that made her want to punch him.

"And you have no right to mislead my mother and my friends because I made you take a few seconds out of your sulk time to actually speak to someone," she told him. His eyes darkened, but she straightened her spine and addressed the room. "If you'll all excuse me, I'm done with schemes and inquisitions."

She stomped from the room leaving three mouths agape and one set in a grim line.

17

Gunnar crossed the bedroom threshold and found Tessa sitting with her back rigid against her headboard and a notebook across her bent knees. Her head whipped around when he came in and closed the door behind him. Carefully, she laid aside the notebook. "What are you doing here?"

He could see the panic swell in her and how hard she worked to drive it back. It was clear she would never conquer this fear of him, not really. "You said to come in."

"No I didn't."

"Yeah, you did." He'd knocked; she'd said come in. He remembered it exactly, it only happened four seconds ago.

Tessa shook her hair back. "I wasn't paying attention. I must have thought you were Connie."

"They left."

She started to slide to the edge of the bed, but paused, blinked. "What do you mean they left?"

Gunnar rolled his hand over, stalling. Given her already guarded state, it would sound too ominous to say he got rid of them. It was easier than he'd expected. A simple matter of pulling Connie aside and telling her he and Tessa needed to talk. He could tell from Connie's breathless sigh and twinkling doe eyes that she was probably conjuring some kind of romantic notion in her mind, but Tessa could straighten it out later. They were gone and that was what mattered.

Tessa regarded him with suspicious eyes. "This is my room."

He waved her off, annoyed. "Yeah, I know."

"You shouldn't be in here."

"I've been in here before."

"You were sick," Tessa said.

One look at her sweet face, glowing pink, told him she not only remembered him here, but in her bed, naked. He couldn't forget it either. It wasn't every day a woman told him she was a virgin.

"That was different," she added.

He hardly heard the words. Thinking of her inexperience made his mind go places it shouldn't; it was easy to lose his train of thought. He blinked before he could forget his reason for being here and stood in front of her at the foot of the bed. He held out the business card he'd found in the kitchen. "Who's Carter?"

Tessa tried to snatch the card from his fingers but he closed his fist around it.

Her fear seemed forgotten as she rose. "Give me that. You have no right to—"

"I don't care."

That stumped her, for a moment. "That is my property and none of your business."

"I disagree," Gunnar told her.

"Well...*I* don't care!"

Gunnar narrowed his eyes in warning, but her gaze flashed right back. Was it any wonder he wanted her?

"The people in my life are none of your concern. You don't see me being immature because Samantha called for you."

"She did?" He looked at her until she dropped that beautiful green gaze to the floor. There was an unusual strain in her voice he couldn't quite...could she be jealous?

Tessa whirled away from him toward the door.

His hand was on her arm in a second. "Where do you think you're going?" he asked. The sudden awareness of how slim her arm was in his grasp caused him to loosen his hold.

"I won't stand here and argue with you," she told him.

"Then let's not argue."

Slowly, he pulled her closer, watching the pulse jump in her neck. She didn't resist when he lowered his mouth to hers.

Gunnar could have sworn her bones liquefied as she melted against him, into him. This was risky. It should stop. She was like a drug, the feel of her an addiction, and he feared if he didn't break it off now, there would be no going back. He drank in a few more seconds before levering her away.

His own ragged breathing drowned out the sound of hers, but her mouth opened and closed, evidence that she too struggled to form a coherent sentence.

Desire snapped in the air between them, and he turned away before it could draw him back.

What was he thinking, kissing her that way? He wasn't—that was the problem. He hadn't recognized how close he was to flashpoint and had allowed emotion to rule. Normally the emotion was anger. It was familiar, safe, he knew how to direct it, what to expect in retaliation.

But this...altogether different. In the short time

he'd known Tessa, she had infiltrated his core needs, forcing him to reevaluate his objectives, making him realize he still wanted things he'd long ago dismissed as impossible: a home, children, stability.

Consequently, he feared things he hadn't before: isolation, failure, dependence. It was too much, too soon. He hadn't lied to her mother, he hardly knew her. Yet she had already influenced him in ways he couldn't express. What would happen over time, six months maybe, when he became more attached and unable to let her go?

When Tessa finally realized who and what he was?

"We can't do this," he told her, looking back.

Tessa stood frozen, catching her breath.

"I won't get us into a situation we'll regret."

"But…"

"You're not ready for this."

The light of battle sparked to life in her eyes, dissipating the haze of longing.

"Neither am I."

"Because I'm a virgin," she said, disgusted.

"Yes." He snapped the word out, but hearing the harshness of it, softened his tone. It wasn't her fault he wanted her. Nor was he pushing her away because of her inexperience—at least not in the way she thought. "You're innocent and I'm not. In any sense of the word."

Tessa crossed her arms. "So it's your plan to keep turning me on and off like a light switch until when? Until you're bored or decide to move back to your house?"

"I didn't mean for this to happen."

"You want me."

It was a simple statement. He couldn't have said why it sounded like a threat. "I do. But it's not going to happen."

"Because you say so," she said with a nod. "Interesting. You didn't want my mother to treat me like a child, but ten minutes later you're doing it."

"This is different."

"Because you know what's best? She thinks the same thing."

Well, what could he say to that?

Tessa raised her chin and went to the door. "Please leave."

She'd given him his escape from the mess he'd created. But for how long? Until the next time they were in the same room together and the scent of her freshly scrubbed skin snared him? Or she walked past and sent him one of those long looks she probably wasn't even aware of? The ones that made his heart spasm and his brain misfire?

He had no intention of going through this again.

When she reached for the knob, he slapped a hand onto the painted wood of the door.

"I asked you to leave." Her voice was laced with nerves and heat.

Patience ebbing, Gunnar hissed out a breath, took her by the arm and sat her on the bed.

"What are—"

"Sit there and shut up."

"Don't tell me to shut up."

"Just…please." Gunnar scraped a hand over the stubble on his head, then jammed his hands in his pockets.

He didn't intend for things to spin this way. When he came into the house, it was with the desire to grab a quick shower before meeting Max and David at McIntosh's. Almost at once, he was being lured by the sound of women's voices singing the praises of a guy named Carter in an overt attempt to interest someone.

Entering the living room, seeing the look on Tessa's face, it became clear she was the intended mark. She didn't look interested, but it irritated him to think she might be. Then, to find the jerk's card with his friendly little message...

In hindsight, keeping her mother and friends here might have been the wiser course. If they were still here, he would be on his way to a friendly game of pool. But jealousy was a newly discovered muscle, and it grew and strengthened when flexed.

He gazed out the window to where the clouds skidded away, revealing a sky of pale blue, in direct contrast to the gloomy gray of his heart. Below was a fenced in yard with thick grass, though browning, and a tall gnarled oak. The kind of yard he would have loved to play in as a kid.

Instead, he'd kept himself occupied in dim hallways and dismal rooms where he'd been forced to wait quietly while his mother entertained her boyfriend of the hour one thin wall away. It was a world away from here. A world away from Tessa.

He glanced at the fresh flowers on the table under the window, a reminder of the kind of woman Tessa was and the fact that she was far, far out of his league. He needed to stop dreaming about what he could never have and end this stupidity now before it got out of hand. And maybe the best way to do it was to force her to see the differences between them.

18

"Are you just going to stare out the window while I sit here? Am I some kind of hostage?" Tessa asked.

"You can't give yourself to someone you don't know," he said, immediately spinning around, assuming she would argue the point. "I don't mean because you're a child, I mean because you aren't that way. If you could you would have already, and this conversation would be unnecessary."

To his relief she remained silent.

"You don't know me, Tessa. Just because I showed you my tattoos and where I work isn't enough to make you shake off your morals and climb into bed with me."

She rolled her eyes.

"Your brother doesn't want me to touch you," Gunnar said. "Believe me, he has his reasons."

"Then why don't you go?"

She started to get up, presumably to show him the door again, but he stopped her with a look.

"Because if I don't do this now, we're going to keep going around in a circle."

"For my good."

He ignored the sarcasm. "Dominic thinks he knows me, too. And he does, better than most people, but he wouldn't let me through the front door if he knew everything I've done."

Tessa's lips tightened. "Dominic would never reject you."

"Not the Gunnar he knows, no," he said, returning his gaze to the yard. "But the Gunnar who turned his back on his family when they needed him? The Gunnar who killed a man?" He heard her soft gasp and closed his eyes. "Dom wouldn't have any part of that guy."

When he faced Tessa, her eyes were huge, puzzled, and sad. She sipped in a small breath. "Your family..."

Surprised her first question wasn't about killing a man, it took him a few seconds to follow her thoughts. "I'm not married, Tessa. I didn't abandon a wife and a house full of kids. I mean my brother and sister."

"Of course," she said. "Dominic would have mentioned..."

He could see her relief. Too bad it would be short lived.

"I find it hard to believe you turned your back on them," Tessa said.

"My point exactly." He came to sit beside her on the bed, hands clasped and hanging between his knees. "You don't know me."

She didn't argue, but he knew she wanted to.

"My mother died when I was eleven—"

"I'm sorry."

"Don't be. When she died I took care of the kids."

"At eleven?"

"I'm the oldest." Gunnar sneered. "I took care of them most of the time when she was alive. I could hardly do worse. I did what I had to do to keep them alive."

It would serve no purpose to tell her how they'd made a home in an abandoned box truck and scrounged meals out of restaurant dumpsters. Or the things he'd done to make money.

"How old were they?" Tessa asked.

He cast her a sidelong glance.

Her hands were folded in her lap.

"My brother was seven, my sister eight," he said, staggered by the depth of emotion the words revived in him. "And one night when I was seventeen I took off and didn't go back."

The story in a nutshell.

"What happened to them?" Tessa asked, her face filled with concern for his family, people she'd never met.

"Child Services put them in foster care."

"I'm sorry."

So was he. It was what he'd tried to avoid until he couldn't hack it any more. It hurt, then and now, to acknowledge that when his family needed him, he'd abandoned them. The fact that neither of them complained made it worse.

He got up to pace, taking a moment to remind himself that telling Tessa was the right thing. It was almost unbearable, this simultaneous hope and dread, recognizing that in a few minutes whatever she felt for him would change forever. He rolled his head in an attempt to release the knots of tension from his neck.

"I couldn't cut being their father so I convinced myself they'd be better off anywhere than with me."

"You were only a boy," Tessa said, with brimming emotion.

"I was never a boy." His tone sounded harsh, but he couldn't soften it with the anger and pain constricting his vocal chords. "While they tumbled around in the system I got into drugs. I guess to numb me," he said, then chuckled derisively. Did it make sense to defend that part of him when he was about to expose much worse? He let the silence prepare them both.

"Don't," he said when he sensed Tessa forming a syllable. "Let me get through this." Gunnar cracked his knuckles and drew in a breath. "I had no way to contact them. But there was a judge who tried to help me. Judge Barrett," he said with genuine affection. "After my third arrest for car theft she got down off the bench and dragged me in her office." He let the corners of his mouth kick up with the memory. "She was tough, but went out of her way to help me. Anyway, she fixed it so I could call the kids once a week. I couldn't bring myself to visit."

He ran his hand down the smooth painted window frame, let it fall away. "I didn't see them face to face for two years, but one night when I was nineteen Samantha called me, crying so hard I could hardly understand her."

A renewed feeling of helplessness surged forth and he gritted his teeth to keep it at bay.

"Samantha's your sister," Tessa murmured.

Gunnar gave a firm nod. "Samantha and Evan were in separate foster homes. Evan did OK in his, but Sam was with a new couple. The wife used her for a slave and the husband was always drooling over her."

This was it, Gunnar settled in his mind, no going back. "This time when she called, she was terrified. The wife was out and the husband tried to rape her."

Tessa sucked in a breath.

He couldn't tell her precisely what Samantha told him. "She locked herself in the bathroom with the phone and begged me to come before he found a way in. She didn't call the cops," he said quietly. "She called me.

"I told her to get out of the house if she could, then I went blank. No rage, no explosion, nothing." His hands involuntarily fisted at his sides. "I don't remember the drive, only pulling up and walking into the house."

Gunnar swung around and stood in front of Tessa. "He was in his underwear, climbing the stairs with a can of beer in one hand and a screw driver in the other. I didn't wait for him to ask who I was, I just grabbed him by the throat, threw him down the stairs and started beating him."

"Oh…" Tessa whispered.

With no effort Gunnar could evoke the sound of bone meeting bone as his fist repeatedly made contact. "He couldn't put up a fight. I could have walked away." He crouched down in front of Tessa and met her eyes levelly. "But something told me to finish him off."

Tessa brought her arms up to hug herself.

"So I killed him."

"But—"

Gunnar shook his head, furious. "No! No 'but'. I killed him because I wanted to. I just clicked off." Tears welled in Tessa's eyes, but he couldn't stop when he was so close to pushing her away.

"I saw Sam in the upstairs window when I left, but I didn't even talk to her."

A tear escaped down Tessa's cheek. "You protected your sister," she said.

Gunnar shook her, gently, but with any luck enough to get her brain back in gear. "Understand what I'm saying to you. It wasn't the first time I wanted to kill or the last, only the first time I did. Lester Watts was a piece of trash, and I wanted him dead, so I beat him to death with my bare hands. That's what's in me."

Even now, Tessa tried to touch him, but he took her hand from his shoulder. Emotions swirled in her misty green eyes, too strong, too real to hide.

He didn't want or deserve her compassion.

"The police...didn't—"

"No witnesses," Gunnar answered. "I saw it on the news the next day. Turned out he'd been molesting children in the neighborhood for years, and they assumed one of them got even. Bad police work if you ask me."

"How did he ever become a foster parent?"

"Good question. But he's dead and that's what matters."

He watched when Tessa wiped the tears away as they fell. If he reached out to dry them she would let him and he wouldn't be able to take that any more than if she slapped him and called him a monster. As much as he wanted her to reject him, he couldn't stand to hear the words.

"A few months later they arrested a drug addict named Harris Barkley. He had a long list of priors including jail time for domestic abuse and happened to live near Lester. He was also a former foster kid of his."

Gunnar couldn't gauge Tessa's reaction. What he took for horror could well be sympathy. "My not being around to visit Evan and Sam worked in my favor. And since Sam didn't tell the police what Lester did to her, they never even looked at me. The cops nailed Barkley for it."

Why wouldn't they when Harris had confessed to

the killing?

The silence grew insufferable after a few minutes, and he thought he knew what it was like for a prisoner awaiting sentencing. He clenched his teeth. His hands and arms felt weighted.

"Is that why—" Tessa began, then cleared her throat. "Why you have nightmares? From the guilt?"

The word sliced him to the core. It could be guilt all right, but not because of Lester. "No. They started after…"

Tessa took a tissue from the box near the bed and dabbed her eyes. Gunnar rose and went to the desk where her Bible lay open. He straddled the frilly chair behind it, hanging his arms over the back.

"My brother was a Christian." He paused, waiting until he could trust his voice to remain steady. "He thought everyone had a chance to make things right, that no one was hopeless." He looked sideways at her. "You believe that?"

Tessa regarded him directly. Of course she did.

"Yeah, well, he died an optimist." Though she didn't speak, he could feel the sympathy emanating from her and mentally pushed away the comfort it would have given. "He tried to save me," Gunnar said, his voice half sorrow, half chuckle. "He's the reason for this." He jerked a thumb toward the angel on his back. "He told me he prayed every day for angels to watch over me. I figured if I had one with me he'd stop. He didn't."

Gunnar took a deep breath through his nose, blew it out through his mouth. "He didn't know what I did to Lester. But one night eight months ago, we had an argument on the phone. About God, as usual," he said, his voice going cold. "Well, I argued. I was drunk and in a bad mood—hard to believe, I know. I figured if I told him everything, he'd see how bad I really was and give up."

"The way you're hoping I will now," Tessa said.

He ignored her. "I ranted and he came back in that quiet way he had. He wasn't like me. He said I still had a chance, and even though I murdered a man I could get to heaven if I was sorry." Gunnar snickered. "Is that true, Tessa? All the years of living like a heathen erased like they never happened?"

"It doesn't exactly work that way."

"Tell me how it works, sweetheart." The sardonic edge was working. Though she stayed put, he could see her withdrawing from him. "Explain it to me," he coaxed when she didn't speak.

A lone tear trailed down her face. "If you sincerely believe in Christ as your Savior the sin is erased, yes, but you can't undo the actions or consequences that result."

Gunnar looked down at the Bible's highlighted pages and resisted the urge to hurl it across the room. "My Savior."

Tessa licked her lips and sat arrow straight. "I'm going to go out on a limb here and say you told your brother because you knew he could show you the way to forgiveness." When his gaze shot to hers, she tilted her head expectantly.

"You think I want forgiveness?"

"Ultimately. It's what everyone wants."

He laughed again, to hide his inner turmoil. "Maybe." He'd heard it all before, including his brother's theory that the reason he knocked redemption was because deep down he didn't think he deserved it.

"The trouble is you don't think you're worthy of forgiveness."

A cold chill slithered down Gunnar's back. She was starting to give him the creeps the way Evan used to, telling him things about himself even he wasn't ready to acknowledge. "Do all you people take the same course? 'Pat Answers 101'?" He cracked his knuckles. "It's amazing how much you sound like Evan," he said, but this time without venom.

Tessa sniffled once more into her tissue before her face iced over. "Did he die in January?" She looked like she might hyperventilate. "Evan Turner?"

"Yeah."

"You said Evan before—I can't believe I didn't put it together. He used to go to my church, the one I go to here. I went there before I moved, but now I go there again—never mind." She stood. "Your last name—"

"None of us have the same last name, or father for that matter."

Tessa looked at him carefully. "There is a resemblance. Around the nose and jaw. I didn't know him well," Tessa said. "But I heard him talk…" She bit her bottom lip. "He said his brother's name was Tom."

Gunnar swallowed the lump in his throat. "Only he called me Tom. It's my middle name. Guess it was easier when he was a kid."

He watched her win the battle over tears and when she spoke it was with quiet reverence. "I was back up from North Carolina for the holidays and when I went to church that Sunday…he wasn't there. Then we heard…what happened."

"He was on his way to my house."

"Gunnar—"

"Don't tell me you're sorry."

The silence grew as his mind returned to the phone call, the monotone voice of a New Jersey State Trooper telling him his brother was dead.

"Did he mention he came to my house every Sunday after church?" Gunnar asked at length.

Tessa said nothing.

"He always brought coffee and donuts, and worked his way around to recapping the sermon, or whatever you call it. I never wanted to hear it.

"That day I called him around four a.m. and woke him. I knew he'd come by later and wanted to divert him so I told him I needed to talk. I should have thought it through," Gunnar mused aloud. "But like I said, I was drunk. So I confessed. Evan said I shouldn't be alone, and he was coming over. I told him not to."

He stared at his feet for a long moment. "Do you know why I came here? I mean the first day, why I came?" he asked.

Tessa didn't reply.

He struggled with the words. "I needed to make the nightmares stop. I can't explain them to you." Gunnar halted, deliberating if he should try. *No point.*

"I tried staying drunk, sleeping pills, keeping myself awake; none of it worked. Then I thought maybe a change of scenery..." He shook his head. "Dominic was the one person I could trust not to ask me a thousand questions or expect me to volunteer information."

"So you've had nightmares since Evan died?"

"The last couple months." He took a deep breath from the current of air blowing in the open window. "I had one here the first night I stayed. And since I'd exhausted my options, killing myself seemed like the best idea."

"What?"

Her face was stricken when he looked at her. "Yeah. Almost did it, too." *Almost.* And it was only reviewing it in his mind now, that he realized how much the voice in his ear then, sounded like the one who told him to kill Lester.

"Call it desperation, quitting...you called it a tantrum, I believe." Watching her eyes, he could almost see her brain piece together the events of that night, and something in him softened. He had to look away. "I haven't brought a gun into this house since."

"But you didn't do it. There's a reason you're here," Tessa asserted. "Do you believe in God?"

"Sure, He's responsible for the chain of miseries making up my life, right?"

"He's the One protecting you." She lifted her hands, let them fall. "He told me to pray for you before we ever met. He loves you."

"He loves *you*," Gunnar corrected. "And you're nothing like me."

"None of us measure up, that's the point of God's grace."

She said it so matter-of-factly he had to stare. "Don't preach to me, Tessa. You measure up, Evan measured up."

"No, you're wrong. The Bible says—"

"Don't tell me what the Bible says!" He ran a hand along his chin. "I'm a sinner, and I'm going to hell when I die. I'm going to fall into one of those nightmares and never wake up. End of story."

Tessa wiped her cheeks with the backs of her wrists. "It doesn't have to be, you have a choice."

"There are no choices, people are what they are."

"People change."

What was wrong with her? He would accuse any other woman of playing mind games. But the deeper he looked into this open book that was Tessa, the more beauty and goodness and honesty he unearthed. So how could she believe they were on the same level?

"I was trouble as a kid and I still am. I'm willing to bet you were a parent's dream," he said.

A shadow passed over her face, but she was quick to mask it.

"A perfectionist, right? Your toys always put away, your clothes folded in the right drawers?"

"I have faults like anyone else."

"Yeah? Tell me one."

Tessa looked at her feet. "I can be critical," she answered.

"Too generic, you're not getting off that easy," he said, his tone uncompromising. "I told you the highlight of my low life, now you tell me some nasty secret of yours."

"Comparing sins isn't going to help anything."

"You're wrong," Gunnar fired back. "If I know you have a few skeletons in your closet I might listen when you talk."

"Do you want to know what I think?" Her eyes glittered with renewed passion.

"No."

"I think you're confused."

The statement took him by surprise. "What?"

"On one hand you want to blame God for your crappy life, on the other you want to blame yourself."

"That makes no sense," he said.

"Exactly. You don't run the world. You can't blame yourself for what happened to Evan, or your sister."

Gunnar's face hardened, his back teeth clenched tight.

Tessa inched closer but didn't touch him. "And you can't punish yourself for things you couldn't control."

The arrow was closer to the bull's-eye than he cared to believe.

"What do you know?" Gunnar growled.

"More than you want me to."

"So you're saying it *is* God's fault?"

"Why does it have to be God's fault?" she asked. "There's good and evil, and God's good, so who's left? And don't say you; you aren't evil."

He imagined Sunday school would have been like this as a kid. "You want me to say the devil, right?"

Tessa set her hands on her hips and stared at him. "I see who you are, Gunnar," she continued as though he hadn't just tried to bait her. "You don't want me to, *and*," she pushed through when he would have stopped her, "you're afraid to want me."

"I don't want you any more than I've wanted dozens of women." What did one lie matter after having confessed to murder? Worse, she knew he lied, making him look pathetic. He continued, anyway. "I've never had a real relationship. One night stands, no strings. That won't change because I met you."

"It has changed. Isn't that why you're acting this way?"

Yes, and he couldn't see a way to handle it. Only misery lay in store for her if she tangled up with him. He would try another tack.

"What are you looking for, a fixer-upper? Someone you can mold into the man of your dreams?" He took a step so that his chest brushed her shoulder.

"Or do you go for bad boys?"

"Now you're being obstinate."

"Am I?" He could hear the uncertainty in her voice. He pushed harder. "You're trying to get me to lose control. Is that what makes you hot, a little power struggle? I can accommodate you there." He grabbed her by the wrists and banded them both in one of his hands before pulling her closer.

Her eyes shone with doubt and sadness, and it brought a vile taste to his mouth. As bad as he wanted her to think him, there were limits to what he would do to make a point. With an unintelligible growl, he released her and walked out.

19

Murder. A terrible word, no doubt. The worst thing a man could do was take a life. Yet despite Gunnar's best efforts, Tessa didn't see the monster he tried to illustrate. She saw a man who deeply regretted huge mistakes, and knowing he deserved punishment, was determined to inflict it upon himself.

Before she heard the heavy footfall of boots or the jangling of his car keys moving along the side of the house, Tessa knew he was leaving and likely wouldn't be back. While one man might use the confession of murder as a key to open a new door of his life, Gunnar used it as a key to lock the door behind him, leaving her on the other side.

The scene with him a little while ago frazzled her nerves. She needed to relax before this evening's service. No sooner had she settled on the bed than her mother called. Once Tessa convinced her Gunnar hadn't sold her into slavery, and promised to call her tomorrow, she closed her eyes and nestled into the pillow. But Gunnar haunted her.

Frustrated, she rolled to her back. Was she romanticizing him, attributing to him some sensitive consciousness he didn't in fact possess? What if he wasn't as remorseful as she thought, and his declaration of guilt was merely the warning he pronounced it to be?

She might simply be reacting to the gravitational pull inherent in dynamic people like movie actors or rock stars. As a girl, she'd been as susceptible as anyone, but now, in the real world, she should be immune to that. She shouldn't require a reaction so powerful it couldn't be overlooked before she was drawn to someone.

As it was, she found it hard just to muster the enthusiasm to accept a dinner invitation. Oh, Tessa dated attractive men—when she dated—but most weren't interesting enough to warrant more than a sigh of relief when they walked her to the door. Which might be the reason she'd had a total of three second dates in her whole life.

Until Scott. Looking back, she couldn't remember what she'd seen in him. They'd dated for a year, but each time they were together had felt like a second date, never progressing in drive or emotion. She had started to believe she was defective.

But Gunnar effectively squelched the worry that she couldn't feel anything for a man. Psychologically, things were murky, but physically...wow! He didn't even have to touch her to have a firestorm of sensations raining down on her.

She wished she could define their relationship. It wasn't a friendship in the conventional sense, and they were unquestionably more than acquaintances. Apart from basic human attraction, kinship might be an apt label for what they shared. Although not immediately evident, she and Gunnar shared a common bond—a sense of disconnection, she from her parents, and he from everyone else.

How did the man exist? So vexed, so explosive. The only time he seemed remotely at ease was at his shop. Thinking back, it astounded her to consider the talent and skill required to transform ideas into substance in such a way. It was purely a matter of time before the whole world discovered Gunnar Mason. At least the Gunnar Mason he wanted people to know.

∂∽✵

Hours later, Tessa woke blurry-eyed in a dark room. The only light was the clock displaying nine fifteen. So much for church. She started to pull up the bedspread and call it a night, when the Holy Spirit suddenly impressed her to pray.

Intercessory prayer was sometimes arduous, often complex, and always necessary. When Tessa felt her eyes droop and the Holy Spirit again stirred her awake, she discerned the need was immediate. She was compelled to turn to Psalm 91, as she had time and again over the past couple of months. The Psalm was all about protection and trust, but whose? Gunnar's or hers?

Gunnar is hurting, God's Spirit said in a calm, assertive voice that was neither scary nor audible yet propelled her to action, this time without argument.

She didn't need to be touched emotionally or see into the spirit realm to trust that things were happening to help Gunnar here in this realm. Nonetheless, tears streaked her face as she walked around the room seeking God's mercy, binding demons and loosing angels.

When she found that praying for Gunnar eventually led back to her, she sat on the bed and dropped her head into her hands. Of course, it would.

A Christian woman should represent modesty and

chastity. But when Gunnar kissed her, lust and recklessness took charge. If he hadn't made her listen to him, there was no telling what would have happened. It was a shocking and humbling revelation that *he* was the one to use reason and self-restraint. And nothing short of humiliating to think that if Gunnar walked in the door this minute, it was possible she could repeat her wanton behavior.

Easy as it would be to fall into the victim role and claim to have been tag teamed by lust and temptation, she accepted responsibility. And prayed for strength. She was going to do a better job resisting Gunnar. She couldn't control which thoughts popped into her mind, but she would decide which ones received her full attention.

Even now pushing aside thoughts of the physical sensations Gunnar caused in her, she wondered what would happen the next time she saw him. She asked God to give her direction and jotted *self-control* on her prayer list before climbing back into bed.

When she went downstairs at eight thirty a.m., it was obvious Dominic hadn't come home all night. He called from work soon after to tell her he wouldn't be home for dinner because he'd be at Gunnar's helping with the finishing touches on his house.

Tessa's stomach sank. Now that Gunnar's house was finished, he had no reason to come around. She might not see him again.

She exhaled through her nose. If she pondered it, she would start to feel sad, so she concentrated on housework, changing sheets and scrubbing the bathrooms. Rather than helping to ease the pressure, however, the activities made her feel obsessive and neurotic.

At nine thirty, Connie came through the front door wearing a navy pinstripe jacket with matching skirt and her hair slicked back to the contour of her head. She looked incredibly professional, very smart.

Tessa was glad for the company, but if she hoped Connie would be a good diversion from Gunnar, she was wrong.

"Spill it," Connie demanded, slinging her purse onto the counter and stretching a wide grin over white teeth.

"Spill what?"

"You and Attila the Hunk. What happened?"

"I'm sorry, it was so embarrassing."

"Embarrassing, are you kidding?" Connie poured some coffee and hitched herself onto the countertop, dangling her feet. "My mother was floored! And she gets a kick out of your mother's ranting."

"I wish I could see the humor."

"I don't find my mother amusing, either. It's a mother-daughter thing."

Tessa pursed her lips, reminded to call her mom. It was impossible to explain, and she had no intention of trying, but she had to at least give her a decent phone call. "What did Gunnar say to you?"

Connie's grin broadened. "That he needed to talk to you. But it was the way he said need, like he *needed* to talk to you." She rolled her eyes heavenward.

"What did my mother say?"

"Well, he took me out here to tell me, but she followed," Connie told her, swinging her legs to some internal rhythm. "She started to grill him, but cool as you please, he walked away. I never saw anything like the way he just shuts someone off."

"Tell me about it," Tessa muttered.

"Your mom was ma-aad. She wanted to go after him, but my mother and I guaranteed her there is absolutely nothing going on between the two of you. I told her he didn't feel well, and he's normally a pleasant person." Connie giggled. "So I understated," she added when Tessa raised her brows.

"Understated."

"OK, I lied, but did I lie about the two of you? Is something going on?" Connie asked.

"Define 'something'."

Connie eyed her quizzically, studying her face, then hopped off the counter. "Were the two of you up all night? You look awful."

Tessa sat at the table. "No. Yes—*I* was up. Praying."

Connie tugged on the hem of her blazer and sipped her coffee. "Hmm."

"He didn't stay here last night." Tessa put a fist on the table, stacked the other on top and capped it with her chin. "It's complicated."

"When a man looks the way he does it's always complicated," Connie said with certainty.

ॐ∽

There were myriad ways Tessa could measure time: hours spent looking at houses with the realtor, number of times she'd reassured Connie the wedding gown she picked was perfect, or how often she'd answered the phone before bed to find her mother checking on her. Five houses, thirteen reassurances, nine phone calls from mom.

Instead, she measured time the old-fashioned way—Gunnar had been gone nine days.

Nine days without hearing the roar of his motorcycle, or the sound of his voice when he granted her a few reluctant words. Nine days without feeling the quickening of her heart when he was nearby, or the warming of her skin when he just looked at her. Nine days without the scent of him lingering in the air near his room, or seeing him come in from work either mildly pleased or angry—there was rarely an in-between.

She thought of him all the time. It had to stop, but how, when Dominic spoke of him, or a black car drove by, or someone called to ask her if she'd seen the cover of Custom Carriages magazine, as Connie did today?

"No, should I have?" Tessa asked. As the name implied, the magazine featured motorcycles. She'd seen an issue once in her dentist's office.

"Only if you want to see Attila the Hunk," Connie said gleefully. "He's on the cover."

Tessa's heart revved to 200 beats per minute. "Really? That's great." She hoped her voice sounded mildly uninterested as she tucked the phone under her ear to finish drying the dishes.

"I'm on lunch. I'll bring it by and let you read it yourself."

"Can't you just tell me what it says?"

"You have to see the pictures. Why didn't you tell me Gunnar builds these things? When I mentioned his name to Mike, he freaked!"

"Why?"

"Are you serious? Mike's a bike nut. He said he's followed Gunnar's career for years. I can't believe he builds these!"

Tessa's mind drifted back to the impulsive trip to Gunnar's shop and her initial impressions of his skill and creativity. She remembered how he'd examined her, even as she'd examined his work.

"What does it say?" she asked, shaking away the mental revival of the kiss that followed. She could hear Connie flipping through pages.

"OK, it says he's the up and comer of the decade. *'Intelligent engineering, refined creativity for the discriminating buyer',*" Connie read aloud. "*'Faultless craftsmanship with attitude and a demand for recognition will carry Gunnar Mason through the decade and into cycle history.'* Wow, your friend is quite the artist."

Tessa was so proud of him she beamed. Now that she'd heard the gist of the article, she would have to see it firsthand. She wondered if he had seen it.

"I'll meet you at the diner," Tessa said.

She raced to the front door, grabbing her bag on the way, pulling up short when she saw the envelope on the floor under the mail slot and her name printed in neat block letters. She opened it and unfolded the crisp white paper, to find a note in the same hand, all capitals.

TESSA,

I KNOW I'M NOT THE EASIEST PERSON TO GET ALONG WITH, BUT THANKS FOR TRYING. I WISH THINGS COULD HAVE BEEN DIFFERENT.

GUNNAR

After rereading the note a half dozen times, Tessa stared at the piece of paper, trying to make sense of it.

Gunnar wouldn't have intended for the sadness to come through in the note. It had. But why write it at all after trying so hard to push her away?

I wish things could have been different.

The logical conclusion was he regretted their bickering and mutual uneasiness and now looked for some kind of closure. She put the note back in the envelope and tucked it in her jeans pocket. One thing was clear; he didn't intend to return. Facing that was going to take some time. For now, she would ignore the hollow in her chest.

But then another notion struck her. Chilled her. What if it was intended as a final goodbye? She pulled the paper back out and reread it. Given her knowledge of a prior attempt, it could be interpreted as a suicide note.

She paced the hall, sat on the bottom step, paced some more. She should call Dominic and have him look in on Gunnar—he would be able to find him. But there was no way to ask Dom to check on Gunnar without intimating some relationship between him and her, or without having to explain why she suspected it might be a suicide note.

Tessa sat, elbows hitched on her knees, chin in her palms. She got up and paced. She waved the note around as she moved, using her hands to outwardly express her inner dialogue—what reasons she might give, what arguments against Dom's inevitable warnings. She wrung her hands, tried cracking her knuckles—but wasn't the pro Aunt Elaine was—then returned to her starting position on the stairs. A man's life hung in the balance. There was no room to worry over Dom's disapproval.

Fighting a shiver of panic, she jumped to her feet and stuffed the note back in her pocket. She had to stop overreacting and put the situation in perspective. And take first things first. Pray. Dominic might not get to Gunnar in time, but God would.

A few minutes later, she was able to calmly reason, which brought her back to her first question, *why*?

Why send a note to make her think of him when Gunnar could have continued to stay away with no contact? Because he wanted closure? Because he felt bad that things were left so badly between them? To ensure her silence concerning what he'd told her? No, no, and no. None of that made sense.

Tessa smirked with sudden comprehension. Only one answer made any sense to her. It was so obvious, now.

Gunnar was changing his mind about them—him and her together.

20

Gunnar shook his head, surprised to be walking through the front doors of the Jesus Lives Family Worship Center. He didn't recall making the decision to come, but here he was being welcomed into unfamiliar territory by a great bear of a man with a red face and hair to match. The man smiled and told him to sit anywhere.

He doubted he'd find answers here, but Evan had believed he'd found them, and Gunnar needed that connection now more than ever. As he walked across the blue-on-blue carpet, he resisted the impulse to look up. If his arrival caused the roof to collapse, he didn't want to be tipped off and have an easy excuse to leave.

Even so, he would have stayed home if Dominic didn't mention Tessa was spending the evening with friends instead of coming to service. Seeing her was the last thing he needed.

Gunnar slid into the last pew. In an effort to avoid eye contact with anyone, he made a pretense of reading the first thing he could find, which happened to be the pew Bible in front of him. He opened the red hardcover and leafed through the fine white pages to where a satin marker peeked from the book of Isaiah. He blinked as the words leapt off the page.

"But the wicked are like the troubled sea, when it cannot rest, whose waters cast up mire and dirt. There is no

peace, saith my God, to the wicked."

No peace. He found it more than a little eerie that a few lines written so long ago could nail his pathetic life so precisely. Could there be any more proof of his wickedness? Tessa would disagree, of course. But they couldn't both be right.

She was a puzzle. There were as many contradictions in her as there were differences between them. As he raced down the wide and bumpy road of the sinner, she cruised the smooth, narrow road of the saint. Everyone knew who had the right of way if those roads should cross.

Christians. The word left a bad taste in his mouth.

Evan had surely resorted to religion, as most people did, to escape the cruelty and despair of an awful life, but what excuse did Tessa have? Where did she come by the insecurity that drew her to religion in the first place? Gunnar contemplated the most logical source—her mother.

He put the Bible back and clasped his hands together on the back of the pew in front of him. With his head bowed he might look like he was praying and be left alone. That was all he wanted.

That wasn't true. He was developing a habit of lying to himself lately. The one thing he desired was the one thing he couldn't have and nothing or no one could substitute.

He had wandered to McIntosh's the other night, but found no thirst for a drink or any of the women who sent him teasing looks as they jiggled to the music. There'd been no urge to slip into the back and get high, or to start a fight and grind out his aggression on some poor guy's face.

He wanted Tessa.

How could he have believed his life wouldn't change because of her? Another lie. His life could now be neatly divided into two parts: before meeting her and after meeting her. She even affected his work. The job was underway and going better than expected, but he was increasingly expending more brain power on her than on the chess project.

He hoped it would pass; knew it wouldn't.

Gunnar looked around as people filed in. Strange people. An old woman with a crocheted shawl draped across hunched shoulders, hummed a slow melody, eyes closed, as she swayed in her seat. A man and woman a few rows up were murmuring avidly, with the woman *amen*ing after practically every sentence, including her own. He thought he heard mention of blood sacrifices. But more disconcerting was the man across the aisle who knelt on the floor with his face buried in his forearms on the pew, weeping.

Gunnar had started rethinking the wisdom of coming here when he felt eyes on him. He looked to find a girl at the end of the pew, staring at him from behind long black lashes. She couldn't have been more than five. Her eyes were almond-shaped and her hair the purest shade of black. She laid one hand on the smooth wood of the armrest and held the other behind her back.

Gunnar couldn't figure children. He couldn't remember ever feeling like one. Growing up he'd only had his brother and sister to relate to, and they weren't much like children, either.

"I'm Miranda," the girl said. She smiled, revealing a gap where one front tooth should be. "You're pretty," she told him.

The declaration left him too stunned to reply, even

if he had words.

Miranda brought the hand from behind her and gave him its contents, a wrapped red sour ball. "Here. I got it from Sister Waters," she confided. "But I'm not posta to eat it because I have a cativy."

"A cavity?" Gunnar suggested.

Miranda moved her head up and down. "But I didn't want to say no. She likes to give us candy."

He was finding the little creature charming, even so, he held back a smile. "Where are your parents?"

"Outside. Want me to get them?"

"No," he answered definitely.

"You look mad," Miranda said, without fear. "Are you?"

Gunnar glanced around the church looking for anyone who might be her parent. He knew enough about children to know they shouldn't be unattended while grilling strangers.

"My mom gets mad at me sometimes 'cause I don't always listen."

He nearly smiled again, this time at the gleam in her eye. She reminded him very much of Samantha. "You should listen to her."

Miranda twisted her face. "I don't like going to bed. I bet no one makes you go to bed."

No one makes me do anything, he wanted to say, but answered instead, "No, but I'm old enough to go without being told, because it's good for me."

Miranda seemed to be considering this. "What about eating candy?"

Gunnar took his time, considering as well. The safest answer he could supply was, "What does your mother say?"

"Are you an angel?" she asked abruptly.

Gunnar stared at her. No one, *no one* had ever accused him of being an angel.

"You look like Evan."

Gunnar felt the words as though they'd been laid to his sternum on the end of a sledgehammer.

"Miranda," someone called, to Gunnar's relief.

A small woman with the same dark exotic looks of the girl, waited by the rear door.

Miranda waved and took a step, but turned back to him. "Do grown-ups get cadi—cavi—"

"Cavities," he finished for her, and nodded.

She reached into his hand and reclaimed the sour ball. "Then you shouldn't have it, either. Bye."

Surprised and reluctantly amused, he watched her take her mother's hand and walk to the front of the church, chattering the whole way.

Gunnar remained alone watching the other pews fill. Thank God they were leaving him alone. People stared at him all the time but tonight the sense of eyes boring into his back agitated him, adding to the restlessness already crawling inside him. He whipped his head around to see who glared at him, but found empty space and the building's rear wall.

A shiver ran across his spine, and he felt an inexplicable desire to leave. He stayed put. Determining what went on here and its appeal to his brother outweighed the impulse to flee.

It shouldn't matter. He should let it be. He couldn't. Any more than he could let Tessa be.

What had compelled him to send her that note?

In all honesty, the magazine article. He tried being blasé, but a feature in the most widely circulated bike magazine in the country really meant a lot. Seeing himself on the cover, reading the article, brought to mind the one person he wanted to share it with. Of course he'd begun mulling over the way they'd left things and the next thing he knew he was sliding a note under her door like a love-sick kid.

He was going soft in the head.

The service started on time, and, with any luck, would end soon. The choir didn't have matching robes but all wore blue skirts or pants and white shirts. Something stirred in him as he listened to them sing, but since it was close inside the small brown and white building, he decided it must be the heat.

A man introduced as Pastor Caswell, was in his forties with dark hair going grey at the temples. He was commanding, not soft-spoken, yet gentle in the way he addressed the people, like a father counseling his children, in everyday language, without drama. Unlike the showmen Gunnar saw on TV at three a.m.

He spoke of Jesus healing ten lepers and one coming back to thank Him, before telling of a woman who met Jesus at a well. Apparently the events were connected, something to do with meeting both physical and spiritual needs. Nothing earth shattering, but Gunnar imagined Evan would have applauded the positive message.

After service, Gunnar lingered near the back. Several churchgoers, or whatever they called themselves, walked toward him on the way out, most murmuring a smiling "hello," but none stopped. No doubt respecting the wish clearly written on his face: *keep moving.*

Miranda waved as her mother carried her by, her sleepy head drooping onto her mother's shoulder.

Gunnar watched the pastor stand by the door and hug or clasp hands with each person who filed past.

When Miranda met him, she perked up, leaned toward him and whispered in his ear. Pastor Caswell glanced at Gunnar and smiled.

A few minutes later, as the band broke down their equipment, three female stragglers discussed an upcoming women's breakfast. In a holder beside the door were a pile of business cards with the church logo and phone numbers. On impulse, Gunnar slipped one in his pocket.

When at last the pastor was free, he crossed to Gunnar and offered his hand.

"Hello. I'm Pastor Caswell. Bob, if you prefer."

Gunnar didn't prefer either, but took his hand. "Gunnar Mason. Evan Turner's my brother."

Bob placed a comforting hand on Gunnar's back. "I'm sorry for your loss. We miss Evan a great deal."

Gunnar was perplexed, partly by the action—strangers didn't touch him—but mostly because he didn't want to punch the guy.

"And Samantha?" Bob inquired. "We met at Evan's memorial. How is she?"

"Good. Do you have time to talk?"

A young man, probably eighteen or nineteen, stood on the altar wrapping a guitar cord around his hand, when he stopped to listen. The three women ceased their chattering to better eavesdrop.

"Alone," Gunnar said.

Bob inclined his head toward a white door. The kid on the altar gave him a quick look, and he returned a brief wag of his pointer finger.

"Bouncer?" Gunnar asked, unconcerned.

"My son, Kyle. He worries."

"You get many fights in church?"

Bob laughed, creases forming at the corners of

shining blue eyes. "It's happened."

He opened the door and waited for Gunnar to enter before closing it behind them. Like the man, the office wasn't what Gunnar expected, either. The chair behind the desk looked relatively new, but the desk looked ready to collapse under the weight of volumes of books and reams of paper. One of the legs was supported by a folded Florida travel guide. The room needed painting and the blinds sagged on one side, but somehow, it wasn't so bad. Better than his own office.

"How can I help you?" Bob asked, gesturing to a threadbare chair in front of the desk.

Gunnar sat but instead of taking his place behind the desk, Bob pulled a matching chair up beside him.

"I'm not sure," Gunnar answered. "I have questions maybe you can answer, maybe not. And I don't know if I want to hear what you're going to say or if I'll believe it, so I don't know why I'm here."

Bob clasped his hands together, letting them hang between his knees. "You can say or ask anything, Gunnar. It won't leave this room."

Gunnar rubbed his palms on the thighs of his khakis. "I'm having a rough time. Since Evan died."

"That's understandable."

Maybe he'd made a mistake. It wasn't like him to reveal anything so personal to a stranger—although he'd done it with Tessa—but going against his better judgment, he'd followed this odd compulsion to come here, and for what? Pat answers he could read in any self-help book? Although he wasn't giving the guy much to work with.

"Did Evan tell you about me?"

"Yes." Bob's face went somber. "Does it bother you?"

Gunnar laughed without humor. "Would it bother you if you were me?" He skimmed a hand over his face. "I'm not ashamed of where I come from, Pastor. Just what I've become. Evan got the same start as me, and he turned into a great guy. What happened?"

Bob leaned closer. "Can I be honest with you?"

Gunnar looked at the man beside him. There was hesitancy. No doubt, Evan had warned the man of his temper. "Go on."

Bob rubbed his thumbs together. "Don't take this the wrong way, but the truth is Evan had his share of flaws and struggles."

Gunnar held his temper in check. He'd spent so much time venerating Evan, he didn't need someone else telling him his brother was imperfect.

"We all make mistakes," Bob said, fisting his hands to make his point. "I've done plenty I'm ashamed of."

"Have you ever killed a man?" He watched Bob shift, uncomfortable. There hadn't been time for Evan to divulge that.

"No. No, I haven't."

"I have." It was irrational, yes, but suddenly important to prove he was worse than Evan. Someone had to believe him. Gunnar rose from the chair and strode across the room. "Is that just a mistake?"

Bob wore a solemn expression. "I don't know the particulars. And I'm not making light of it, Gunnar. What I'm saying is to God sin is sin."

Gunnar sat on the edge of the desk and tried to grasp what Bob was telling him. "So, if I hit you in the face it's sin?"

"Right."

Gunnar leaned slightly forward. "And if I don't

stop hitting you till your blood is spattered on these walls and you stop breathing, it's the same thing?"

Bob was a good-sized man, but his eyes said he was no fool. He cleared his throat before speaking.

"Sin is sin," he said. "Of course the consequences would be different. You'd go to prison, and my wife and kids would be awfully upset." He gave a nervous chuckle. "But repercussions aside, the Bible says we've all sinned and fallen short of the glory of God. That means everyone, not just murderers."

Gunnar crossed his arms. "What I did was no mistake. It was deliberate. What's God's view on that?"

Bob waited a moment, then moved to the door, opened it a crack and spied out. He closed it tightly and returned to his seat. "Maybe you should tell me the whole thing."

Gunnar related the grisly truth—the whole truth this time, including the fact that Lester Watts had raped Sam. Every so often, he glanced at Bob to see if he was taking mental notes to use against him later, but saw only interest and compassion reflected in attentive blue eyes. The same things he'd seen in Tessa's eyes, yet somehow easier to receive from this man.

When he finished he waited for Bob to speak.

"Well," Bob said, and scrubbed a hand over his chin. "I'm afraid if you're looking for absolution, that's God's department. But I will say if it bothers you, and it seems to, that's a good thing. It doesn't mean you're off the hook, but at least you have a conscience." He paused. "If you don't mind my asking, why aren't you in prison?"

"Another guy confessed."

"Are you saying an innocent man took the blame

for something you did?"

The pastor's look of concern gave form to Gunnar's feelings. His conscience had been stretched to the limit in this area.

"He swears he killed Lester," Gunnar said. "Look, I didn't want this. When I heard someone confessed I went to a friend—a judge—and told her I did it. She didn't want to hear me. She let me read his whole file. He claimed he heard noise coming from Lester's, found him near death, then stuffed a rag in his mouth and suffocated him before stealing some stuff from his house."

"And you don't believe him?" Bob looked confused.

Gunnar didn't respond. He'd been so sure Lester was dead.

"Was a cause of death given?"

Gunnar nodded. "Asphyxiation."

Facts were facts, but it didn't make sense. Harris Barkley had opportunity, motive, and all the right answers, but...

"What are the odds he would be there at the exact right moment?"

"Gunnar, you didn't kill him," Bob said. "You're in the clear. It was by God's grace and mercy that you didn't end up in prison for the rest of your life."

That should be good news, but the guilt didn't lessen. He knew in his heart that had he known Lester was breathing, he would've finished the job.

Gunnar took a good, hard look at the man across from him. He noted the same kindness he'd seen from the altar in the same no nonsense manner, telling him that while Bob might not have all the answers, he wouldn't lie to him.

"You don't believe anyone's hopeless, either."

Bob laughed, a cheery, genial sound. "If that were the case I'd be doomed. And I have no plans to go to hell when I'm done here."

No, you don't want to go there, Gunnar thought, lowering his gaze to the floor. "I want to ask you something."

Bob opened his hands, as if welcoming it.

"What would you tell a woman in your church about getting involved with me?"

Taken by surprise, Bob blew out a breath. "Honestly?"

Gunnar kept his expression impassive.

"I would remind her that the Bible tells us we shouldn't be joined with unbelievers, and there are reasons for that," he said, looking Gunnar in the eyes. "This is our life, not just something we do on Sundays. We walk the path every day. If she's going to get serious with someone, it's important he's walking in the same direction she is, with God. And by God I mean the Father, the Son, and the Holy Spirit." Bob paused as Gunnar shifted his feet on the beige carpet. "It isn't personal."

"I understand. And I agree." Gunnar was first to hold out his hand. "I appreciate your time."

He could see why people would be drawn to this man, and probably the church. Bob was sincere and encouraging, and who didn't want that? Unfortunately, the man didn't live in the real world.

Bob held onto Gunnar's hand until he met his eyes. "Gunnar, God wants to make your life whole. He's protecting you from death because He's not finished with you."

Gunnar pulled his hand away and took a few steps

back. "What did you say?"

Bob took a cautious step back. "God is trying to speak to you. Not the way I am," he added. "To your heart. All you have to do is listen."

When Gunnar slammed through the doors into the parking lot, his mind was in a spin, his temper on the rise. Pastor Caswell knew of his suicide attempt. He didn't say as much, but he knew. How?

Only one person in the world could have betrayed his trust. Gunnar didn't want to believe it, but much of what Bob said sounded like the same drivel he'd heard from Tessa—too much to be coincidence.

Part of him was disappointed that she would expose him so easily. The rest of him was furious. It would take a substantial dip into his reserve of control to keep from throttling her. It wasn't a good idea to see her right now. Maybe ever.

21

"Don't be mad!"

Tessa looked at the receiver, unsure she'd put the right end to her ear. She heard a voice, so she must have. The room came into focus a little at a time.

"I'm sorry, you all worked so hard, but it was a spur of the moment thing."

She recognized the voice as Connie's but for the life of her, Tessa didn't know why she would be calling her this early on a Thursday. It was Thursday, right? "It's six o'clock. What are you saying?"

"We eloped!"

"Who?"

"Me and Mike! We drove to—"

Tessa's brain clicked on. "You what?" She sat up and flung the quilt to the foot of the bed.

"We're in love!" Connie declared.

"No kidding."

"We didn't see the point in waiting."

"That's great, Con," Tessa said with as much gusto as she could assemble at this hour.

"Are you mad? You're mad." Connie's voice was repentant, but she giggled, elated.

"No, I'm happy for you. But the wedding plans..." Tessa sighed, tamping down the selfish part of her that was tempted to gripe. So she missed out on her best friend's wedding and the chance to make herself crazy planning a bachelorette party. So what?

She could hear Mike laughing in the background, evidently tickling Connie, causing her to yelp and snort and fumble the phone.

Tessa smiled. "I'm happy for you."

"Really?"

"If it's what you both wanted, of course." Tessa yawned and wrestled her robe on with one hand while Connie jabbered into her ear, recounting the romance of it all.

"I want you to come to dinner tonight," Connie said.

"Already?"

"Yes, our parents are going to be there."

Tessa stopped in the middle of the stairs "You told them, right?" She could hear an intake of breath through teeth. "Connie?"

"I want you there when I tell them."

"Oh, no," Tessa shook her head emphatically even though Connie couldn't see. "I refuse to be in the middle of a family feud."

"I need you for moral support."

"You have a husband, now," Tessa pointed out.

"He needs support, too."

"That's why he has you."

"You're my best friend," Connie countered.

Shoot. The best friend card. Tessa waited several seconds for a retort to come to mind. Defeated, she threw up a hand. "What time?"

"Seven."

"Do you need me to bring anything?"

"Yes, your reason and enough patience for the rest of us," Connie answered. "Oh, and it couldn't hurt to pray," she added, before disconnecting.

When Tessa entered the kitchen, Dominic looked up. He dropped one of the sleeping bags he carried to open the back door. Gathered on the floor were two oil lanterns, two collapsible chairs in sling bags, a pot and a box with assorted other camping paraphernalia. Fishing rods leaned against the wall, a tackle box on the floor beside them.

"Going somewhere?" Tessa asked.

Dominic sent her an infectious grin, tossed the bags onto the grass outside the door and hefted the box. "Up to Unity Point with Pauline. I took a few of my sick days. There's a note," he said, directing his gaze to the table.

"Ah." Tessa pulled the tie on her robe tighter and took the rods from the wall. "I smell marital harmony in the air."

"We don't want to get ahead of ourselves," Dominic said. "We want to see if we can be alone for an extended period without killing each other. If not, there'll be no witnesses."

"You won't have to worry about killing each other. You'll freeze to death first."

"Well I'm planning on staying inside and keeping warm."

"So why bring these?" she asked, raising the poles.

"They're for show. I don't want to seem over-confident."

Tessa followed him outside and took a deep breath of the dewy autumn air. "I'm telling you, marital harmony."

"I hope you're right." Dominic took the rods from her and angled them into his car. "Why don't you have shoes on? Why are you up at all?"

Tessa stepped on a stone, then picked her foot up

to rub the impression it left. "Connie called."

"I thought I heard the phone. I was in the basement."

"She and Mike eloped." She hadn't absorbed it fully.

"Cool."

She followed him back into the house. "She wants me to come to dinner tonight for moral support. They're going to break the news to their folks."

Dominic sobered, laid a hand on her shoulder. "Want to borrow my gun?"

Tessa hugged Dominic. "No, thanks. You have a wonderful time." She kissed him on the cheek. "I'm going for a run, and I may see if I can paint those back rails. I hear it's supposed to be warm today."

"What's with some women? You don't mind getting all dirty, but when us guys are dirty you won't touch us."

"One of life's great mysteries."

Dominic kissed her cheek. "See you Sunday night."

"Tell Pauline I said hello."

❧❧

Dominic was right, she didn't mind getting dirty. It didn't bother her that her hands and nails were speckled with latex paint. She was happy to be outside enjoying the fine weather. The neighborhood was quiet, with most inhabitants at work or school, but more than that, she relished the peace in knowing that God was intervening in her life, always. Knowing she didn't have to be in control in order to be happy removed a lot of the pressure.

That reminded her, she should call her mother.

Facing the house with her back to the sun, she went back to work, opening her senses to her immediate surroundings, taking it all in. She didn't need to turn to know that a pair of birds were flitting through the bushes to her left, or look up to see it was a squirrel clicking and chattering in the tree overhead. Nor did she need to turn around to know it was Gunnar's shadow blotting out the sun.

She laid the paint brush across the top of the open paint can, stalling while her heart completed a slow flip, and twisted to look at him.

"Oh, hey." She hoped her voice was nonchalant, not swelling with the mixture of relief and embarrassment. The first, that he was OK, the last, recalling their final exchange in her room. He looked good, all tough and tempting.

"You should be using oil paint out here."

Tessa wrinkled her nose. "I don't like the smell." She got slowly to her feet. "I'm afraid you missed Dominic."

"I'm looking for you."

He was angry—*angrier*—than usual.

Tessa rubbed her palms down the thighs of her old jeans. "Me?"

He stood watching, waiting. "We need to talk." As he did once before, he walked into the house in front of her.

Tessa smirked at his back. He most likely wanted to discuss his change of attitude. It couldn't be easy on him coming back this way after what happened the last time they were together. She followed, almost walking into him when he stopped suddenly inside the back door.

"I saw Pastor Caswell," he said. "But you probably knew that."

"No, why would I?" she asked, moving around him to the sink to twist on the faucet. "Wait, you saw Pastor...my pastor?"

"I assume you discuss everything with him," he said, ignoring her query.

Tessa squeezed a small amount of dish soap into her palm. She detected a note of accusation. "Why don't you tell me what you're getting at?"

The ringing of the phone prohibited him. He folded his arms and waited while she rinsed paint and bubbles down the drain and took a clean towel from a drawer. He continued to wait as she dealt patiently with a telemarketer. No sooner had she hung up than the phone rang again.

"Hello," Tessa answered.

Gunnar swore. "Does that thing ever stop ringing?"

"Is that Sir Hunkalot?" Connie asked Tessa through the line.

"Yes."

"Wow, way to go. I'll talk to you later."

"No—" Tessa started, but the line was already disconnected, leaving her alone with Gunnar once more.

"Can we go somewhere?" he asked, taking the phone from her and hanging it up.

"You're the one who wanted to come in here."

"Yeah, now I want to leave."

He fell silent again, during which time she noticed he wasn't just angry; but troubled. She hoped it wasn't the nightmares.

"OK," she agreed.

Tessa followed Gunnar to the end of the driveway. But when she saw his car parked at the curb, she stopped. No way was she taking a drive with him. Not with the mood he was in.

A car drove by blasting Led Zeppelin from blown speakers. "Want to take a walk?" she asked, facing him.

Gunnar grumbled and placed a hand on the small of her back, urging her forward. She couldn't have said why she found it sweet even if he was walking so fast she had to half-run to keep pace.

Two boys with skateboards breezed by, craning their necks as far as possible to examine Gunnar.

"Whoa, that dude's huge!" Tessa heard one say.

"It's a nice day," she said, looking up at Gunnar's dismal expression.

He kept moving.

A police car passed and tooted the horn. Tessa waved at Kevin Moore, one of many boys she'd gone through school with who went on to become a police officer.

"Are you going to say anything?" she asked Gunnar.

"I'm thinking."

She was about to tell him he should have thought it out first, when he pulled her behind a fat oak.

"I thought I knew," he said. "But when I get this close to you I want to..."

Kiss you, her brain finished for him. She trembled at the dark intensity in his eyes. She waited for his lips to meet hers.

"...choke you."

"Excuse me?"

"I don't handle betrayal well."

"Excuse me?" she repeated, clueless.

"Is there a problem, Tess?" Kevin asked through the passenger side window as he glided his cruiser to the curb.

Tessa didn't see the car swing around, but apparently her disappearance behind the tree wasn't missed. "No, Kevin, we're fine."

The cleft in his chin deepened when he smiled wryly. He lifted his wire frame sunglasses to better assess the situation, and Gunnar. "You're sure?"

"She said she's fine," Gunnar ground out.

Tessa saw Kevin stiffen in his seat. He was perhaps seconds from getting out of the car. "Be quiet," she told Gunnar, and walked to the car and leaned in the window. "Wow, that's something," she told Kevin when he took off the glasses to reveal his newly acquired scar.

"Yeah, that's what I get for breaking my fall with my face." He gingerly touched a hand to his brow. "Fifteen stitches."

"Poor baby," Tessa said sympathetically. "But chicks love guys with scars."

The sound of skateboards fast approaching made Tessa spin around.

"You're Gunnar Mason!" One of the boys hollered.

"Oh man! Your bikes are the hottest!" The other chimed in.

Gunnar organized his features into something resembling tolerance, but when Kevin got out of the car, he visibly braced for confrontation.

Kevin stepped forward, his thumbs hooked in the leather of his belt. "You are Gunnar Mason," he said, surprised. "You do great work."

"Wait here," one of the boys ordered. "I have to

get Matt!" With that he was off at a dead run.

"Why aren't you guys in school?" Kevin asked the remaining boy.

"We were at the dentist."

"Him, too?"

"Yeah. We're brothers." He handed Kevin a slip of paper. Kevin read the dentist's excuse printout, nodded, and handed it back.

Eyes wide, the boy appraised Gunnar. "How'd you get so big? Man! You do steroids? Can I have your autograph?" he asked with unabashed enthusiasm.

"I, uh, don't have a pen," Gunnar said, patting his pockets.

"No problem," Kevin answered, reaching into his breast pocket.

Gunnar took the pen. "Paper?"

"Sign my shirt!" the boy said. Gunnar crouched a little and pulled the back of the shirt straight. "Could you make it say 'To my friend, Squirrel'?"

Gunnar dropped his hand. "Squirrel?"

"My nickname."

"I don't have any friends named Squirrel. What's your real name?"

"Livingston."

Gunnar snorted, but stopped just short of a laugh. He signed the shirt with bold block letters, To Squirrel—Gunnar Mason.

"Can I get one of those?" Kevin asked, holding out a folded piece of paper.

As Tessa stood watching a man she'd known most of her life awed by another man, she understood Gunnar's celebrity for the first time. It was odd, but the few things she did know about him were things typically reserved for intimate relationships, none of

219

the everyday stuff that composed an individual's life. She knew he had killed a man—murdered, by his own admission—but didn't know his favorite color. She knew he tried to take his life, but had no idea where he lived. It was bizarre.

At the sound of running feet, Tessa turned. The other boy was back, an older boy lagging behind.

"Chris, I got his autograph!" Livingston boasted, aiming a thumb at his back.

"I told you it's him, Matt." Chris folded his arms. "You never believe me."

"Mr. Mason." The new arrival's voice was a reverent hush.

He was taller than Tessa and gangly, around sixteen. His midnight blue eyes, shadowed and deeply set in a gaunt face, looked as though they had seen far too much for their years.

Gunnar offered his hand with none of the reservation she'd seen with other people. "Call me Gunnar."

"I'm Matt. Wow, I can't believe I'm talking to you," he said, through labored breaths.

Tessa could see Gunnar was uncomfortable with the accolades, but he was gracious and tolerant while they quizzed him, Kevin included. She sent Gunnar a smile that he didn't return. Whatever the reason for his anger, he wasn't ready to let it go.

"You ride?" Gunnar asked Matt.

Matt looked wistful at the idea of riding a motorcycle, but gave a negligent shrug. "Next year, maybe…"

The sentence hung in the air like a pendulum, and Tessa let out a small relieved breath when Gunnar picked up the significance of it.

"Next year you'll be what, seventeen, eighteen?" Gunnar asked.

"Seventeen," Matt replied, his breathing slow and even now. "I was going to get a dirt bike."

Gunnar looked pained. "You're not a guy who'd settle for a dirt bike, are you?"

"I see a lot of injuries from dirt bikes," Kevin said, joining in the camaraderie. He let out a long, slow whistle. "A lot of injuries."

"My sister's boyfriend gave me a ride on his," Matt said.

Gunnar groaned. "You should come to the shop and try a real bike."

"No way!" cried Chris. "You're going to let him ride one of your bikes?"

"Can we come, too?" asked Livingston.

"No," Gunnar answered. He took his wallet out and removed a business card, handed it to Matt. "You call this number when you want to come. If you need a ride, I'll pick you up."

"Man, you're so lucky!" Chris said, spinning in a quick circle. "Mom's gonna freak!"

Tessa hoped he meant that in a good way.

"Can I bring my mother?" asked Matt.

"Does she like bikes?"

"No, but she'll take me."

"Sure, bring her," Gunnar said. "We have to go." He took Tessa by the hand and began walking back toward her house, removing the choice to follow or not.

She looked back to see Kevin get in his car and drive away. The three boys stood in awe, but knew better than to tag after.

"Hey." Tessa tried to dig her heels in but to no

avail. "Why don't you stop and tell me what's wrong? And what does my pastor have to do with it?"

He remained silent, barely glancing at her before he pulled her onto the porch.

"Didn't you just say you didn't want to be here?" she asked.

He released her at the door.

Rather than make a scene, she followed him inside to the living room. She sat on the arm of the couch, waiting as he paced like a large unsettled cat.

"OK," she said after a full minute. "What's going on?"

"Your pastor said something to me that couldn't have come from anyone but you."

"Why were you speaking to my pastor?"

Gunnar aimed an incensed glare at her, but continued to tread the carpet.

"Look, why don't you tell me what I'm being accused of?"

"He told me God's protecting me from death because He's not finished with me," Gunnar snarled.

And he was upset why?

"So?"

"So I know what he meant and he knew I knew. The more I think about it the more I know."

Tessa shook her head. "What?"

"He knows I tried to kill myself," Gunnar snapped. "And the only other person on this earth who knows that is you, Tessa. You!"

She felt the full load of it for the first time. He had entrusted her with a secret so personal and devastating and...*he thinks I betrayed him*. Given this insight, she couldn't blame him for being mad. She stood, determined to defend herself. "I didn't say anything. I haven't spoken to anyone from church."

"He heard it somehow."

"I didn't tell anyone. I wouldn't."

He stopped with his back to her and hooked his thumbs in his back pockets.

"Gunnar, please believe me, I didn't say anything."

"I told him what I did to Lester."

Shocked, she stepped forward, wanting so much to touch him. "Why?"

"I wanted to see what he would say."

"And what did he say?"

"That's not the point," Gunnar rounded on her. "How does he know what I didn't tell him? It isn't possible he was taking shots in the dark." He ran a rough palm over his lengthening hair. "The words he used weren't specific, but he knows. I can't explain— Tell me if you find some humor in this," he said when her mouth curved upward.

Tessa sobered. "No." She went back to the couch.

He was waiting for some explanation. He wasn't going to like it.

"God must have told Pastor." She opened her hands out to the sides when he fairly growled. "There's no other way to explain it."

"There's another way, and that's not it," he declared, jabbing a finger into the air between them.

Tessa's hands tightened on her thighs. "OK, let's have it."

He glared silently.

Her hackles rose, but she waited a breath before answering. No matter how angry she might be for being falsely accused, Gunnar was justifiably offended. "You told me and no one else. I told no one."

"So you say."

"Yes, and I'll keep saying it because it's true."

"Then someone was listening."

Tessa gave a shrug of agreement. Someone was listening all right. "I believe God told Pastor—"

"Come on—"

"And He told you that Pastor knows."

"God doesn't tell me anything."

"It's no wonder. You don't listen to anyone!" she fired back.

Though he remained still, she had the sense of movement, as if his body was coiled with energy waiting to be released. She had never seen him any other way. Even in sleep, he seemed ready to spring into action at the smallest sound.

A swell of compassion engulfed her. "Would you come here and sit?"

"I don't want to sit."

"Please."

He came to her, but instead of sitting, hunkered in front of her as he had when he'd told her about Lester. He rested his arms on his knees.

"If I find out you betrayed me..." He stopped.

Was she supposed to pick up the threatening tone? There wasn't one.

"I would appreciate it if you just told me," he finished.

"Gunnar, for the last time, I didn't say anything." She looked at him closely. Either he didn't believe her, or there was more bothering him. *Wait...* "Would you honestly rather believe I betrayed you than believe God is intervening in your life?" She saw the answer in his eyes. *Unbelievable.* "I'm afraid I can't put you at ease, there." She touched a hand to his shoulder. "God is helping you. He told me to pray for you before we even met, and He kept you from killing yourself."

"Why intervene now?" Gunnar asked. He took her hand from his shoulder and held it, though there was nothing affectionate or gentle in the gesture. "Why wait until I'm thirty-two years old to get involved when He could have done it years ago?"

No answer would satisfy with his heart so hard, so she gave his hand a squeeze. "Why don't you ask Him? And listen for an answer."

22

That night Gunnar listened. He didn't hear anything but the ticking of the grandfather clock in the hallway. Perhaps because he didn't expect an answer to a question he didn't believe was heard in the first place. The only thing he felt was empty, like much of the house he wandered.

He walked into the master bath and splashed water on his face. The house was finished, more or less, but he accepted it would never be a sanctuary. Changing the interior of the house didn't change what was inside him. Buffed oak floors, mahogany handrails and Italian tiles couldn't replace memories of his past or take away the turmoil of his present.

No peace for the wicked, he reminded his reflection in the vanity mirror.

He dried off and went back to the bedroom where the smell of paint lingered. He lay on the king-sized sleigh bed and breathed it in along with the odors of raw wood and varnish. It was a far cry from Newark and the stench of urine and decay he'd grown up with. He would never forget the smell of poverty. He swore he would never return to it.

His financial future looked bright. By his own standard—the one that mattered—his work was a success.

The public agreed, which made business lucrative,

but he wasn't fueled by the grasping, gluttonous desire for wealth. Creating with his mind, building with his hands, was his salvation. He didn't need millions of dollars or hundreds of women. He couldn't care less about commanding the masses or saving the planet, and though he wanted to dominate the bike world, his primary goal was to dominate his circumstances. To be in control.

And he was.

Well more often than not. Tessa was a continual reminder that control was cagey.

Gunnar closed his eyes and pinched the bridge of his nose. He'd lost ground since meeting her. He was ruthless with his body, pushing it harder, making it stronger, yet it involuntarily reacted to her whenever she came near. As for his mind, he was proud of his ability to focus on a task to the exclusion of all else. But lately, with startling regularity, his mind had begun to generate unwanted thoughts of her.

Then there was his heart, the least vulnerable of all the targets. It had been breached, that much was fact. To what extent, he feared he might not comprehend until it was too late.

He had to concentrate on business, filter Tessa out. The relocation of the shop could be a great distraction, but he was dragging his feet. He needed to accelerate the pace, for a number of reasons.

Mason Custom's reputation was unfolding beyond hardcore bike enthusiasts. What started as a cult following had gradually ballooned to the point where people frequently recognized him on the street, and with the magazine article it was getting worse.

Yesterday, he'd pulled into the shop lot to find a gaggle of girls armed with cameras and cell phones, snapping pictures of anything that moved. It made him mad. Maybe he'd install an electric fence at the new place.

But there was that kid Matt he'd met on Tessa's street. There was something honest and pure in his eyes that tugged at Gunnar. Also something haunted. Gunnar couldn't be called a humanitarian, but what would it hurt to spend a few hours with the boy, see what made him tick?

He stared at the ceiling and sank into the down comforter. It felt good to get off his feet. Too good. He could be asleep in five minutes, and while that would normally be a good thing, he fought it. The nightmares hadn't recurred in about a week, but something else nagged the back of his mind and wouldn't let him rest: *What if?*

Oh, he had a good firm grip on reality but *what if? What if* God was there? *What if* He heard him? It wasn't rational but...*what if?*

Gunnar had no experience with this kind of thing, but he wanted to give the prayer business another try and didn't want to be asleep if an answer came. He'd already asked God why his life was a mess, but a simpler issue might yield a quicker response.

Gunnar linked his fingers behind his neck. Would he be able to distinguish a response from God from his own reasoning?

This time there needed to be a clear-cut request requiring a black or white answer, no grays. But what?

If You're there show me a sign.

No, there were too many ways around that.

Move this lamp.

Nah. He doubted God did parlor tricks. Of course, Gunnar's mind countered, God probably wasn't doing anything better, seeing how He didn't appear to be involved in the weightier matters of protecting children from abuse or ending world hunger.

He sifted through a hundred subjects, all of which seemed stupid or unreasonable.

"I don't know what to say or ask," Gunnar said aloud. "Why don't You start?"

When his cell phone rang, Gunnar bolted off the bed. On the second ring, he snatched it off the table, but only stared at it. He waited until the next ring to answer. Of course, he was being asinine, he realized. God didn't use the telephone.

"Hello," he answered, perturbed that his hand shook.

"Gunnar, Max. I got a message for you," the surly voice announced, muddy and broken. Must be driving.

"Yeah, what?"

"A guy named Bob called the shop when I was lockin' up. Says he's trying to get in touch with you, asked me to relay."

Gunnar pushed his voice past the drumming of his heart and tried to sound casual. "Thanks. How's the rook coming? Any luck with the oil tank?"

"Dave straightened it up. It's gonna be a real sweet piece when it's done. Hey, see you tomorrow."

"Yeah." Gunnar inhaled deeply, released it in a steady stream. *Bob...Pastor Caswell.* There was nothing mysterious or otherworldly about Bob calling the shop. Mason Custom wasn't a secret, anyone could get the number. The timing could be explained, too. Bob had to have called Max *before* Max called here, and that was *before* Gunnar told God to talk to him. Coincidence.

See? It all made sense. But what did Bob want? Gunnar took the church business card off the small night table where he'd laid it. He'd considered throwing it away but hadn't been ready to sever the one remaining connection to his brother.

The most logical explanation for Bob's call was that Tessa had called him, wanting to correct the misunderstanding. And Gunnar did believe it was a misunderstanding. The circumstances of the pastor saying the right thing at the right time were odd, but he would stake his life Tessa told the truth.

Forgoing deliberation until he punched in the phone number and asked to speak with Pastor Caswell, Gunnar trod a line back and forth, waiting for him to come on the line. What could the guy have to say? Why should he care? He was going to hang up, when Bob's voice boomed in his ear.

"Gunnar, thanks for returning my call. I doubted you would."

"I almost didn't."

"Well, thank you. I know you're a busy man so I won't keep you. I want to extend an invitation to YANA tomorrow night." Before Gunnar could ask, Bob explained. "YANA stands for You Are Not Alone. It's a counseling session for men, here at my home. We get together and share our good news, bad news, grievances, whatever."

"And you thought I'd be interested," Gunnar said, trying to assimilate such an idea.

"No, but I wanted to run it by you in case," Bob answered. He hesitated before he continued. "I also offer private counseling. No fee."

"No thanks."

"Gunnar, if it's a matter of trust—"

"Since you brought it up, how did you know God's protecting me?" he added sarcastically.

Bob's reply was quick and direct. "God told me you tried to take your life."

Despite already knowing the answer, Gunnar found his mouth forming the words. "Did He tell you via Tessa?"

"Tessa? Silano? I didn't know you were acquainted."

"Yes." There remained no reservation in his mind—Tessa didn't call Bob tonight.

Bob's silence told him he was piecing together this new information with what he already had.

"Can I give you a bit of advice?" Bob asked.

Gunnar lowered to the floor beside the unlit fireplace. It was dark and cold. "Sure."

"For a Christian, faith in Jesus Christ is the foundation of our lives. It's the center, and everything else revolves around it. If it doesn't, it won't belong."

"Careful, Pastor, you're starting to make it sound like a cult." Gunnar made no effort to keep the rancor from his voice.

"No, it's a real relationship with a living God." Bob paused. "I don't want to get preachy. I'm saying, whether or not you believe it, Tessa does. She loves the Lord. She won't get involved in a relationship with you."

She already had, but Gunnar wouldn't tell her Pastor about the sparks that threatened to ignite them both whenever they were together. Not him alone, the cynical infidel, but good, sweet, faithful Tessa as well.

"If she did get involved, what do you guys do, excommunicate her?"

Bob laughed, and, though it wasn't intended, made Gunnar feel foolish. "No, she can do what she wants, but I believe she would be miserable trying to make a go of a relationship with an unbeliever."

Gunnar pressed his back into the wall and crossed his bare feet.

"If you want," Bob interrupted Gunnar's brooding, "I could give you a brief rundown of what we believe, when you have time."

This time Gunnar nearly laughed. "Are you trying to save me?"

"Wouldn't be much of a preacher if I didn't, right?" Bob chuckled. "I just want you to better understand what she believes and why, so you'll—"

"Leave her alone?"

"I was going to say you'll be better equipped to decide if you want to pursue her," Bob answered. "But I don't want to put any pressure on you. I bet you do enough of that yourself."

"I appreciate it," Gunnar said dryly.

"Look, the offer is always open. YANA is every Friday, seven to nine. Though some nights we stay and talk long after. I live in the brown house behind the church. Any time you want to talk, just call or swing by."

Gunnar mumbled his thanks and clicked the phone off dissatisfied, depressed, and a little irritated. He suddenly had energy to burn and at the moment, the best way he could think to do that was go to the shop where there was plenty to be done. The chess set was progressing but that was only one of many clients.

On top of those, Biketoberfest was fast approaching and Mason Custom would be taking several bikes to Daytona, including the Tessa inspired bike.

All of the parts for Tessa's bike had been fashioned and fitted together for the mock up, and now it had to be disassembled so the parts could be shipped off to chrome, paint, and powder-coat. The engine was being specially crafted in Germany. No roaring and rumbling for that, no, the engine and exhaust would echo Tessa in its quiet precision.

23

Tessa walked down the wide slate steps of the church with renewed inspiration and an audio copy of the service in her bag. The message on commitment and perseverance was timely—a confirmation that the time had come to arrange her life in some kind of order. It was time to start *doing* rather than simply *being*. She had a good start in that area; she was meeting the realtor at eleven.

The sky was heavy with clouds of varying shades of gray massing in layers to the west, but Tessa refused to let the weather chase away the pleasant mood that had followed her from Connie and Mike's "announcement dinner."

It was touch and go for a few minutes after the elopement disclosure. Tears flowed—more than a few—but in the end, everyone wore a happy face. Connie and Mike were united in wedlock. They loved each other. Tessa already knew that, but watching them together, really paying attention, had moved Tessa to tears of her own.

She wanted to belong to someone, and she wanted that person to belong to her. Not in ownership, but in trust and acceptance. When passion faded, as she believed would happen eventually, Connie and Mike would still *belong* to each other. Was anything more wonderful?

Grandma Isabella used to tell her that the boy she would marry was out there somewhere living his life as she lived hers. She'd said he would spend his years learning to be a good husband so that he would be ready when the Lord brought them together. Tessa had believed it then, and she believed it still.

Of course, in all her romantic daydreams the man had always been represented by a faceless hero...until recently.

Now that man had come to be distinguished by dark brows, usually vee'd in a scowl, above depthless compelling eyes that held secrets she could scarcely comprehend. His mouth was firm, often drawn into a hard, angry line. His jaw, sturdy and indomitable, his chin slightly dimpled. His nose wasn't perfectly sculpted and straight, but fit his face. An incredible face.

Tessa quickly assured herself that her subconscious was merely borrowing Gunnar's looks for a template until the real thing arrived. Her husband would be kind and gentle, temperate and loving. The opposite of Gunnar Mason. She couldn't picture a quiet Saturday morning with Gunnar, scanning the newspaper at the kitchen table or walking out of church arm in arm.

The idea was ridiculous and she chuckled aloud, looking up as her foot met the sidewalk. The sound stuck in her throat when she saw him standing across the street.

"What are you doing here?" she asked, crossing to him, even as she willed her mind to believe the tingles racing along her spine were caused by the unexpectedness of seeing him.

"Looking for you."

She looked around as the rest of the congregation continued to pour from the building. She waved at some, smiled at others, before moving away in an attempt to thwart any idea they might have of approaching. Gunnar wasn't good with people.

"Oh? What for?" she asked.

He pushed away from the car. "I was trying to get in touch with Dominic, but he isn't answering his cell."

"He's camping, probably no signal."

"Yeah. I have something for him and wanted to drop it off at the house. Thought I should ask you first."

"That's not necessary," Tessa answered. He watched her steadily, and though it might be wiser to step away, she moved closer. What could happen in front of a church? "If you have it with you, I can take it."

"I don't."

"Well you can drop it off whenever you like."

"Will you be home later?"

"Later?" She was planning to come back for the evening service.

"If you have plans…"

She heard the faintest trace of displeasure and surmised he expected her to tell him what she would be doing. It was a behavior she had no intention of encouraging. "Give me a call later and see if I'm in. Or you can leave it on the porch."

"That won't be possible." He took a step forward. "I wanted to bring it by the other night, but no one answered when I called."

So much for nothing happening in front of a church. She felt confined even outdoors. She shifted her feet so it wouldn't be so obvious that she was putting distance between them.

"You didn't leave a message," she said.

"I hate answering machines."

When he kept staring at her, she started walking. "When did you call?"

"I don't know, the other night."

"If it was Thursday, I was at Connie's. Well, Connie and Mike's, now. They eloped."

"She pregnant?"

"No!" Tessa stopped short. Unwilling to engage in a dispute for his amusement she ignored the challenge and kept walking. "She's not pregnant." She jerked her shoulder in a light shrug. "They just didn't want to wait to belong to each other."

"Didn't they already? Isn't that why they got married?"

The truth of his words gave her pause, and she had to agree. "Yes." But she never expected him to see it that way.

"Would you elope?" he asked.

Her reply was ready before the word *elope* was finished. "I want the man I love to stand with me in front of God and family."

"That doesn't have to be in a church."

She shot him a look before realizing he was genuinely interested. "I always wanted a traditional wedding."

Gunnar frowned at her. "What is it with women and ceremonies? So will you be home?" he asked before she could answer.

Moving as far from him as the sidewalk would allow, she walked toward her car. "Um, maybe."

Gunnar fell in step with her. "I'll be leaving it on my way out of town, so if there's any chance you won't be home I have to know."

"Dominic should be back around ten."

"Too late."

"Well, what time is good for you?"

"Around seven."

She could still make church. "Yes, I'll be home. Where are you going?" she asked before she could help it.

"Maryland. Business." He hooked his thumbs in his front pockets. "Going to miss me?"

Even if the question hadn't been so odd coming from him, the easy smile playing at the corners of his mouth was enough to entice a smile from her. "If I were?"

He searched her face carefully. "I might make it a point to come back."

He must be joking, but the idea that his return might be uncertain made Tessa's nerves skitter, reminding her it wasn't wise to be in his company too long. When they reached her car, she unlocked it and tossed her purse and Bible bag onto the front seat. A girl's voice called out.

"Angel!"

Tessa arched a brow when Gunnar returned a tentative wave. "You know the Wongs?"

He cut Tessa a sidelong glance. "As a matter of fact, just Miranda."

Very odd. "Why does she call you angel?"

"I have no idea."

Tessa studied him before favoring him with a full smile. "She's right."

He wrenched back as though dodging a blow. "What?"

"You do remind me of an angel." When he stared

at her, horrified, she laughed. "Not the little chubby babies you see on wallpaper and greeting cards. Angels are actually extremely intimidating. The Bible says they excel in strength. In fact, their first words to humans are usually, 'Fear not'."

He looked more pleased with this definition and turned with her to watch Miranda's father fasten her into the car seat.

Gunnar looked back at Tessa. "I have a lot to do before I leave tonight. I'll see you later."

Tessa watched him walk to his car before getting into hers. She was wondering if there would always be such strain between them, when Connie's words came back to haunt her. *Sexual tension.* They weren't so funny anymore.

༄ఌ

Max stopped the trailer in front of Tessa's house and put on the flashers. The motorcycle behind it came around to the driver's window.

"Be right back," Gunnar said, and rode the bike around to the back of the house. A light burned in the kitchen so he set the bike on the stands and knocked on the back door, spinning the key ring around his index finger.

When Tessa opened the door, he could only stare.

Her feet were bare, her t-shirt, a few sizes too large, hung over the hips of loose-fitting jeans. She wore no make-up and held a potholder in one hand. Her hair swung loose, shiny, and straight as rain, the way he preferred it. He had a fleeting suspicion she wore it this way to torment him, knowing he would picture it the whole time he was away. Stupid. She was completely guileless and would wear it this way solely because she liked it.

But he would think of it.

"Come in," she said, when he hadn't spoken. "I have something on the stove."

"I, ah…" *Speak, you idiot*, he told himself. "I have to go, Max and David are waiting for me in front."

"Oh." She looked disappointed.

"I could use a drink," he said.

"Why don't you ask them in for a minute?"

"No."

She didn't argue, but cast him a look. "Help yourself," she said, pointing toward the refrigerator.

Whatever was cooking smelled great, but when his hunger stirred, it wasn't due to the aroma that wafted toward him when she opened the lid of a simmering pot.

He swallowed, riveted as she held a spoon to her naked mouth, tasting her concoction, licking the residue from her lips.

Every muscle in his body tensed.

She was magnificent. He couldn't blame Randy for saying so, more than once, but it was a good thing he'd made him stay behind. To keep up with production, Gunnar told him, but mostly for the idiot's own protection.

Gunnar didn't care how much he needed Randy's hands on the chess project; if he said another word about Tessa being hot, he was gone, first to the hospital, then to unemployment.

Tessa replaced the lid on the pot and swung her hair behind her shoulder. "So you're going on business?"

"Yeah." He grabbed a drink out of the refrigerator

and placed the keys on top. The soda can opened with a small explosion, and Gunnar downed half the contents as he took in the room.

There was linen on the table, candles in holders waiting to be lit, a vase holding fresh flowers. Probably making a special meal to welcome Dominic back from his trip. Gunnar couldn't see the sense in it, but it was the kind of thing she would do. "Too bad I'll miss Dom."

Her expression brightened. "He called earlier to say he and Pauline were staying one more day. I guess they're getting along."

Gunnar's already rigid body went on alert. "Then what's this?" he asked, using his finger to indicate the scene on view.

Man, he hoped it was simple male ego that had him hoping she wasn't expecting a male dinner companion. If not ego, he was in deep, deep trouble. He finished off the soda.

"What?" She followed his eyes and blushed with color. "Oh, I'm celebrating."

When he lowered the can to his chest she was looking at him curiously, her green siren's eyes wide and shining.

She looked nervous, but why? Was she expecting that Carter guy?

She nipped at her bottom lip, looked away.

Or could there be a more immediate cause? Maybe it wasn't nerves at all, but attraction. Testing, he moved an inch closer. She moved an inch away. He captured that alluring, crystal gaze with his, held it, until she looked away.

How could he slip right back into this sensual rhythm with her when he'd spent the last two weeks trying to forget her?

"Celebrating?" he asked, struggling to keep his voice casual.

"Yes." Tessa took a dishrag from the oven handle and wiped a red spot from the stovetop. "And I want to thank you."

"Me?"

"Mm-hmm. For helping me commit to starting my business."

His brow furrowed as he pulled up the memory. Right, the morning she made him French toast. "The inn."

"I met with a realtor," she said. When she smiled, delighted, he could have sworn he felt the impact of it. "There's no use waiting once you know what you want."

Tessa licked her lips. Gunnar's stomach tightened like a fist.

"You look good," she said unexpectedly. "You're sleeping OK?"

She was stalling for some reason.

"I don't get much chance to sleep, but at least I'm not afraid to go to bed." His rusty laugh did little to end the awkward vibe in the room. "You were saying? The realtor?"

"Oh." She paused, the smile widening. "I bought a house!"

Without warning, Tessa launched herself at him. He caught her with one arm and had barely enough time to put down the empty can before her lips were on his. It was a quick kiss, but he felt it to his toes, and when she looked into his eyes, his heart lurched to a stop before thundering off.

They had kissed before, but this time there was no

faltering. He wrapped her in his arms and took the initiative.

A squeak lodged in her throat, but she kept pace with him, as they moved as one, breathed as one, until by mutual consent, they slowed the kiss and eased apart by centimeters. He was glad she didn't pull away quickly, fearing the effect breaking it off at once might have on his system.

When she laid her head against him his chest contracted painfully.

"If I thought we could finish this, I'd cancel my trip." His voice was a gruff whisper as he defied his need to stroke her hair and hold her close. Gently but firmly, he shifted her so that the contact was limited to his hands on her arms. He needed to gain some distance and fast. He took a deep breath.

"So you bought a house," he said, trying to lead the conversation back to its origin.

The extended silence told him she was pulling her wits back together as well. He marked the small victory. For all the good it did.

"Well, nothing's set in stone," she said. "There'll be inspections and closing and all that, but it's terrific! Wait till you see it."

"Aren't you diving in a little fast?" he asked.

She beamed up at him. "I don't understand all the steps yet, and it's a little nerve-wracking, but mostly it's exhilarating, the not knowing."

He couldn't help the smile, or the pride he had in her. "And you're celebrating." He noticed now the single table setting. "Alone?"

"Yup. But you can join me in a toast." She went to the fridge and took out a bottle of sparkling cider. The sound of a horn made them both freeze. "I forgot you have to leave right away."

He would have given anything if she would ask him to stay. He could always send the truck on ahead and follow later—no.

"Not until I have a drink with you." He got the glasses and poured for both of them. "To your new business." He tipped his glass to hers. "And to you."

"Thank you. And good luck in Maryland."

He set his glass on the counter. "I have to go," he said, then took her hand and walked her to the front door.

He paused with his hand on the knob. "When I get back, we'll celebrate together. Maybe have dinner."

"I'll look forward to it," Tessa said. She clasped his forearm when he opened the door. "Wait, weren't you supposed to leave something for Dominic?"

"It's in the yard. The keys are on the fridge."

"Keys?"

He didn't respond, as with great reluctance, his fingers separated from hers. She was still at the door, glass in hand, when he climbed in the truck and slammed the door.

"Something wrong?" Max asked him.

"Just drive."

24

Blue skies and sunshine marked the first day of Tessa's new life, for that was what she considered the fifth of November. As of this morning's closing, she was legally responsible for a house that would, in about twenty years, be hers. She'd spent the day working on the revamp. It was hard, tedious work, but the repetition did little to put Gunnar from her mind or ease the sting of disappointment that came each time she remembered he was back from Maryland. Had been for weeks, according to Dominic.

It shouldn't upset her. So he hadn't kept his promise to take her to a celebration dinner; what could she expect, really? No doubt he'd found someone to keep him entertained, to share his interests and his bed while he was away. Tessa knew what happened at those bike shows; she'd been online.

Tessa pulled behind Dominic's house and spotted his motorcycle swathed in a white cover near the back fence. She didn't know which surprised her more, Gunnar giving it or Dominic accepting it. He'd already ridden it longer into the season than was normal, but with the weather changing, he would soon be storing it for winter.

When she saw Gunnar's car her body reacted immediately. The night he'd left for the bike show she had thrown herself at him—literally—and she'd dwelt on it ever since. If she closed her eyes, she could feel his hands at her waist, his lips on hers.

If she at least believed he was having as much trouble forgetting their last kiss as she was, that would be some reparation, but she didn't. Instead, he'd used his innate ability to shut her out. And that was exactly what she needed to do with him.

She forcibly dislodged the memory. Wanting to replay that scene with him was dangerous. And pointless, since he had, in essence, rejected her. Oh, he'd told her he wanted her, and it might have been true at the time, but apparently, his interest had cooled.

She sighed. The whole scenario was an exercise in futility. Whether he wanted her didn't matter because she shouldn't want him. He was an unbeliever. Was it any wonder they couldn't come together? God must be trying to show her something.

She sat in her car for a full minute deliberating whether to drive around until he left, but time wouldn't permit it and neither would her pride. Rejection wasn't pleasant, but she would not play into his hands. He would expect her to be uncomfortable or to flutter and fawn over him, coyly asking why he hadn't called. And he would love every second.

Not on his life. She strode purposefully toward the house.

Dominic's face was in the refrigerator when she came in. "Hey," he said.

"Hey," she replied.

Spying Gunnar, her stomach hopped once and plunged to the floor. He sat at the table, his long legs jutting into the center of the room, his black hair longer than last she'd seen it but still short. She hoped her casual smile would distract him long enough for her to force air into her lungs. He didn't draw his legs in when she walked by but sent her a long, studying look.

"How's the house coming?" Dominic asked, as he set cold cuts and iced tea on the table.

"Great. I got a lot done today," she said, automatically raising a hand to her stiff neck. "Too many hours looking up on a ladder, but it's worth it."

"I told you I'd be there first thing tomorrow. Why couldn't you wait?" Dominic asked.

"I enjoy the work. And I want to get it done A.S.A.P. I've waited too long to do this, already," she said, speaking of her decision to open the inn.

Dominic shrugged. "Want a sandwich?"

"No thanks, I have to shower and change," she answered, refusing to look at Gunnar. If he wanted to pretend nothing happened, so would she. "I'm going to dinner."

"Dinner? You should be going to bed," Dominic admonished, layering turkey and ham on bread.

"I have a date." She saw no need to mention it was with Connie and Mike. Because she was aware of Gunnar's eyes hot on her back, she couldn't resist adding more. "Don't wait up."

She walked away smug, but by the time she reached the landing at the top of the stairs she felt petty and sulky.

It didn't stop her from going to the closet after her shower and picking the hottest dress she owned, the one guaranteed to have the jaw of that impervious Gunnar Mason plummeting to the floor.

She wasn't conceited, but her mirror image didn't lie. She looked great, clad in sparkling, curve hugging royal purple. With the addition of four inch black heels, she shot from great to sizzling. Satisfied, she flipped her jacket over her arm and set off to singe Gunnar.

She stopped half way down the stairs. Since when was she the sort of woman who seduced men? One answer came to mind—since meeting Gunnar. And, she surmised, since it was out of character for her, it must be his influence.

Tessa found Dominic alone on the living room couch surfing channels on the TV and munching a bowl of corn chips. There was no sign of Gunnar, but she hid the disappointment with a smile.

"Wow," Dominic said, taking her in. "You look fantastic."

"Thanks." Girlishly thrilled, she gave him a slow spin.

"You want to borrow my gun in case your date gets out of line?"

"You're always too ready to loan me your gun. Isn't that against police regulations or something?"

"Want to borrow my pepper spray?"

She leaned down to give him a kiss. "I'll be back early."

Dominic chomped a chip. "What happened to 'don't wait up?'"

Tessa gave a quick look into the empty kitchen. "It's not a real date, it's dinner with Connie and Mike."

"No blind date, set up kind of thing?" he asked.

"No." She paused, suspicious. "Why?"

Dominic grunted. "It's my experience that as soon as a person—a female person—gets married, she wants all her friends to experience the same wedded bliss. It drives them nuts to see anyone single when they're so *happy*."

The increasing acrimony in his tone set off a

warning signal. Must be having another tiff with Pauline. "I could stay if you want to talk, dinner's no big thing."

Dominic dismissed her with a quick shake of his head and leaned forward to reach his iced tea on the coffee table. "I'm fine. When I know what women want I'll be better than fine. I might also be dead by then. Besides, it would be a waste of that dress to sit here with me."

"You're sure?"

"Go have a great time," Dominic said. "Bring me back a doggie bag."

"I'll see what I can do."

❧

Tessa gave the maître d' her name and looked around for Connie and Mike. She spotted them seated in the middle of the room, but they could have been alone for all the attention they paid to those around them. She watched them, fingers entwined, heads bent close, and was genuinely delighted for their happiness. But when the maitre d' touched a hand to her arm and smiled cordially, she felt a lump forming inexplicably in her throat.

"I'm sorry," she said, taking a napkin off an empty table and dabbing it under her eyes to prevent a flood. "Rough day."

Yes, but hardly the cause of her tears. She wanted to be here with Gunnar, anywhere with him. She'd expected to reduce whatever feelings she carried for him to annoyance and jealousy by now, but seeing him tonight threw her a curve and she was pining.

Pining. Her. Choking on the revelation, she moved

steadily forward.

When Connie waved at her, Tessa cleared her throat, squared her shoulders and found her smile. She would be darned if she would pine for a man who kissed her senseless one day and the next pretended she didn't exist.

"Don't be mad, don't be mad," Connie chanted, rising to greet Tessa as the maître d' seated her.

The last time Connie told her not to be mad she'd announced her elopement. What now? "Why should I be mad?"

Connie scooted into the chair beside her. "I had no control over this."

Tessa gawked at her. "What's the matter with you?" Her gaze followed Connie's to the sturdy form advancing toward them.

Tessa turned to Mike, searching his face for any sign this was an elaborate joke, but he only cocked his head, waiting for the scene to play out.

"Tessa." Carter greeted her with outstretched hands, and before she could stop it, was pulled to her feet into an enthusiastic embrace.

"I'm sorry," Connie mouthed behind him.

"Carter," Tessa said, confusion warring with irritation as she pulled from his grasp.

"When I heard you were going to be here I said to myself, Carter, you have to go this instant."

"And so you did," Tessa replied blankly.

"Here is your proof," he said, gesturing down the length of his body with stubby, fingers. "I don't usually eat this early, but would I be a fool to let this opportunity pass, or what?"

"Definitely a fool," Connie said dryly.

Carter pulled Tessa's chair out further. "I hung up

with Aunt Vivian, jumped in my car, and came right here," he said, with the tone of a child bragging of some grand accomplishment.

"Mom is full of surprises," Connie said.

"Remind me to thank her," Tessa said, gritting her teeth when Carter pushed her chair in, bending to kiss her cheek in the process.

"That dress is sensational," he said, eying her like the blue plate special.

It was going to be a long evening.

25

Gunnar didn't expect the house to impress him. It did. Aesthetically speaking it was in rough shape, but it appeared structurally sound and was a good size for an inn. Adequate to accommodate enough guests to make a profit, yet still be manageable. If he had Tessa pegged, she would try to do it all instead of hiring help.

He took his tools out of the trunk of his car and walked up the steps. A few gave a little under his weight. Closer inspection revealed dry rot. They needed to be replaced first thing. He took a tape measure from the toolbox, a pad from his back pocket, and a black marker from behind his ear and started making notes.

"Gunnar!"

Gunnar walked down the steps and stood on the front lawn, well, dirt, in order to see Dominic leaning out an upstairs window. "Yeah."

"When you come up, bring the step ladder. It's in the foyer by the stairs."

Gunnar continued measuring. Who knew his miserable past would be useful in any way? The experience he'd gained the summer he worked on Ryan Forsythe's construction crew came in handy. He'd been fourteen, but looked the nineteen he claimed to be. Ryan had believed him, or pretended to. It might have been a long-term gig if Gunnar hadn't threatened one of the crew with a nail gun.

He looked up from the porch deck to see Tessa's car pulling into the rutted driveway. His heart gave a jolt. Their eyes met, held, but she looked away in time to circumvent the fence post.

She was out of sight long enough for him to assume she had crept through the back, but then she appeared in front of him dressed in sweats, a long sleeved shirt, and sneakers. That lush, chestnut hair was tucked underneath a white, paint flecked cap.

"Hello," she said. "Dominic didn't tell me you were coming."

"Do you want me to leave?" He sounded cross and defensive but couldn't help it. She'd made sure he heard her say she was going on a date last night, and he bet all her hair wasn't hidden away, then.

"No," she said after a minor hesitation.

She paused, waiting for him to speak, but he didn't think he could trust himself to say something nice so kept silent.

"I could use the help," she said finally. "Thanks." She walked past him into the house and closed the door.

Man! How could she be so indifferent to seeing him again when he'd thought of nothing but her since she planted that kiss on him? He rubbed a hand over his face. Who was he kidding? He'd thought of no one but her since their first meeting. When she walked into the kitchen last night he'd been dying to grab her and take that pretty, sassy mouth of hers, but she'd looked right through him as if he was nothing more than vapor.

On top of that, they'd had plans to get together

and celebrate the house and he'd stood her up, more or less. Didn't that mean anything to her?

It was possible her date had been keeping her busy in his absence. The fact he had no right to be jealous ticked him off more than she did.

Gunnar gave in to the urge and punched a hole in the top step. Yeah, it needed to come off anyway but it was stupid. Some of the skin on his knuckles was scraped off and it started to bleed a little. Good. The sting would remind him to stay away from Tessa. Self-preservation, he decided to call it. He wiped his hand on the bottom of his shirt and went inside to bring Dominic the ladder.

Resting the ladder on his shoulder, he began his ascent when he had to ask himself…what was he trying to preserve? Gunnar Mason, a man he reviled? His way of life, composed chiefly of loneliness and temper? Why preserve something that should have been destroyed years ago? Disgusted, he pushed away the thoughts.

He heard Dom and Tessa upstairs conferring about crown molding in one of the bedrooms. He leaned the ladder on the wall outside the door and returned the way he came.

❦

Tessa remained hidden all morning, which suited Gunnar fine. He kept to his part of the house, putting up drywall in the library, and she kept to hers doing whatever. Occasionally he heard her exchange a few words with Dom. Around one o'clock, when her car started and faded into the distance, he should have been able to relax, but his shoulders were in knots.

Dominic poked his head in the door. "Come on, let's grab some lunch before Tessa gets back. How 'bout Angelo's for pizza?"

"You go. I want to finish here; my time's limited." Gunnar applied more joint compound to the seam of two new pieces of drywall.

Dominic came into the room and looked around. "Nice job, she'll be happy." He chuckled. "She went to pack some stuff. You believe she wants to sleep here tonight?" Gunnar took the room in. "Upstairs," Dominic said. "She's rushing the whole thing if you ask me, but she has her own mind."

Gunnar remained silent.

"What's bothering you?"

"What are you talking about?"

Dominic gave him a questioning look. "Never mind. Hey, I'll bring you back a sub."

When Dom left, Gunnar scraped the edge of the putty knife into the can of compound. What could be bothering him? That a woman he wanted was dating someone else? Or that he wanted this woman more than any before? Impulse made him take out his phone and dial Samantha's cell number. She was almost certainly delving deep into a patient's psyche so he would keep it brief.

After five minutes of superficial small talk he realized he had nothing to say—nothing that he was comfortable saying—and hung up. For the best. He never discussed women with his sister. She would be all over him, prying details, and trying to psychoanalyze him. He wasn't ready for that.

Gunnar hadn't realized how hungry he was until Dom came in and pitched him a white paper bag smelling of heaven.

"Meatball sub," Dom informed him and handed him a can of ginger ale.

"Thanks." Gunnar tore the bag open from top to bottom, unwrapped the sandwich and began to devour it, pausing once to guzzle from the soda can.

"Hungry?"

Gunnar grunted.

Dominic gave a stiff nod. "So, are you going to tell me what's wrong?"

"What do you mean?"

Dominic leaned casually against a bare wall and folded his arms. "I couldn't help noticing your knuckles are all tore up. Coincidentally, there's a crater in the front step the size of a fist."

Gunnar crumpled the garbage into a tight ball and tossed it onto a pile of debris in the center of the room. "Shooting for detective?"

"Funny."

The sound of tires crunching gravel halted further interrogation and the men looked out the window.

Below, Tessa opened the back door of her car, which was loaded to capacity with boxes, bags, lamps, and a chair. Her desk protruded from the trunk.

"How did you get that in there?" Dominic called to her.

Tessa smiled and hefted a box onto her knee.

"Be right there." When Gunnar followed, Dominic turned. "Doesn't look like much, I'll get it."

Fine with Gunnar. He had some cleaning up to do before he slipped away. Maybe he would lend a hand if he found any free time next week, but he would try to arrange it when Tessa would be elsewhere. He moved back to the window—not to catch a glimpse of her—and saw the desk bouncing up the front path with Dominic underneath.

Gunnar intercepted him on the staircase. "Where does it go?" he asked, transferring the desk from Dominic's shoulder to his.

"Up. Third door on the right. Thanks."

Gunnar followed Dom's directions and placed the desk in the center of the room. Tessa would move it where she wanted it. He turned to go as Tessa pushed a box across the threshold with her foot.

"Thanks," she said when she saw the desk.

"No problem."

She moistened her lips and came all the way into the room. "I really do appreciate all your help. I know how busy you are."

Gunnar wished he could pinpoint what it was about her that pulled at him so strongly. But right now, he couldn't keep from going to her any more than he could keep his heart from beating.

She looked like a helpless child, swaying a little, with her hands clasped in front of her. He fought the impulsive need to take her in his arms and hold onto her.

"What do you want from me?" he asked, his voice low and thick with resignation.

Tessa blinked bewildered eyes at him. "I don't understand."

No, she didn't. She wasn't manipulative. She wasn't forcing him to choose or playing games to illustrate the emptiness of his life without her. She was simply being Tessa. She stared at him wordlessly as he waged his private inner war, forced to recognize his greatest fear—that this growing hunger for her might just unhinge him.

He was reluctant to break the spell keeping her in

this spot, but he had to ask. "Don't you want to know why I've been avoiding you?"

He cringed inwardly. Did he really want to admit to her that she was filling his thoughts? And that it scared him enough to make him keep his distance until he could figure it out? He would also have to admit he had yet to figure it out.

Tessa looked at the floor. "It's none of my business."

He took her hand and gave it enough of a squeeze to make her look up. "No?"

"I assumed you were busy with other things." She tried a careless movement of her shoulder.

Seeing all he needed to in the simple gesture, Gunnar's mouth relaxed into a half smile. "You mean you assumed I was busy with a woman." His smile broadened when her eyes lit with that familiar spark. He suddenly felt at an advantage, something he hadn't felt in weeks.

"Only one?"

"Well, you said yourself I'm very busy," he joked.

Tessa pulled away, but he blocked the door before she could go. Outside a car door closed and footsteps drew louder.

"Tess, you want this in the kitchen?" Dom called up the stairs. "It's marked cookbooks."

"Yes!" she called back. Gunnar reclaimed her hand.

"What do you want from me?" she asked, using his earlier question.

"I want to be with you," he replied, surprised how effortlessly the statement fell from his tongue.

But when those green eyes blinked, then fixed on him, his surprise was quickly replaced with self-derision. It wasn't fair of him to drop that on her. And how could he expect her to believe it after the way he'd treated her?

He could use the excuse that this was all new to him, so he didn't have a suitable course of action prepared, but to just say the words, *I want to be with you*...stupid.

A noise in the hallway had Gunnar stepping back, releasing her hand.

"You two going to help me or do I have to..." Dominic slowed his steps when he came into the room in time to see them parting. "...do it myself?" he finished when they both looked at him.

Tessa ran her palms down the front of her jeans. "I'm going to see where I put that box of linens."

Dominic watched her go.

Gunnar stood calmly, waiting for Dominic to round on him as soon as they were alone.

"What do you think you're doing?"

"You mean with your sister," Gunnar said flatly.

"Yeah, with my..." Dominic's voice was rising, and he paused to get it in check. "Yes, with my sister."

Gunnar looked him in the eye, telling his friend he would stand his ground, though he hoped it wouldn't come to a physical confrontation. "Talking."

"You were touching."

"Yes."

"Why?"

"I like her," Gunnar said in simple terms. "And for reasons I can't piece together, I think she likes me."

"She doesn't know what she likes," Dominic snapped. "She has no experience."

"How do you know?"

Dom's face hardened to stone. "If you laid a hand

on her—"

He took a solid step forward, but Gunnar kept his arms at his sides. He could take Dominic, but they were well-matched combatants and he had no desire to brawl right here on the floor.

"Give me a break, Dom, she's what, twenty-five, twenty-six? She may not have been around the block, but she knows the neighborhood."

Gunnar barely had enough time to register how wrong that sounded before he was rocked back on his heels. He'd underestimated the speed and accuracy of Dominic's right cross. Deciding he deserved it, Gunnar held his body in check before he could fire back with one of his own.

"I let you live in my home and this is how you repay me?" Dominic asked, his body tensed for action.

Gunnar touched the back of his fist to his throbbing lip. "Whoa," he warned, holding his other hand up when Dominic approached again. "The first one was free, the next one'll cost you."

"What are you doing with Tessa?" Dominic demanded.

"We were just talking."

"About what?"

"None of your business."

"She's my sister."

Gunnar moved a bit further out of reach. "Yeah, and you don't want her with me, I get it. But I didn't ask for your approval."

"You better," Dominic retorted.

"Tessa isn't a girl anymore, bro. She's a woman. Not the kind of woman you'd picture me with, I'll give you that..." Gunnar looked out the window to where Tessa was wiggling a huge box from the front seat of her car. "But I like her."

Dominic stood, flexing the hand he'd just used to punch Gunnar. He relaxed his posture slightly. "You like a lot of women."

Gunnar lowered his head. Yes, another reminder that his past would always haunt him. But he couldn't change his feelings for Tessa, and if it meant being selfish to grab hold of her, so be it. Coming to that conclusion was unexpected, and to be pondered at a later time.

"Have you seen me with, or heard me mention other women since I met your sister?" He could almost see Dominic replaying the days in his mind before his lips bent.

"And the bike show?" Dom asked. "There's no way you looked, but didn't touch."

Gunnar almost smiled, flipped his palms upward. "You're gonna believe what you want. And I know you don't want to hear this, but she's all I think about."

Gunnar scowled, reflecting Dominic's expression. "I want to be with her even though we don't belong together." He ventured a foot closer. "You think I'm stupid? But you said yourself she has her own mind. Even I don't know why she gives me the time of day."

Dominic shoved his hands in his front pockets. "And that's it, no matter what I say?"

"You want to punch my head in, don't you?"

"If you make her unhappy, I'll kill you," Dominic warned in a deceptively calm voice.

"I can't promise it won't happen," Gunnar answered. "But I'd rather die than hurt her."

Dominic slapped him on the back, none too gently. "We'll see."

Both men looked toward the doorway as sounds

of Tessa struggling with the box drifted up. More relieved than he wanted to divulge, Gunnar met Dominic's eyes directly. "Still friends?"

"We'll see about that, too," Dom answered, but gave him a half-cocked grin.

Tessa dropped the box at the top of the stairs. "Thanks for nothing," she huffed. "Come on, break is over. You bring this in there," she told Dominic, who headed to the box. "And you bring in the rest of the boxes. I've already carried them onto the porch," she told Gunnar. "What happened to your lip?" she asked after a closer look.

At once aware of the puffiness and the taste of blood, Gunnar looked from her to his attacker. "Guy stuff," he answered innocently.

"Idiots," she said in disgust and walked away. "And what happened to the front step?" she called back.

26

Maybe Dom's right cross, rattled his brain more than he wanted to admit. That would explain why Gunnar saw Pastor Caswell standing beneath the porch light wearing a Houston Astros hat and yellow Adidas.

Seeing the movement at the window, Bob looked up and waved.

Gunnar flicked the curtain back in place and swung the door open.

"Hello, Gunnar," Bob hailed. "I hope I didn't catch you at a bad time."

"How did you get my address?" Gunnar asked, before stepping aside to let him in, remembering too late he hated company.

"I went by Tessa's," Bob answered, automatically sweeping the hat from his head as he entered. "Her brother gave me your address. Nice guy."

Well, that was one opinion. Gunnar shifted his sore jaw. If Bob noticed his swollen lip he gave no sign. "What do you want?" He didn't mean to sound inhospitable, really.

Bob smiled. "Well, I tried to reach you at work, but there was no answer this time of night."

"What's so important that you tracked me?"

Transferring his hat to the other hand, Bob reached into his inside jacket pocket, took out a small, tan book and handed it to him.

Gunnar turned it over in his hand. "What's this?"

"It's Evan's prayer journal."

Gunnar's stomach clenched, and he closed his hand around the leather cover. Silent as a ghost, he moved into the living room.

Bob trailed behind. "I was straightening up the den after the meeting tonight and came across it in the rack with some old magazines. I guess it got lost in the clutter."

Furniture for the living room hadn't been a priority, so Gunnar lowered himself onto a large crate, and stared down at the book. Bob's feet shuffled nearby.

"I thought you should have it. But if you want to give it to your sister, that's your call," Bob said.

Gunnar's fingers caressed the leather grain.

"I didn't read it," Bob said. When Gunnar looked up Bob met his gaze evenly. "I would tell you if I did. I did peek inside to see whose it was. We give them to people when they get baptized. The name is written on the inside cover," he said, waggling a finger at the book.

Gunnar returned his gaze to the book. Maybe if he stared hard enough he would be able to read the words without opening it.

"Coffee?" he asked after a minute.

Pastor Caswell followed him into the kitchen where there were chairs and a table.

"Remodeling, huh?" Bob asked, taking in the spacious room. "What a nuisance that can be. We renovated our house in Maine before we came here. We loved that house."

"So why aren't you in it?" Gunnar nodded toward

a chair, which Bob took, hanging his hat on the back.

Bob's eyes lit with humor. "God doesn't check with me before He does anything. Sometimes He has other plans." He shrugged. "I don't always agree with Him, but it's always for the best."

Gunnar let the comment slide, not wanting to start an argument after the man was good enough to bring Evan's journal. "I don't have cream," he said. "Or milk."

"Black's fine."

"I have sugar somewhere."

"Don't go to any trouble."

"Are you always so agreeable?" Gunnar asked, irritated.

Bob chuckled. "Not if you ask my wife."

Gunnar took two mugs from a box on the counter and brought them to the sink to rinse. "Can I ask you something?" he asked, shaking the excess water out. "What made you become a pastor? You don't strike me as the type."

"Oh, you don't want to get me started on myself. According to some members of my flock I can be long winded."

Gunnar crossed his arms, waiting.

"God," Bob said after a moment. "He didn't force me to be a pastor, but you know what I mean."

"No."

The smile faded from Bob's lips and he sat erect in his chair. "All right, let me see if I can answer that." He paused. "I got saved at twenty-nine. Kind of a late bloomer," he said, when Gunnar's brows shot up.

"Not a church kid?"

Bob shook his head. "Far as you could get. My father was an alcoholic. Mean as a viper. I hated him until the day he died. Even after. There are times I struggle with residual hatred when circumstances come up that remind me of him." He looked Gunnar dead in the eye. "After you told me what happened to your sister I prayed a lot. For her and you, and myself."

Gunnar lifted his chin, a sign of solidarity, though he didn't see the connection to Samantha.

"When he died, I moved in with my grandmother," Bob continued. "I was fifteen, she was seventy-six. So we didn't see eye to eye on anything."

"Let me guess, an old church lady?"

"Wrong again. My father inherited his mean genes from her." Bob laughed. "Scariest woman God ever put on this earth. She was my catalyst to make something of myself, so I could get out. Books were my escape, no matter the subject, anything that took my mind off what happened to me—thanks," he said, when Gunnar set a full mug in front of him.

"So it followed logically that school became a refuge. I buried myself in academia and after-school activities to elude her. Fortunately I had a fair share of brains so when I won a full scholarship to CSU, I ran and didn't look back."

"Where was your mother?"

"I never knew her."

"Wish I could say the same for mine."

Bob propped his ankle on his knee and draped an arm on the back of the chair. "On the surface it seems people have children for the solitary purpose of messing them up, but there's always a plan."

Gunnar kept his one word opinion to himself. "You were saying?"

"Right. During college, I went nuts. I did more

coke and slept with more women than all of my friends combined."

Gunnar's brows shot up once again. "You?"

"Don't look so shocked," he told Gunnar. "I didn't hang with Bible-toters back then, and I didn't always look like this," he said, patting his softening middle. "I was in a rock band. I used to be hot."

Both men laughed.

"In fact, I met Tara in a bar after a gig. My wife," he clarified. "She introduced herself one night when I came off stage, and we've been together since."

"So, God's plan included sex, drugs and rock n' roll?"

"Uh, no, that was my plan, but I'm getting to that," Bob said. With a smile of remembrance, he sipped his coffee. "Sometimes on a trip to the past I sit and visit with my pre-salvation days."

Yes, this guy was easy to talk to and easy to trust. But it didn't make them friends.

Bob set down the cup. "OK, so I met my wife, and two months later she's pregnant."

"Now I am shocked," Gunnar rebuked him jokingly.

"You should've seen me. And she was a wreck! Twenty-two years old, only knew me a short time, and bam, she's pregnant. Add to it the fact that she comes from a large conservative family, and you have trouble, squared."

"This gets better, right?"

Bob nodded. "The night she told me, I visited this church in my neighborhood, just in case there was an infinitesimal chance of a miracle, like it was a mistake and she wasn't pregnant." He rolled his eyes at his foolishness. "And I wasn't even high at the time.

"I listened to the preacher explain how Peter stepped out of the boat onto the stormy sea and how Jesus saved him from drowning. I related, so I asked Jesus to do the same thing for me."

"You remember that?"

"When your life changes, it sticks with you," Bob related soberly.

Gunnar wondered what Tessa was doing. "And then your life got all happy," he said, sitting across from Bob.

Many emotions filtered through Bob's blue eyes before he finally answered. "Some people feel a change right off the bat, some don't. I did. I felt…clean," he said, smoothing a hand down his chest. "It's a cliché, but it was like my whole life started fresh. Aside from the band, I had a real job in an office supply company, a new car, but it didn't mean anything. I saw the big picture all at once, and whether I had season tickets to the Garden didn't matter. I used to be ambitious," he said with mirth.

"Going into the church I thought having a baby was the worst thing that could happen to me, and coming out, it felt right. To that point, my level of commitment went as far as maybe we'd get an apartment together, but by the time I picked Tara up the next day, I had a ring in my pocket."

"Sounds like you were brainwashed," Gunnar said.

"I call it soul washed," Bob said. "Anyway, I could suddenly recall sitting in my room, praying as a kid, asking God to give me a wife one day who would love me. Oddly enough, my upbringing made me want to be married and have kids of my own. I guess for the stability."

Marriage was a four-letter word in Gunnar's mind. Until he'd met Tessa, anyway. "Was Tara a Christian?"

Bob's lips curved. "No, and she didn't know what to do when I told her. She was just getting to know me, and then she had to get used to a completely different guy and decide if she wanted to marry him." He got up to top off his coffee. "And I didn't make things easy. I started preaching at her, telling her she needed to repent. I had no idea what I was talking about, but I knew if I was saved, the mother of my child should be, too."

If Gunnar knew women... "She didn't take it well."

Bob sipped the scalding coffee before answering. "She said I'd lost my mind. But she called a Christian friend and talked to her. What I couldn't do in a month, God did in a day, through someone else, and Tara accepted Christ." He returned to the table with a big grin. "Of course I like to say I planted the seed and her friend watered it."

"Ego?"

"Seriously, yes. At the time," Bob added. "Now, I won't take the credit, or the blame, for anything spiritual. That's God's realm, not mine."

Gunnar turned the mug around. He wanted to ask about the evil side of that realm.

"Don't misunderstand," Bob continued. "Salvation doesn't make life perfect. In fact, it often makes things harder."

"So, why a pastor?" he repeated his original query. Having seen the church building in need of repair, the modest home—he'd driven by a few times—Bob didn't do it for the money.

"Ah." Bob took another mouthful of steaming coffee, before continuing in his steady, unhurried cadence. "It happened that getting saved that night left me with more questions than answers. For the first time in my life, I was aware of something greater than myself, and I couldn't understand how that could be. I felt the reality of it, but how could Jesus come into me all of a sudden and do what He was doing? Why hadn't I felt it before? It didn't make sense. Things don't just change your heart, right? There had to be a logical explanation. So I jumped into the Bible with both feet. When I finished reading it through—"

"You read the whole thing?"

"It was a book, so I read it. When I finished, I read every book I could find on the Bible, Jesus, meditation, world religions, UFO's, anything that might remotely explain my experience. I read, cross-referenced, read and cross-referenced some more. I had stacks of books, folders of printouts; I even corresponded with all the popular preachers.

"But one day I prayed before I opened my Bible. I asked God to reveal Himself to me, and I found the answers where they were all along, in His Word. Except now, I read the words with my heart instead of my head."

Gunnar hoped he didn't look as at sea as he felt.

"You don't follow, and that's OK," Bob told him. "Because you can't follow with your intellect. I got saved through faith, and I found the answers through faith. It turned out the logical conclusion I was looking for had nothing to do with logic. It was Jesus."

"Jesus."

"The reason He can do what He does is because He is Who He is." Bob opened both hands and leaned back in his chair.

Torn between frustration and hope, Gunnar

leaned forward in his. "That's an answer?"

"Best one I have for you." Bob wagged his head. "I can quote you Scripture and verse, show you in the Bible where it says Jesus is God, and the atonement for our sins, but that isn't how I know. That only confirms what I know." He paused. "To answer your question, once I learned the truth, there was nothing else for me to do but dedicate my life to Him and tell as many people as I could. I guess I still haven't mastered it. I mean, right now, you're looking at me like I climbed out an asylum window."

"I believe you," Gunnar said. "That you're sincere," he amended, unwilling to commit to anything. "But you're right, it doesn't make sense."

"That's the beauty of it. It's so astounding, so incredible, that if it were an intellectual thing most of us would be doomed."

Gunnar rubbed the back of his neck. "You mean hell."

"Do you believe in hell?" Bob asked.

"If anyone should, it's me. I've been there."

Bob's face sobered as he studied Gunnar's expression. "You don't mean that figuratively," he said.

He trusted Bob, but pastor or not, the guy probably thought he was a nut.

Then Bob reached across the table and touched his arm briefly. "I was once chased out of a house by a demon in a red dress, and I don't mean a bad date. Believe me, you don't want to mess with the dark side."

"It's messing with me." Gunnar rose with his mug, but stopped in front of the coffee pot with his back to Bob. "A few months ago I started getting nightmares."

He turned to face the man who might have answers for him. "They're closer to abductions. It's hard to say, since I think I'm going to them, not the other way around."

"You mean an out of body thing?"

"No, my whole body is there. I feel and smell everything. When I get back, my sheets smell of smoke." He paused. "I can't prove it."

"You don't have to, I believe you."

"There's more."

Gunnar related each incident in excruciating detail, moving through his escape to Dominic's house, the episode there and his suicide attempt. When he finished he took his place at the table and waited for Bob's response.

"Wow," Bob said. "That's like…biblical."

"What?"

Was Bob mocking him?

"Well if you died and went to hell, that would be one thing. But you're experiencing it and living through it and only God could, or would, do that."

"God?" Shock was the least of Gunnar's instant emotions. "Why would He do that?"

"He's most likely allowing it to happen as a warning. You have a call on your life."

"A call?"

"Yes. Glad I'm not you," Bob said, making the sign of the cross.

"Are you trying to make me feel better?" Gunnar asked, aware of a new sense of dread slithering around him. "Cause it's not working."

"God's got a plan."

Gunnar banged a fist on the table and made Bob jolt. "Stop talking in riddles and tell me what's going on!"

Bob aimed a finger at him. "For the devil to be tormenting you, trying to coax you into suicide, means you must be a threat to him, alive."

"How?"

"I don't know. Don't get all upset," he continued when Gunnar ground his teeth. "I believe God must have a plan in store, and you're going to be pivotal. I already told you, He isn't finished with you."

"You're nuts. Why me?"

"Maybe not you," Bob said. "Maybe someone you'll influence in some way, maybe one of your kids."

"I don't have kids."

"Yet," Bob answered pointing a finger skyward. "But someday down the line. You need to be here, whatever the case. But as you stand, you're a target and without God's protection..."

"Protection? Are you kidding? I wanted to kill myself to keep it from happening again."

"You realize, that had you succeeded, you would have ended up there permanently," Bob said.

Yes, Gunnar did realize that, after the fact. This was crazy. Gunnar raked his hands over his face. "You just said He protected me."

"He did, and He might still, but because you're under someone else's umbrella."

"Riddles..."

"You aren't saved, correct?" He looked to Gunnar for confirmation.

Gunnar made an impatient gesture with his shoulder.

"Well, people argue this point, but I happen to believe the power of God is limited for you. Until you give your life to Jesus and let Him be your Lord, anything He does for you is more or less a…spill-over, a benevolent token you aren't entitled to."

"Entitled? But, aren't we *all* children of God?"

"We're all His creation, and He wants to do great things for us, but we all have free will and often don't discover what He has for us because of bad choices. He'll try and steer us toward the truth, but He's a gentleman and won't press. He has to be invited.

"It's like when you have a son and he comes to you one day and says, 'I want to go to the movies with my friends. I need twenty bucks and a ride.' You say OK but when you get outside, all of his friends are gathered around the minivan with their hands out. Now you may give them all a ride, because it's a big van, and hey, they're all going to the same place, but only your son is getting twenty bucks." He sipped his coffee, looked into Gunnar's eyes. "Because he's yours."

Gunnar understood the allegory, but didn't get the correlation to his problem. "So…"

"Someone must be praying for you. Because *they're* asking Him, He's answering, and you're reaping the benefit. That's also probably how the devil knows to target you. He doesn't know the future beyond what the Bible says, so I'm guessing something's giving you away. An increased angelic presence, maybe."

Gunnar stood. When he'd first learned Tessa was praying for him, he'd been ticked. Now he was freaked out. "But if I'm pivotal in some way, isn't God *supposed* to protect me?"

"Not necessarily. His plan may include you, but like I said, we all have free will and if you don't want to join in, He'll have to get somebody else." Bob paused. "The trouble is, even if you make up your mind to participate, you have to stand on your own. The devil can't violate you that way once you're covered by the blood of Christ."

"Wh—"

"No rituals," Bob interjected. "Not the way you—. Let me start again."

For the next half hour, Pastor Caswell laid out the plan of salvation, starting with the Old Testament.

To Gunnar's surprise it didn't sound so far-fetched, anymore.

Bob's words rang true; it wasn't logical, but it made sense.

"Tessa's praying for me," he told Bob later.

"She's a faithful woman."

"Yeah," Gunnar murmured. "I wish..."

Bob tilted his head expectantly.

Gunnar felt stupid, but he told the man so much already. "I wish she'd come to her senses and have nothing to do with me."

Bob eyed him sympathetically. "But at the same time you're worried she will."

Gunnar looked at his hands, so much larger and rougher than Tessa's. Hands that had been cut and broken. Hands that had known the flesh of countless women. Hands that had murdered.

"We agree I'm no good for her."

Bob's finger was quick to jab the air between them. "I never said that. I said believers shouldn't join with unbelievers and that Tessa would be miserable if she did."

"It's the same thing."

"It doesn't have to be."

Gunnar's mouth twisted into a cynical half smile.

"Isn't that some kind of blackmail? Get saved, get the girl?"

Bob laughed. "If it were possible to blackmail people into salvation I would need a bigger church. Boy, I could tell you some things. But in order to be saved it has to be about you, for you, and the plea has to come from you. It doesn't take if there are ulterior motives. You can't get saved to spite the devil, or to make the nightmares stop, although I believe they will."

Gunnar narrowed his eyes.

"I'm going to pray for you," Bob said.

"Thanks," Gunnar murmured, but when Bob dragged his chair closer and reached toward him, Gunnar ducked out of the way. "You mean now?"

"No time like the present," Bob said, clapping a hand onto Gunnar's shoulder.

Gunnar was more than a little uncomfortable as Bob bowed his head and asked God to be merciful and send defending angels. When he prayed for God to send His salvation, Gunnar's flesh erupted in goose bumps.

The cell phone at Bob's hip rang. "My wife," he said, holding the phone at a readable distance. "Hello."

Gunnar got up to put his mug in the sink, and paused to look at his reflection in the window glass. "Ulterior motives," he murmured.

"I'm afraid I have to go," Bob said, the faintly lined plane of his forehead deeply grooved with concern.

"Problem?" Gunnar asked.

"One of the older sisters in the congregation is being taken to the hospital," Bob answered, taking his hat, and edging toward the doorway.

"Can I do anything?"

"No, thank you. She's in pretty frequently, it isn't life threatening. You mull over what I said." Bob walked toward the front door. "We'll talk."

Famous last words, Gunnar remembered, closing the door. Which reminded him of the initial reason for Bob's visit.

He returned to the kitchen and picked up Evan's journal, but didn't open it. He would try it fresh in the morning. He already had too much on his mind.

27

Tessa stretched her arms toward the kitchen ceiling, simultaneously wincing and smiling as muscles she couldn't pinpoint screamed to be left alone. It felt wonderful. She was more sore today than yesterday, but never more proud of a task. She couldn't wait to get back to it, but she'd designated today to recuperate while she scouted for kitchen supplies, maybe do some shopping online.

Hanging her feet on the bottom rung of the chair, she reviewed her supply list. The equipment she already owned was good quality, but insufficient to meet the demands of a growing enterprise.

"There's a restaurant supply place on Hammond Avenue in Fairfield," Dominic said, looking over her shoulder at the list. "The owner's a friend of Pauline's."

"Anybody die there?"

"Not to my knowledge."

"Thanks, I'll look into it."

"Hey, have I told you how proud I am of you?" he asked.

Tessa looked up at him.

"I mean it," he said. "It takes guts to start from scratch, especially when it means going against what people think you should do."

By "people" he meant their parents, who had

made some less than encouraging remarks concerning her business venture. She thought it had rolled off her back. Until tears welled in her eyes. "Thank you."

Dominic kissed her cheek. "I talked to Dad yesterday. He wants me to tell him if you get into any trouble."

"You wouldn't."

"No. Because you won't be getting in any."

Praise and confidence—it was too much to take in all at once. The phone rang and she wiped her tears with her knuckles as he answered.

"Hello. Yeah. It's for you." Dominic handed her the phone. "Gunnar."

What? Gunnar was calling her?

And Dominic wasn't making an issue of it? This was odd. She'd suspected whatever guy stupidity they were up to at the inn yesterday was related to her talking with Gunnar, but since it wasn't like Dominic to keep things inside, she decided she was wrong. This seemed to confirm it. Thankfully.

She appreciated her big brother watching her interests, but she could do without his *suggestion* that she defend her heart from Gunnar, or worse, his trying to do it for her. She wasn't convinced it needed defending. It could be simple infatuation.

No. Her heart disagreed. There was much more to their attachment than the dreamy affection of adolescents. Standing with him in that room yesterday, feeling her nerves tighten and tingle from nothing more than his eyes on hers, she was keenly aware in some deep place inside that no one else would make her respond so. He must have felt it, too. He'd told her he wanted to be with her, and now he was calling her instead of running in the opposite direction. That was monumental.

"Hello," Tessa said into the phone.

Gunnar sounded a little cautious. "I stopped at your place and you weren't there, so I figured I'd try Dom's."

"I stopped by for breakfast," she said, neglecting to mention she'd cooked it.

"Don't you have a cell phone?"

"Had one. Lost it in a flood," Tessa said. I've been meaning to replace it, I just haven't made time."

"What're you doing now?"

"Not much, why?"

"We should get you a phone."

"You want to go with me to buy a cell phone?"

Dominic looked back at her, but kept silent.

"Yeah," Gunnar said. "Wait there, I'm on my way."

☜☞

Tessa was overjoyed with her new phone. She was currently loading it with candid shots of Gunnar's less than willing face, and the price was terrific. The salesman had started firm, but after a short walk with Gunnar to the end of the counter and back, Tessa was able to buy the best phone with the best plan for half what she'd expected to pay.

"One smile," she said, leveling the tiny lens at him across the fast food restaurant table.

"Give me a reason to smile," he said.

"Being in my presence?" His lips twitched, but she wasn't fast enough. "My shining personality?"

"Would you put that thing away?" Gunnar took the phone from her and set it on the table. "Thanks."

"You're too handsome to be shy." He almost laughed, but she didn't reach for the camera. "So why were you looking for me this morning?"

He hesitated. "I wanted to ask you to dinner."

Tessa glanced at the plastic tray in front of her.

"In a restaurant," he said.

"So why haven't you?"

Gunnar shifted his feet under the table. "I'm getting around to it."

He fidgeted with his keys, sat taller in his seat, looked at her, looked away. If Tessa didn't know better, she'd say he was anxious. The idea seemed outrageous.

"You don't have to be nervous with me," she said, laying her fingers lightly on his hand.

Puzzlement creased his brow as he looked into her eyes. "I'm not a stone wall, Tessa. I get nervous when it matters."

Tessa's heart swelled, then melted and filled her body with warmth. No one, in her whole life, had paid her a lovelier compliment. He looked away, but not before she saw something in his eyes she hadn't seen before. He was brooding—always, agitated—definitely, yet underlying it all there was this gentle hesitation.

"Will you have dinner with me tonight?" he asked, quietly.

"Yes." She could see some of the tension drain from him, smoothing the lines on his forehead.

"Seven?" he asked.

"Fine." Tessa took her phone back. "You want my new number?"

"Already have it," Gunnar said, tapping a finger to his temple.

"What if I didn't want you to have it?" she teased.

"We'll never know." Gunnar stood, dumped the garbage in the trash and placed the empty tray on top of the can. "I have some free time tomorrow if you need help around your place."

She smiled, beamed actually. It was sweet of him to offer. Dominic told her how hard Gunnar was working and that the transition to the new shop was approaching sooner than originally planned. She walked through the door he held open, touching his hand as she passed.

"My cousin Seth is coming tomorrow after church."

Gunnar took her hand and pulled her back when she would have walked on. "So?"

"So you have your work to do."

"Tomorrow's Sunday," Gunnar retorted.

Tessa didn't flinch at the note of annoyance in his voice. "Thank you, but you'll be in the way." She tried to keep her lips straight at the look of insult on his face. "We're going to finish my room."

"I'll come Monday."

Tessa looked up and to the side, considering. "Well, if you help me, you have to let me help when you move your shop."

Gunnar smiled indulgently. "You want to help me move tons of equipment."

Tessa yanked her hand away. "If you're good enough to offer help so am I."

"It's not the same thing." When her brow rose, he groaned.

"I don't expect to haul a motorcycle on my back, but there are things I can carry," she said. "Your whole office has to be packed up, files, coffee maker, pencils."

"I appreciate it," he said with grudging calm.

"But?"

He took her hand back and brought it to his chest, leaving her no choice but to come closer. "No but. I'll tell you when, and when I do, don't complain I'm working you too hard."

She smiled, accepting the agreement.

"Or that I'm a little grouchy."

She snorted. "Grouchy? That's how you describe yourself?"

His eyes darkened, lids lowering slightly before he bent to take her mouth with his.

They stood in a fast food parking lot, but at that moment, she could have been anywhere in the world. The shadow of giant golden arches falling across her face could have been that of a leaning palm; the start and stop of car engines as patrons came and went, the pleasing serenade of exotic birds. But the warmth flooding her didn't come from a foreign sun, rather from his hands as he splayed them across her back.

He drew away, swiping his tongue over his bottom lip. "You won't complain will you?" he asked.

She tossed her head, as much to clear it as in reply. "I'm not much of a complainer."

He opened the car door for her, and she shrugged her jacket off before getting in.

"What happened to your arm?" Gunnar asked when he got in.

Tessa glanced at the long, purplish-yellow bruise on her left forearm. "Oh, nothing."

Gunnar didn't start the engine. A warning prickle danced across her shoulders and it occurred to her to tell him she'd hurt her arm working on the house, but there was no reason for her to lie, especially about a thing so trivial she'd forgotten it.

"It's only a little bruise."

"What happened to your arm?" he repeated, firmly.

"I banged it into a table," she said, riled now. "I told you it's nothing."

More tenderly than his voice belied, Gunnar lifted her arm for inspection. "If that were all there was to this, you wouldn't be so evasive."

She resented his thinking he could demand an answer. She also resented questioning whether she owed him one. She wrenched away and he let go.

"That's how it happened, as a matter of fact," Tessa said. "Carter had my hand—"

"Carter? The guy with the 'thinking of you' card?" Gunnar's eyes flashed hot and the muscles worked in his jaw, yet for all his power and rage, she felt in no way imperiled.

"You're making more of this than it is," she told him.

He faced her fully, resting his forearm on the steering wheel. "Why don't you tell me what happened?" he said with a humorless smile.

Tessa laid her hands in her lap, confident reason would defuse him. "Carter was holding my hand—"

"Why?"

"Are you going to let me tell you?" She rolled her eyes. "He was pretty lit up and trying to talk me into a nightcap at his place." If she weren't so exasperated, she might find it funny, replaying the silly things Carter had said to her, promised her. "I thanked him but declined, and he persisted."

"Persisted?"

"He didn't try anything," she answered quickly.

After what happened to Gunner's sister, she could understand his protectiveness, but enough was enough. "But he's hard to discourage, so I jerked my arm away and smashed it on the edge of the table." She rubbed the spot.

Gunnar gritted his teeth. "I don't want him around you."

Tessa flattened her spine against the seat. "It was an accident, Gunnar. He was very apologetic. He even made the waiter bring me ice."

"If he comes near you, he dies."

All the air seemed to be sucked out of the car. Could he sit here and calmly announce to her that Carter would die if he came near her? With his history?

"You can't threaten to kill people!" She jabbed a finger in his direction to make a point but tucked it away, not wanting to equate boldness with physical aggression.

"Tessa," he said, calmly.

"Don't 'Tessa' me. You can't tell me what to do."

"I'm not telling you what to do. I'm telling him what to do."

Tessa let out an appalled wave of breath. "You can't push the world around. Carter happens to be the cousin of my best friend."

"I don't care."

"You're overreacting, and I told you he was drunk."

"I can't believe you went out with that bozo."

Tessa wiggled her finger back and forth. "I didn't go out with him." Gunnar tilted his head, puzzled. "I just happened to meet him at the restaurant the other night," she said.

"Thursday night?" he asked.

She nodded.

"Thursday night you said you had a date," he reminded her.

Tessa moved her hands in a helpless motion. "Technically. I met Connie and Mike. Carter...showed up."

"You purposely made me believe you were meeting a guy."

Despite the shame, she raised her chin. "I lied."

"You lied?"

Tessa avoided his eyes. "I wanted to make you jealous. I was furious that you didn't tell me when you came back from Maryland and—"

"Whoa, whoa. Furious? You do know that's overreacting."

"I was mad. I—"

"You said furious."

She wanted to be spiteful and tell him she'd made it up, but playful mockery had replaced his rage, and she decided to take it as a blessing and leave it be. "All right, furious, and a little hurt." She met his eyes briefly. "We were supposed to celebrate. It was important to me."

"I'll make it up to you." Gunnar ducked his head, forcing her to meet his eyes. "And I won't kill Carter."

That made her giggle, and after sending her a long look, Gunnar started the car and drove her home.

28

Standing in front of her open closet, Tessa held a hand to her belly to settle the mass of bees swarming there. She couldn't understand why her nerves were wound so tight. She was familiar with the dating ritual; there was no mystique to the notion of a man taking her to a quiet restaurant, maybe a movie, or dancing. But tonight nothing would be familiar. She would be with Gunnar.

Stopping for a burger this afternoon had been easy, no pressure, just two people who happened to be hungry at the same time. But tonight would be a date. She wanted this, right? At least she had before realizing there would be mood lighting and awkward small talk while they waited for their food.

She considered canceling, but with what excuse? That she'd had time to dwell on it and let her fear get the best of her? That he was so potently male she found it hard to breathe when they were in the same room? What if she choked on her appetizer?

Tessa stopped in the center of the room, pushed her palms toward her feet and took a long, cleansing breath. Her mind was running away with her, and it had to stop.

In less than a minute, she pressed past the nerves and returned to sifting through her clothes. She debated pants vs. dress for a ridiculous length of time before selecting black pants and a blue silk blouse.

By the time she finished dressing and working her hair into a sleek knot, her bout of nerves passed, and she actually looked forward to the evening. She dropped her cell phone inside her purse, pulled on her jacket, and walked outside to wait. It was six fifty, and if she knew Gunnar at all, he would be punctual.

Tessa sniffed the sharp scent of burning wood and looked up at Frieda's chimney, next door. Hazy fingers of smoke reached out, extending to join passing clouds and temporarily dim the glory of the glittering white stars.

At the sight of Gunnar's GTO, a sentiment assailed her, so powerful she wanted to cry. Not nerves, but intense expanding warmth throughout her chest. Her brows pulled together in perplexity trying to make sense of it.

Approaching on the narrow path, gaze on hers, Gunnar appeared to be trying to make sense of her. He stopped at the bottom of the steps. "Something wrong?"

She flashed him a diversionary smile. "No, of course not."

As he guided her to the car with a gentle hand on the base of her spine, Tessa wondered if she would ever get used to the spontaneous jets of sensation his touch aroused.

"Where to?" she asked, when he'd buckled into the seat beside her.

Gunnar plucked two tickets from his visor, handed them to her. "I don't know if you like plays."

She read the title of the Tony Award winning play, a play for which tickets were harder to acquire than one of Wonka's golden ones. "My mother tried to get tickets to *Alvin's Nemesis* for the last three months. How did you get these?"

A wicked smile his only answer, Gunnar turned the key in the ignition and flew into the night.

He kept quiet, giving Tessa time to herd her scattered thoughts. Meditating on nothing at all might be safer than focusing on her initial reaction to seeing him tonight. It was certainly better than dwelling on the aura of power radiating from him as he masterfully navigated the route leading east. And under no circumstances would she contemplate the beauty of his hands gripping the steering wheel or how they felt when he touched her.

With a silent sigh, she forced her senses to concentrate on the tangible things: lights from business signs and traffic signals sweeping across the car windows. The escalating buzz of a small foreign car engine entering the highway. The changing pitch of tires as blacktop gave way to a stretch of concrete before claiming the road once again. Inside the car, a green hue colored the dashboard. She looked away when she saw the speedometer climb past seventy.

The car smelled of expensive leather, which, she noted, came in part from the supple red leather seats, but also from the bomber jacket Gunnar wore. Taking him in at a sidelong glance she noted he was wearing black pants instead of the jeans he usually wore, and loafers rather than his customary boots. She couldn't wait to see what he wore under the jacket.

When he flicked a glance her way, she shifted in her seat and cleared her throat.

"Are we in a hurry?" she asked, tipping her chin toward the speedometer.

"Not particularly." He changed lanes smoothly

and accelerated.

The quiet returned, broken only by the steady hum of tires on pavement and reverberating off the shiny white walls of the Lincoln Tunnel.

❧

As the critics declared, the show was outstanding, but looking across the restaurant table at Gunnar, Tessa was hard pressed to remember much of it. Slashes of black drew together above his inscrutable eyes but as candlelight shimmered in their fathomless depths, it wasn't romance reflecting back at her.

Before the show, she'd sensed the strain vibrating off him, but there hadn't been time to have a real conversation. Now, when the waiter left, Tessa tentatively touched Gunnar's hand.

"Are you going to tell me what's on your mind?"

Gunnar moved his hand away and leaned back in his chair. "Yes."

Tessa sipped her water, put the glass back down and met his gaze, waiting.

"Your pastor says I'm marked for death."

The abruptness of the announcement left her momentarily speechless and quite unsure she'd heard correctly. "What?"

"He thinks the devil's trying to kill me."

She looked closely for any sign of humor, but Gunnar didn't have a sense of humor she was aware of.

"Why does he think that?" she asked.

"I told you I have nightmares, right?"

Tessa nodded.

Gunnar ran his finger along the edge of his

napkin. "Well, it goes a little beyond that."

Tessa listened, enthralled, as Gunnar described in terrifying detail what he suffered in the night. A few things made more sense—his hostility for one—and she now had a better grasp of what pushed him toward suicide. How had he coped so long with the torment?

"I'd say Pastor's right," Tessa said, when he finished.

"Great."

The waiter arrived with their plates, then disappeared. "You said when you had the gun to your head—" she shivered inwardly "—it didn't feel like you. It felt like you were being driven." Gunnar met her eyes across the table. "I believe you were."

"Demons, right?" he asked. "Can they do that?"

"They can't pick up your gun and shoot you with it," she said. "But they can be persuasive."

"Yeah," he grumbled.

Tessa glanced around the small room. To an eavesdropper the conversation would seem like mumbo jumbo, and ordinarily she wouldn't care if strangers thought her "out there" or weird, but she kept her voice low in consideration for Gunnar's privacy.

"When was the last time you had one of those dreams?" she asked.

"It's been a while. Thank God." He made a sound exactly between a chuckle and a snicker. "I mean that."

This time when Tessa reached for his hand he left it under hers, turning it upward to lightly grip her fingers. "But you don't think it's the end," Tessa said.

He topped her thumb with his and rubbed gently. "It's like they're constantly hovering. Waiting for the right time."

Tessa refused to acknowledge the chill that swept through her.

"I know when they come for me, I won't be able to stop it," Gunnar said. "And one of these times they'll pull me back there and I won't come out."

Gunnar released her hand, picked up his fork and started eating, leaving Tessa feeling helpless and inadequate. She knew the words to speak to him, she believed them with everything in her, but she couldn't help him if he didn't believe. Nevertheless, she had to speak.

"There is something you can do," Tessa said, her voice thick with resolve.

"Sure, get saved, spite the devil. That's an interesting doctrine you guys have: revenge through salvation."

"I don't want to push Jesus on you, Gunnar. I just hate to see you in pain." And she hated to think he might be taken from her. Leaning back, Tessa took up her fork. "You have to decide for yourself." She hoped her voice belied none of her anxiety.

Gunnar was quiet, pensive. "OK, aside from all that, here it is. The reason I wanted to go out tonight, other than getting your take on all this, is to see what's going on between you and me."

The surprise likely showed clearly in her eyes, so she blinked and lowered her brows a fraction. "You and me?"

"Whatever is happening between us," he said dangling the fork from his fingertips. "Lust, attraction, call it what you want, but I need to know where I stand in relation to this Jesus thing."

His directness, the blatant demand in his question

brought her up short. There was no use denying she wanted him, but could she set aside all she believed to be with him?

No.

Could she force him to change his life in order to have her?

No.

Unfortunately, the answers to those questions brought her no closer to answering his. "I can't answer that," she told him.

His eyes met hers with mysterious force for an instant before he answered. "I'm not going to try to sway you to the dark side, but I want to stick around and see what happens. As long it takes.

"Tell you the truth I don't know how I want it to go," Gunnar said. "One minute I'm positive being with you would be the worst thing that could happen to either of us."

When she opened her mouth he silenced her with a look.

"The next minute, I'm hoping we can work it out. I don't know what to think because I can't trust who's thinking it anymore. I used to know who I was, what I wanted. That's changed."

She could say the same, but did this like-mindedness weigh for or against pursuing a relationship? "Let's take it one day at a time and go from there."

They finished dinner in silent agreement to do just that. During dessert and the drive home they talked about plans for her inn and his shop, but her mind was engaged elsewhere, in thoughts of death and demons and in keeping Gunnar alive.

When Gunnar walked her to her front door, he

made no attempt to kiss her, so Tessa stood on tip toe to kiss his cheek, thanked him for the lovely evening, and went inside to face a long night of meditation and prayer.

∽∾

After Sunday morning service, Tessa waited by the back table and skimmed through some of the pamphlets and bulletins until Pastor Caswell was free. When he came to her, he beamed a broad smile and slipped his hands into the pockets of his gray suit jacket.

"How is Gunnar?" Bob asked.

Tessa wasn't surprised Bob understood why she lingered. She made a face, twisting her lip to the side. "That's tricky."

"Ah. Come into my office so we can talk."

Tessa took a chair and set her Bible and purse on the chair beside her. Bob took a post behind the desk.

"I saw him the other day," Bob began.

"So I heard."

At her tone, Bob crossed his arms over his chest. "Hmm."

Tessa twisted the ring on her finger. "He told me you said the devil's after him."

"Do you disagree?"

"Unfortunately, no."

Bob pressed his lips together, and Tessa could tell he was deliberating whether to speak.

"I didn't butt my nose in where it wasn't wanted," he said.

Tessa gave a delicate grunt. "You wouldn't have spoken to him at all unless he wanted you to."

"He is a strong-willed man." Bob laughed

"Yes." She paused. "I don't know what to do. About *us*." She used her fingers as quotation marks.

Bob leaned forward, brows lifting. "That isn't my place."

"I can use your advice," she said.

"All things accounted for, I like Gunnar, I really do," he said, with a touch of surprise. "He's direct and honest. It's hard not to admire that. However, he's unsaved and tormented, not at all the ideal situation for you. I told him the same thing."

She closed her eyes and when she reopened them, focused on a large water stain on the drop-ceiling tile. "I'm falling in love with him."

Bob's understanding eyes and gentle smile urged her to speak freely.

"Even with all I know—and you can rule out the bad boy thing," she said. "He's a good man under all the aggression and rage."

Pastor Caswell folded his hands. "Does he know how you feel?"

"No." She hoped he didn't. "And I don't want him to, it'll only complicate matters. I don't want to influence him one way or the other. One day I think he feels the same, the next he's pushing me away."

"Well, you're familiar with the pitfalls of pursuing a relationship with him so I won't preach."

"Actually, that's why I'm here. How do I determine if the pitfalls are there to warn me off a thing that could ruin my life, or to deter me from something great?" She grabbed a handful of her hair and let it fall behind her shoulder. "Things used to be black and white, right and wrong, but with Gunnar, things I would ordinarily take for a huge warning flare, well...it isn't that simple."

"Because of your affection for him?"

Tessa thought before answering. She remembered God's prompting to pray for Gunnar months before they'd met. Of His telling her to let him stay even after he'd threatened her. "No, at least in the beginning."

She folded her hands and told him in brief about the incidents.

"Hmm," Bob said at her conclusion.

"Am I being deluded?" she asked. "Is it one of the enemy's tricks to pull me away from God?"

Bob's brow furrowed. "It would be clearer if Gunnar were saved."

But he wasn't, and she couldn't—wouldn't—seriously consider a relationship with a man who didn't share her faith. It made her more determined not to give up on him. He would find Jesus and together they would find happiness. Amen.

"I have a lot of thinking to do," Tessa said finally. "In the meantime, I'm worried."

Bob came around the desk to stand in front of her. "Our focus needs to be on protecting him as best we can and praying he comes to stand on his own spiritual feet. If he doesn't, I'm afraid the outcome will be inevitable." Pastor Caswell took Tessa's hands and joined forces to change the course of Gunnar's future.

29

In the fifteen-minute drive to the new shop, Gunnar was cut off three times, almost run off the road by a tractor trailer and given the most offensive finger by a sixty-something woman in a red Jag. Oddly enough, he had no desire to chase down any of these people and make them regret their behavior, which he would have done only a few weeks ago.

So much had changed since then. This shop for one, he acknowledged, walking the fifty feet from his parking spot to the shop door. The move started slow, but once the major equipment was relocated, it took a matter of three days for the transition to be complete. As threatened, Tessa helped, but to his surprise, she'd been an asset. She was stronger than she looked.

When he entered the main area of the shop, the first thing he saw was Matt and Max, welding visors flipped up, leaning together over a piece of metal held between them. Since Matt's first visit with his mother a few weeks back, he came around almost every day, and to Gunnar's astonishment, he didn't mind.

Last month, if anyone told him he would enjoy the company of a sixteen-year-old boy he would have called them crazy to their face. His only excuse could be that Matt was more mature than other kids. He had to be, with what he'd gone through—having leukemia in remission and losing his father just last year. It was enough to conquer most adults.

His mother, Dorothy, was taking a chance letting him spend so much time around the guys at the shop, but for the most part, they behaved, even treated the kid as a kind of mascot. He was a fast learner, good with his hands, and filled with ideas.

Gunnar tried to look only mildly interested in Matt's progress as he passed. Max turned away as Matt lowered his visor and applied the welder to the metal. For a few seconds the air was filled with what sounded like a supercharged bug zapper.

"How's this?" Matt asked Max after he'd raised the faceplate.

"Nah. You see the hole? You held it too long. Try it again."

Matt shrugged. No bad feelings, just back at it.

Gunnar resisted a smile. *Gonna have to start paying him*, he thought.

Matt and Max shut their visors so Matt could join two new pieces of scrap metal with the spot welder, one concentrated electrical pulse at a time. When he finished to Max's satisfaction, Gunnar called him aside.

Bringing his refined work with him, Matt handed it to Gunnar for inspection. It was good. Gunnar nodded, handed it back.

"Your mother told me you have some more free time coming soon," he said.

"Christmas break."

"She said it would be OK if I drag you with me to the International Motorcycle Show on the twenty-eighth, but I wanted to ask you—"

The boy's arms flapped and his eyes bugged out, but it was his sudden inability to breathe that worried Gunnar. Gunnar anxiously scanned the space for somewhere to sit him, when Matt finally exhaled.

"You're not serious!" Matt said.

"Yes, I am."

"The IMS?"

"In New York. We'll be staying a few days." Hoping to hide his pleasure in the kid's excitement, Gunnar marched to his office.

"I don't care if it's across the world, I'm going to the IMS!" Matt said, bounding like a dog at Gunnar's heels, until he reached his office and closed himself inside.

The new office was a depressing battleship gray with a single window five feet off the ground. He planned to have the room painted before he became used to the dismal atmosphere. He jotted a memo to hire someone and moved to look out over the paved lot.

On the other side of the flat black expanse were fields of brown grass and a stand of pine trees. Directly beyond, a sky-blue water tower announced in thick black letters that it served Boonton, U.S.A. He'd never heard of this town until the property came up for sale two years ago. Parts of it were historic, with hundred-year-old houses butting up alongside new structures, and while the center of town boasted more antique shops than he'd ever seen at once, it was generally a nice area. Best of all, his shop was out of the way enough not to draw more than a glance from hurried shoppers on their way to Mega-Mart, the big draw in this quarter of the county.

That reminded him, his printer was low on ink. He'd have to brave the holiday shoppers and...better yet, he'd send someone else. Gunnar went to his desk to write down the specific unit and opened the drawer for a pad. Evan's journal lay on top.

He took it out and opened it, stilling any emotion as Evan's words stared back at him from the pages. Pages filled with requests for mercy, protection, and forgiveness—for his brother.

There were notes on answered prayers and page after page of thanks for blessings bestowed. Gunnar snorted. Too bad Evan hadn't been blessed with long life.

His third time through the little tan book brought Gunnar no closer to understanding Evan's relationship with Jesus. Or Tessa's, or Bob's, for that matter. He read the words, but he didn't get it.

Gunnar replaced the book in the drawer. He'd spent his whole life ignoring God, and in that secret place where even he scarcely ventured, hating Him. Recently he'd been forced to not only think about Him, but talk to Him as if He were capable of answering, and if so, cared to.

Even if God was "out there," how could Gunnar trust his life to Someone who had fumbled it so badly to this point? And not with his alone, but with Evan's and Samantha's? Why would anyone want a relationship with that God? He closed the drawer. He'd wasted enough time thinking about it.

He turned over a sketch of a work-in-progress and scribbled a note on the back reminding him to change the tailpipe design, then set it aside and moved on to the rough draft of the bishop bike. He wasn't happy with this one. It required more detail, but his mind was focused on other things.

He and Tessa were dating. For about a month and a half. He believed that was the term for this seeing each other, doing things together—a practice they'd established with some regularity. He didn't have any experience in the traditional dating arena and was learning the basics one awkward step at a time. He enjoyed the whole dinner and a movie thing, though he hadn't worked up the enthusiasm to endure a double date with Connie and what's-his-name. He liked having Tessa to himself, whether they watched TV at his place, or drove to the mountains to stand in the freezing cold and look at the stars.

In keeping with their agreement to take things slow, he kept his hands off her, but it was killing him. She was a highly responsive woman. Each time she sucked in a breath when his hand brushed hers, his muscles tensed in anticipation. When he had to terminate transmission of signal, and issue new orders to his body, to be a gentleman and respect her virginity, it meant one more sleepless night.

It was normal to picture her in her faded jeans and a tight little t-shirt or to remember her at the kitchen sink, elbow deep in soapy water. No problem. Moving to the next step, imagining her in a steaming tub wearing just bubbles, took no effort at all.

Beyond pubescent fantasies, he was getting to know her as a person. He liked that she was bright, interesting, and paid attention. He even liked her crabby side, which surfaced after speaking to one of her parents. No doubt, she would discuss her family issues with him if he asked, but he sidestepped it, having nothing to offer on the subject of parents.

For all Tessa's wonderful traits, he acknowledged that the focused and earnest part of her frightened him a little, with regards to their relationship. It meant, if at any point, he wanted to act the coward and bail, she wouldn't let it happen. Part of him was glad because it would force him to give it a chance and see what could come of it. The rest of him felt like he was standing on the gallows slipping his head through the noose.

He slapped the drawing on the desktop and began to walk the perimeter of the room. He'd already reflected on the idea of self-preservation and found it flawed. It wasn't about being trapped or changed. As always, it came down to his imminent destruction and the fear of taking her down with him.

He'd watched Tessa make monumental decisions—buying a house, starting a business—but when it came to him, he found it difficult to trust her judgment. If she'd married her high school sweetheart, or had a string of past lovers, maybe he could put more confidence in her ability to look at this relationship objectively.

Physically, he fascinated her, made her body heat and hunger. Emotionally, he triggered her need to be wanted. He might hazard to say that spiritually, she found him a cripple in need of healing, a sinner in need of salvation; and some women loved a challenge.

But suppose he took her to bed, sank into her and let her sooth his soul for a night? A weekend? What then?

He already knew. She would expect commitment. He could be faithful, he didn't want anyone else, but how could he give her the 'happily ever after' every woman wanted?

Gunnar rubbed a hand over his face. He couldn't work, couldn't sleep, couldn't breathe! It was all Tessa's fault. His life was void before meeting her, but at least he'd known his own mind and been capable of focusing on the simplest task. She'd robbed him of his morbid attentions to death and ruin, and replaced them with questions and ideas he shouldn't even consider.

Should I keep pursuing her? I'm no good for her. Will it work? We're too different. What would it be like to spend every day with her? Birthdays? Christmas?

It made his head spin.

And what about Christmas, now that he thought of it? He wanted to get Tessa a gift. What? The last time he bought a gift for a woman was…never. Great. He couldn't think and now he had to shop.

"Shoot!"

And that was another thing. He never said "shoot." His language had cleaned up noticeably, and he couldn't even pin it on Tessa. Not really. She never asked him to change. It was just sort of happening.

He let out a frustrated growl. It was too much to take.

"Bad time?"

Gunnar spun to find Dominic stepping into the small area. Just what he needed. "Just hashing through some stuff."

Dom picked up the bishop sketch. "Incredible."

"So what brings you here?" Gunnar asked, taking his seat, rocking back and folding his hands across his stomach.

"Wanted to stop by and chat," Dom said. He laid down the sketch.

"You want to chat."

"Don't see you much anymore, not even at the gym."

"I work out at home when I have time," Gunnar said.

Dom nodded, a slow movement that told Gunnar he was weighing his next words. "You come here to get something off your chest?"

Dom rested a hip on the edge of the desk. "To ask you something."

Gunnar signaled the go ahead with a jerk of his chin.

"What are your intentions regarding my sister?"

Gunnar narrowed his eyes. "Isn't it your father's place to third-degree me? Or are you here as a cop?"

Dom kept his voice even. "I'm concerned. Tessa is happier than I've seen her in a long time, and you're part of the reason."

"I can see why you're worried."

"She's getting serious. I want to know if you are," Dom said.

Gunnar let out a breath that seemed to come up from the floor. He hated being this on edge around his best friend.

"Do you really want to hear this?" he asked.

Dom raised his chin, the muscle in his jaw clenched, obviously bracing for news of his little sister's love life.

Gunnar lifted his hands, let them fall to his thighs with a slap. "I'm in love with her."

"Man."

Gunnar watched Dom's face, trying to decipher his reply. The way he'd pushed it out, with force but no increase in volume, Gunnar could take it to mean, *"Man, that is serious"* or *"Man, now I have to kill you."*

"So...?" he said when Dom continued to look stunned.

"What do you want me to say?" Dom asked.

"You tell me, you're the one who came here."

Dom adjusted his position, hiking his ankle onto his knee.

With each second counting as an opportunity to speak, and him not taking it, Gunnar grew more irritated.

"I don't expect you to be happy," Gunnar said. "But you can't change what is, bro, neither can I. Believe me, I tried to talk myself out of it."

"So you regret it?"

"Yeah." Probably the wrong answer, it had Dom squinting his right eye. "I'm not built for relationships, you're right about that," Gunnar said. "And I don't want to be a husband, or a daddy, or coach pee wee football on the weekends, so tell me what I can do to get her out from under my skin, and I'll do it."

Dominic propped his hands on his thighs. "Why don't you find some women?"

Gunnar deflected the sarcasm with honesty. "I can't."

Dom's eyebrows rose to considerable heights, irking Gunnar all the more and propelling him to his feet to resume his fitful motion.

Dom swiveled on the desk to keep him in sight.

"I'm serious," Gunnar said. "Tell me what to do that I *can* do, not the impossible, like mess around with another woman."

The silence stretched as one man paced, the other following the track with his gaze.

Finally, Dom asked, "So you think she loves you, too?"

Gunnar stopped and pressed the heels of his hands to his eyes. "I think so, I don't know, I'm afraid to find out." He heard Dom snort, but when he looked over his friend was sober faced. "Did you ever have your heart handed to you?"

"Yeah," Dom said. "The worst thing I ever felt in

my life." He broke into a grin. "But I wore away her defenses until she agreed to marry me."

Gunnar couldn't manage a smile.

"Let me put it to you this way," Dom said. "If she ran to you and confessed her undying love, what would you do?"

Gunnar's reply took no thought whatever. "Fall on my knees and thank God she wasn't smart enough to run when she had the chance." He hung his thumbs from the pockets of his jeans. "I tried to make her, but she's immune to reason."

"Most women are," Dom agreed.

"I've told her things I haven't told you, and she still answers my calls. Is there something wrong with her?"

"She's stubborn."

Gunnar managed half a chuckle. "Stubborn doesn't cover it."

"She's also sweet, and it's easy to hurt her." Dom shrugged. "If she sees enough in you to make her risk it, you can be sure it's there."

A minute later, when Gunnar stood in the chilled air watching Dom drive off, he felt bad that he'd lied to his friend. Truth was, he did want all those things he'd denied.

30

Tessa circled January first on the calendar with thick red marker. The day Blossom Inn would officially open. Although it wouldn't receive its first reserved guests until Valentine's Day, New Years was symbolic of a fresh start, and never more so for her, than this one.

If she couldn't see it with her own eyes she would never believe so much could be accomplished in so short a time, but thanks in large part to a crew of men Gunnar sent one weekend, all that remained was deciding on drapes and linens. In time, she would need to hire some help, but for now she could handle it.

Gunnar agreed to be present at her opening party on New Year's Eve, but she hadn't told him that in addition to Dominic and Pauline, and Connie and Mike, her parents would be here. In her defense, when she'd asked him she hadn't yet asked them. Besides, he would assume she would include her parents on such a special event, wouldn't he?

Some of her excitement leached out. Christmas was less than a week away, so there was no sense ruining it for him, but she would have to tell him before he left for the motorcycle show in New York. That way, he would have plenty of time to mentally prepare. She knew him well enough to know she could count on him.

It was sad that most people would never dig past his outer skin, calloused by years of neglect, and find the real man underneath. She had, albeit with God's prompting, and discovered the blessing, the man that mentored a sick boy, and took time away from his business to help her start her own. The man who often looked at her as though she was the only person in the world.

He didn't find her frigid or out of step with reality for wanting to retain her virginity and though they wrestled with mutual desire, he didn't pressure her. For the first time in her life, she felt understood. It was liberating.

Tessa grabbed her purse and ran outside. She had to hurry to pick up Gunnar's Christmas present before meeting her mother for lunch. But as she buckled her seatbelt, Tessa was suddenly besieged by a sense of import strong enough to have her hands fumble. It was a grave awareness that her actions today could have everything to do with her future happiness. Oddly, she didn't relate it to trepidation over meeting her mother, but rather to impatience over giving Gunnar his gift.

No doubt the expectancy of their first Christmas, together. Well not together, she thought, as she went on her way. She was spending the day with her family. He was spending his with his sister. But this Christmas, they were a couple.

In less than five minutes, she ran out of the jeweler's, carrying the blue and green foil-wrapped box. The silver bow was too garish for Gunnar's taste, but she couldn't resist; it was Christmas! She did, however, resist the urge to drive to Gunnar's and have him open it now.

She couldn't believe how eager she was to give

him the sterling silver dog tag and chain, not because he liked silver—which he did—but because the tag was engraved with Psalm 91:15. She wasn't a supporter of blessed holy water, or Jerusalem sand, or prayer cloths, sold on late night TV, but hoped whenever he glanced at her gift, he might meditate on the words and be reminded she was praying for him.

When her cell phone rang at a red light, she flipped it open.

"Hello."

"Hey," Gunnar replied.

"Oh, hi! I was just looking at your Christmas present. I can't wait to give it to you."

"I'm calling you for the same reason," he said.

"Oh?"

"Since I won't be back until the day after Christmas, do you want your present before I leave, or when I—"

"Now!"

Gunnar laughed, a deep rumbling sound that came through the phone and cheered her. "Fifteen minutes?" he asked.

"I'm not home," she lamented. "I'm actually on my way to have lunch with my mother."

"I could meet you after."

"Great. Around three?"

"I'll be there."

❧❦

Watching the wispy vapor of his breath evaporate, Gunnar did his best to loosen the knots in his shoulders while he waited for Tessa to open the door. He must be nuts to give her such a gift, but the choice had more to do with seeing her face than practicality. If she didn't want it, he'd just have to keep it, although he had no idea what he'd do with it. Tilting his neck to the right, then left, the vertebrae cracked and settled into place. The door swung open.

"Hey."

"Hey," Tessa answered, smiling.

Her hair was pulled back in a ponytail, revealing the long curve of her throat and the pulse beating at its base. He shifted his gaze to hers eyes, so clear and fascinating. He could stare into them indefinitely, and might have, if she hadn't stepped back to invite him in.

"No, come with me," he said, taking her hand.

"What? Where? I need my coat."

Gunnar simply towed her. "This'll only take a minute." When they reached the bottom of the steps, Gunnar moved behind her and covered her eyes. "Trust me."

Obedient, Tessa allowed him to lead her toward the driveway.

"I didn't wrap it," he told her, bringing her to a halt.

His hands slid from her eyes and she opened them. Bouncing in the back seat of Gunnar's car was a tan and black German Shepherd puppy.

"Oh!" Tessa squealed. She grabbed the handle and before the door was open all the way, the animal burst forth and launched itself at her, dancing on its hind legs and pawing at her thighs. She sat on the ground and gathered it in.

"You wanted a dog, right?" Gunnar asked, hesitant.

Overwhelmed by warm breath and a lashing pink tongue, Tessa laughed as the puppy pounced on her, jabbing her in the ribs and abdomen with his oversized paws. "How old is he?"

"Uh...three, four months I think the guy said." Gunnar crouched beside them. "I should have asked you first."

The sound of his voice so near drew the pup's attention, and Gunnar found himself the new object of affection. And not the pup's alone.

"I can't believe you bought me a puppy!" Tessa threw her arms around Gunnar's neck, knocking him into a sitting position. Elbowing the dog's wet nose gently from between them, Tessa planted a huge kiss on Gunnar's cheek. "You are the sweetest man in the world!"

As the puppy lavished affection on both of them, Gunnar pulled Tessa onto his lap and joined his mouth to hers. He didn't care that it was freezing or that they were being bathed in puppy saliva. Or even that they were outside in full view of her neighbors.

The squeaky belt of an approaching vehicle brought them to reason, and Gunnar automatically grabbed the puppy's collar. He helped Tessa off him and stood, scooping the puppy with one hand and offering her the other.

Tessa stood on her tiptoes and kissed Gunnar on the mouth. "I love you," she said.

The breath caught in Gunnar's chest, making it impossible for him to exhale for the length of time it took Tessa to take her gift from him and carry it, tail wagging, into the house.

There were moments, secret moments he'd entertain for a few seconds at a time, when he would imagine Tessa saying those words. In his mind, his reaction fell somewhere between denial and fear.

Denial, because even in his fantasy he couldn't accept being loved, fear because he knew he would mess it up. Mess her up.

But in this moment, with the taste of her fresh on his lips, he felt humbled, not in the unworthy sense—although it was true—but like a force greater than both of them was smiling on him. He felt blessed.

He sucked in a gulp of clean air. He wasn't going to spoil this by reasoning she had said it flippantly, in elation. Nor would he dwell on all the reasons she shouldn't love him, or convince her that she didn't understand what love was. He hadn't either, until he met her.

He meant to grab hold of her with both hands and hang on.

Tessa had left the front door open, expecting him to follow, but he needed to sit. Lowering himself to the edge of the porch, Gunnar let his clasped hands hang between his knees. Inside, he could hear her murmuring encouragement and discussing names with the young dog.

"Samson?" Gunnar heard her ask, then she giggled, evidently charmed by the puppy's response. "OK, Ernest? No, that's too stodgy for you, isn't it?"

Her voice took on that high playful tone reserved for babies of both the animal and human variety, and Gunnar's heart rolled over in his chest. She'd professed her love for him; he would do the same, somehow, some way. What next? Marriage? Children?

His insides shuddered. Instinct had him attributing it to fear, the normal reflex for men who wanted an excuse to cut and run, but it was much deeper than that. It was the fear those things *wouldn't* happen.

"Gunnar?"

He turned to find Tessa standing in the doorway. "Are you all right?" she asked, coming to sit beside him.

He smiled, still an awkward activity. "Yeah. Where's the dog?"

"In my office," she said. "I don't suppose he's housebroken?"

Gunnar cast a worried glance at his GTO.

Neither spoke for a minute, the world strangely quiet, until Tessa cleared her throat.

"About what I said..."

God, don't let her take it back, Gunnar begged, silently.

"I didn't mean to blurt it like that." She took his hands in hers, folding her delicate fingers over his larger, scarred ones. "I wanted to..."

He was hesitant to be relieved. Was she recanting, or wasn't she?

"Well it's out now. I love you," she said. Gunnar angled his body toward her. "And it has nothing to do with the puppy or how great you kiss or—"

"You love me," he said, switching hand positions so that his covered hers.

Tessa gulped and went on. "And you won't talk me out of it, or tell me any more nonsense—"

"I couldn't talk myself out of it." He grinned, when her protest died on her lips. "I love you, Tessa."

"You...what?"

With the initial terror passed, he was enjoying this, partly because he hadn't thought himself capable of love, much less of saying it openly. But more so because he didn't plan on ever saying these words to another woman, and wanted to make the most of it.

"I don't know the extent of it yet because it hits me in waves day after day, but I love you," Gunnar said.

Tears filled Tessa's eyes.

He hadn't had time to brace for his own reaction, and now he had to deal with hers. "Tess, please, don't cry."

"I'm happy. I cry when I'm happy."

He nodded and threw an arm around her, pulling her to him. "Yeah."

Tessa sniffled into his chest, then pulled away, and stood. "Come inside, it's freezing! And I want to give you your present."

The puppy yapped excitedly at the back of the house, but Tessa ignored him, leading Gunnar to the front parlor. She'd done an amazing job with the place, he noticed, taking in the warm lighting and fluffy furniture. Well, most of it was fluffy. There was one skimpy piece of furniture posing as a couch, the kind you'd expect to find in a movie set in the turn of the century.

His eyes came to rest on the large old-fashioned mirror above the gray stone mantle. More specifically to the two subjects captured within its gold frame. Seeing him and Tessa together this way, her hand in his, gazing up at him with such blatant love, made him feel stupid for not having seen it before.

His chest squeezed tight.

"Sit," she said, directing him to the skimpy couch.

Gunnar did, with the silent hope it would hold his weight. Tessa disappeared into the foyer and came back with a small wrapped box.

"Before you open it I want to tell you I'm not trying to push God on you. I thought you might like it and...well, open it." Tessa sat beside him fairly vibrating with eagerness.

Before the wrapper was off entirely, Tessa reached over to help him with the lid. He pulled the box out of her grasp.

"Do you mind?" he asked. "I didn't muscle in when you were opening your present."

Tessa's brows lifted. "Mine wasn't wrapped."

"But you opened the car door yourself."

She gave a resigned huff. Gunner removed the lid and pulled out a thick silver chain. Dangling from it was a silver dog tag. He held it in his palm and silently read the small words engraved on it: *"He shall call upon me, and I will answer him: I will be with him in trouble; I will deliver him, and honour him." Ps. 91:15*

He must have been silent a while, for when he looked up she was watching him, concerned.

"I didn't mean to upset you," she said quietly, and laid a hand on his arm. "I just want you to have it with you. It's important to me."

"I'm not upset," Gunnar lied. He was, but not with her. How could he explain to her that reading the words, he'd felt the weight of each one? Or that this wasn't the first time lines from a book written thousands of years ago seemed to speak to him? "I ah, didn't expect this."

"You don't like it," she said, her voice dashed with hurt and uncertainty.

Gunnar seized the tag in his fist. "I do. I do," he repeated, this time with a small curve of lips before touching them to hers. "Thanks for worrying."

He didn't think she believed him, but she smiled.

"Look at the other side," Tessa said.

He did. And there it was, engraved, permanent, in case he was tempted to think his mind had played a cruel joke: *To Gunnar, Love Tessa*. His name and hers, with love right between them.

"You can read the whole Psalm if you want—some other time," she added quickly, when he moved to speak. "But if you ever want to I can show you how to find the chapter and verse in the Bible."

Gunnar already knew how. He'd bought a Bible last week and had been fishing through it. He slipped the chain over his head. "Show me."

In the short time it took her to retrieve a Bible from the next room, he read the tag again. The effect wasn't as acute this time, but when she sat and revealed the whole chapter, Gunnar was struck anew. Particularly by one line that read: *Do not be afraid of the terrors of the night...*

The mantle clock bonged the hour. He wanted to stay, but Samantha was expecting him. He'd picked some time to draw closer to his sister. With regret, he got to his feet. "I have to go."

The puppy howled.

Gunnar winced. "I should have asked you first. Puppies can be a lot of trouble," he said, following the noise to Tessa's office.

"Well, he won't be," Tessa said. "He's going to be sweet and well-behaved."

They opened the door to find the puppy shaking his head furiously from side to side as he trounced his prey—a striped chair cushion.

"Keep telling yourself that," Gunnar muttered.

Walking into her office Tessa gasped. "You stop that this instant!" she demanded of the pup.

He looked up, paused, returned to his activity.

"Don't you dare!" she said, aiming a pointed finger at him.

Her warning came through loud and clear, and the cushion was immediately abandoned.

Gunnar tossed the remains on top of the desk. "I'll replace it."

"He's my responsibility," Tessa said, and with a slow breath, regained her composure. "You, little one, are going to behave," she told the unrepentant fur ball.

Looking up with what Gunnar thought surely looked like a grin, the animal thumped his tail on the floor. Tessa sighed.

"I'm glad you wanted him today," Gunnar said. "I couldn't leave him alone and Sam would kill me if I brought this monster to her house."

Tessa's lips arced. "I'll ask Dorian to give me some pointers," she said.

"Dorian?"

"A friend of Dom's. He's with the canine unit."

Gunnar took a step closer, putting his body between Tessa and the pup. "How well do you know this Dorian?"

"Enough to know he's a real sweetheart."

Gunnar slipped his hands around her waist. "Is that so? And what does this Dorian look like?"

Tessa gave him a full on smile that expanded inside him like liquid sugar.

"He's almost your height, handsome, very macho," she teased.

"Macho?" he asked, nuzzling at her ear.

She giggled. "You know the type, loaded with testosterone, a real man's man."

He kissed her mouth, her jaw, her neck. "That type has one thing on his mind," he said against her throat. The dog whined, and Gunnar took Tessa's chin to keep her from looking down. He kissed her bottom lip. Her eyes fluttered closed. His muscles tightened.

"I'll keep him at a safe distance," she murmured, breathless.

Gunnar reclaimed her lips, this time with no great finesse. He was demanding, hungry, taking what he wanted. She met him equally, a fact, that, when it registered, had his mind reeling and his body straining. Temptation coiled, intensifying in power around him, and if he didn't get free instantly, there would be no escape.

Breaking the connection was hard, but once accomplished, he nevertheless held her to him like a lifeline. His reserve of control was quickly diminishing. He couldn't keep his hands off her much longer.

After a minute he spoke. "We're realistic people, Tessa. We'll be together, it's inevitable."

She nodded under his chin.

"But the time isn't right, and it has to be. It has to be perfect."

The warmth of her breath on his neck as she looked up at him was intoxicating. He'd never let a woman this close to him in so intimate a way. Tessa was a treasure, and he thanked God he'd been the one to find her.

"I'll be back before you know it," he said, easing her to arm's length.

Trying to lighten the mood, he gave her a quick, friendly kiss. "And do me a favor, don't name this guy Floppy or Goofy," he said, bending to rub the elated pup behind the ears when it slapped its huge front feet on his thigh.

"What do you think of Bartholomew?" She giggled, when Gunnar made a face.

He pulled the office door closed behind them, and

walked her to the front door. "Merry Christmas."

"You too," Tessa said, brushing a finger down his cheek. "I love you."

It was already easier to hear and easier to say. "I love you, too. Don't forget it."

He walked to his car, sending her a half smile before getting in. Half was all he could manage, because he didn't want to leave, but also because somewhere between the kiss and the car, a feeling came on him, like that of a heavy cloud descending. His mind automatically turned to Evan, and death, and the long drive to Samantha's. The temperature continued to drop, the roads were icy…

Tessa stood on the porch watching him back down the driveway, but he couldn't bear to look at her.

31

Christmas get-togethers were meant to be enjoyable, with the roasting of chestnuts, the clinking of glasses, and the spirit of hospitality permeating as candles flickered, and carols played softly in the background. There was excellent food to tempt the palate, decorations to please the eye, and the collective illusion that peace could come, if not to the world, at least to those gathered around the table.

Three heated exchanges, two aspirin and a partridge in a pear tree later, Tessa went to her room wondering when resentments and elevated voices had become part of the holiday tradition. She should have expected it. In the weeks preceding Christmas, the whimsy of wishes and expectations had colored her memory of past holidays with a rosy tinge and sentimental sweetness. Come Christmas dinner, however, when confronted with the reality of temper and manipulation, she'd spent most of her time marveling that she'd become enmeshed in it again.

She couldn't even fall back on naiveté. Whereas, she'd hoped her parents would steer clear of the subject of Gunnar, or that they would accept the path of her life and be happy for her, deep inside she'd known what this evening would bring.

Her mother was a control freak, her father an opportunist, and they could hardly let their only daughter leave without first subjecting her to a barrage of questions, insinuations, and cutting remarks.

Not naïve, Tessa corrected, as she flopped onto the bed with her clothes on. Spiritually lazy. She loved her parents, she really did, and she had to take responsibility for her lousy relationship with them. She was the one who knew Jesus. She had the power to change the situation, but though she'd prayed about it most of her life, she'd never given it the specific attention it required. It was always more of a nuisance than anything else.

Well that needed to change. Now. She began by asking God to forgive her bad attitudes of unforgiveness, laziness, and resentment, and in just five minutes she felt as though something had changed. Some things were like that, just that quick.

The comforter smelled of dog. She scrunched her face and rolled onto her back. Krueger—the puppy's new name—needed a bath ASAP. She shouldn't snuggle him on the bed anyway, it would spoil him. She felt momentarily panicked that he wasn't here before she remembered Connie and Mike had taken him for the night. Good practice for parenthood, Connie joked.

It wasn't the dog Tessa wished to hold onto, anyway. She missed Gunnar. If he were here, she would have made an excuse to the family and hidden away with him. She would have enjoyed the day and her nerves wouldn't be stretched so taut. Nor would she have this impression of approaching calamity.

Fortunately, she knew from experience—weeks of studying for finals, months of preparing a case, past holidays—these feelings weren't premonitions, but residual effects of stress. She was physically and emotionally exhausted, that was all.

An hour later the dreadful thoughts persisted. So she prayed until sleep overtook her.

☙❧

The feeling of impending doom he'd had since leaving Tessa remained throughout his visit, and finding sleep evasive for the third night, he'd packed his gear, apologized to Samantha, and headed out. He wished he could nail down what it meant. The worst thing that could happen would be to lose Tessa. Was that it? Because he wouldn't let that happen, no matter what.

His mouth dipped into a melancholy frown as he manipulated the silver tag between his fingers. He'd memorized the entire Psalm and read through much of the New Testament while at Sam's. He'd even called Pastor Bob to help clarify a few things. He wanted to understand. If it was important to Tessa, the woman he loved...

Wow. He'd told a woman he loved her, and meant it. To quote Judge Barrett, "one for the books." At home he hauled his duffel bag onto his shoulder and went straight to his bedroom. Hopefully sleep would follow. Gunnar was exhausted, but dropped the bag next to the bed before moving past it to the balcony. A little fresh air couldn't hurt.

All around him nature stirred, from the rustling of leaves disturbed by the breeze to some small animal kicking up the underbrush near the side fence. It was probably a "duh" moment to a ten year old, but he had only recently understood that Someone was responsible for everything he saw, touched, ate or smelled. Everything. He believed it now as he never had. And he believed God was the Someone. How had he missed it all these years?

He leaned against a pillar. Maybe he hadn't missed God as much as turned a blind eye. He'd thought God didn't see him, so why pay Him any mind? But now that he'd taken some time to seriously consider Jesus, he couldn't deny Him any longer.

It made Gunnar sad to think of the time wasted in anger and pride. He might not have lived a life of holiness— he still wasn't sure what that was— but he would have been able to appreciate life. The people in it.

The corner of Gunnar's mouth kicked up. He didn't know much about the hereafter but wondered if there was any way Evan could know his thoughts at this moment. Or if he knew his prayers were being answered, that Jesus was making His Presence felt in Gunnar's life.

He felt ashamed to have fought against Jesus for so long only to be proved wrong. He would laugh at his own stupidity if not for the sense of loss, not just for his past, but his present.

If he had his way he would ask Tessa to marry him today, but he knew her answer. No. And he didn't blame her. She deserved the best and he wasn't it. But with God's help he was going to become a man she could be proud of, a man worthy to be hers. Lover and husband may be out of the question for now, but friend was in his grasp. He would be with her any way she agreed.

He looked out over the valley to the north, at the white lights of the city shimmering in the frosty air, and was put in mind of a verse he had read just this morning: *Jesus wept.*

Jesus loved the people even though they didn't deserve His attention, much less His compassion. And He died for them, the believers and the skeptics, the righteous and the unrighteous, the followers and the runners. They all had a moment of reckoning, where they had to decide whether or not to believe Jesus was Who He claimed to be.

For Gunnar it boiled down to this night, and now this moment. When faced with the truth of the Man, Who forgave repeatedly, even as He was dying, Gunnar could do nothing but respond.

He had no eloquent words, only trust that God could interpret what he wanted to say. Instinct had him kneeling before the Creator, the God of the universe. With eyes closed and arms spread wide, he petitioned.

"Here I am, Jesus." He felt embarrassed talking out loud this way. But not enough to stop.

"I'm not the man I want to be, not the man You made me to be, but with Your help, I can be all those things. I've messed my life up so bad and I'm tired of it, so I'm giving it to You. Forgive me, Jesus. Take charge of my life and make it something You can use."

Gunnar stayed put a minute, trying to gauge the after effects. He remembered Bob's testimony of feeling cleansed after giving his life to the Lord. That was exactly how he felt now. He wasn't compelled to fall on his face or dance and shout. He just felt new… refreshed…born again, like the past really was behind him and the road ahead, unobstructed.

He took a deep breath as he got to his feet. It was a little surprising that tears stung his eyes, but they came no further as his breath caught suddenly, a heavy stone of emotion lodging in his throat. Funny, he thought, he did feel like shouting. Instead, his words came out a reverent whisper.

"Thank You," he said to the heavens.

There was someone else he had to thank. He reached for his cell phone. It was after eleven, but there was a YANA meeting tonight so Bob might still be up.

"Hello," Bob answered on the second ring.

"Say happy birthday."

"It's your birthday?"

"Yes. The first day of my new life. With Jesus."

The shout on the line had Gunnar pulling the phone away from his ear. When he repositioned it on the other side, he heard Bob spreading the word to his wife.

"Awesome!" was Tara's excited reply from somewhere beyond Bob. "Welcome to the family!"

"How do you feel?" Bob asked.

"Honestly I feel incredible. I don't know what I was waiting for."

"Timing is everything."

After a few minutes of Q and A, and planning to get together for lunch tomorrow, Gunnar hung up. He couldn't wait to see Tessa, to tell her of his decision, but he had to tell her in person and now wasn't the time. He expected her to doubt his motivation at first. She didn't know he'd been thinking so seriously about handing his life over to Jesus, or that he studied the Bible every chance he got. He'd kept that from her.

But the morning would bring a new start with her as well. No more secrets or things left unsaid. This was a new life and starting it on the right foot was essential.

He thought he was too wired to sleep, but soon after hitting the mattress, he was out cold.

෧෧

The sound of his own breathing ripped through his ears like a saw blade cutting through steel and Gunnar bolted upright. His eyes stung and though the room was dark, he squeezed them tight. This horror was different from the others, more like a nightmare, but still terrifying. He had been in a cold, dim room, but not alone. Tessa was there, and she was fighting an unseen presence to get to him. She fought and screamed, and then she was dragged away.

A cry—of protest or despair—bubbled from his throat. It didn't matter that it was too late; he let it out. Eyes still closed, impulse had him reaching for the tag around his neck.

Then he heard it—a sound in the next room. Gunnar froze. They had followed him from dream to reality.

"You can't have me!" Gunnar yelled. "I'm not going!"

"Well, what do we got here?"

Gunnar stared in the direction of the voice and tried to focus on the shadows. Two forms, one short, one tall, advanced through the doorway to stand at the foot of his bed. He couldn't see their faces for lack of light.

"The guy's nuts," one of them said.

"Don't move," ordered the other.

The air burned Gunnar's lungs as he gulped it in. "I'm not going. You tell Satan I'm not going," he said, swinging his legs off the side of the bed.

"Don't move!" the voice hissed.

Gunnar tried to make sense of this. The voice was

human. Their silhouettes compact, not jagged and bulky. These were flesh and blood beings. Even realizing he wasn't alone in his room, Gunnar's pulse had nowhere to go but down.

"You on something, dude?" the smaller man asked.

"He's crazy," the other said. "Let's get what we came for and get out."

Gunnar licked his parched lips. "What do you want?"

One of the shadows signaled the other and the lights came on, blinding Gunnar anew. He blinked, willing his eyes to adjust.

"Where's your cash?"

Cash? He was being robbed, in the middle of the night. In his own home.

"Where!" the tall man repeated.

Gunnar's brain fired instantly. They thought he was crazy; he could use that. "I have money," he said.

"Yeah? Well you tell me where it is." The smaller man made a show of raising a nine-millimeter pistol to Gunnar's eye level. "Or you're going to be wearing your brains for a hat."

"I have money," Gunnar repeated, automatically absorbing details.

The taller guy was white, brown hair, and a tattoo of a wolf on his neck. He wore a blue fleece jacket and jeans with holes in the knees. The shorter guy was black, wore a down vest and thermal shirt with gray work pants. But their eyes stood out—not the color, but because they held no fear. Both of them looked as if they had all the time in the world, and that worried Gunnar.

"Hey, nut job," the taller said, stepping closer.

"Tell us where the money is."

"Are you the devil?" Gunnar asked, staying in character.

"If you don't get me some cash, I'm your worst nightmare."

Hardly. "I'll get it, it's here," Gunnar said, pointing to the duffel crumpled on the floor.

"Watch him," the taller said and started hauling drawers open.

Gunnar stooped and undid the drawstring on the bag. He thrust his hand inside, felt around, made contact with his weapon.

"I'll help myself," the short man said, coming forward to yank the bag away.

Gunnar was faster.

In a blur of hands and a hail of gunfire, three hearts hammered frenetically.

One stopped.

32

Tessa snapped to wakefulness. The phone was ringing. She glanced at the clock. Froze. It was almost four a.m. Nothing good happened at four a.m. Dominic came first to her mind, and she was flooded with relief when she heard his voice in her ear. Relief was short-lived.

"Tess, get dressed and be on the porch in two minutes. I'm on my way there."

His voice sounded grave and carried with it terrible dread. Had Pauline been in an accident? "What's the matter?"

He paused only briefly but she knew before he said it.

"It's Gunnar."

"Oh, no!" The blood drained to her feet, and she grabbed onto the side of the bed to keep from sliding to the floor.

"He's alive, Tess. He's alive."

Tessa must have done as he asked, throwing her coat on over the clothes she still wore from dinner, because the next thing she registered was being belted into the seat beside Dominic in his cop car and racing to the hospital. She stared unseeing at the blurred scenery. Neither spoke. Her vocal chords were frozen, which suited her, since her only thought was, *don't ask for the truth and he won't tell you Gunnar is going to die.*

When Dominic pulled into the emergency entrance he faced her. "He's alive," he said, giving her arm a gentle squeeze.

"But barely," she said.

He took her hand in his. "We don't know that." He gave it a squeeze. "I'm sorry, Tess. I know the two of you were—"

"Are," she declared sharply. She wouldn't let Gunnar go without a fight. She wouldn't accept his death. No one would decree for her when things were finished between them, not Dominic, or even Gunnar. God wasn't finished with him yet. Hadn't He told Pastor that?

"I love him," she said through the tears that seemed to be there all along. "And he loves me."

"He told me," Dominic said.

He got out of the car, automatically flashing his badge at the approaching security guard.

Inside, nurses hurried, carrying charts and trays or wheeling blood pressure machines. Everyone wore a stethoscope around his or her neck. In a room by the entrance, doctors barked orders as medical staff whirled around one another performing a technical ballet.

When Dominic went to the desk to inquire about Gunnar, Tessa peeked into the room. There was blood on the floor. It would have horrified her if she thought it was real but the human body couldn't carry that much blood so it must be fake, a triage training prop.

"Tess, back here." Dominic took her firmly by the shoulders and started pushing her toward a wall of tastelessly upholstered seats.

"Stop, I want to…" She could see glimpses of the body of a man coated in that fake red blood, except smeared on his skin, staining the sheets beneath him, it became suddenly obvious that it was real. It was grisly and mesmerizing at the same time. She heard more orders being given and squishing sounds when the staff stepped through the fluid on the floor. The odor was potent, even out here.

Before she turned away she glimpsed a calf, and a snake and dagger.

"Gunnar!"

"Tess, no!" Dominic grabbed her before she reached the door and held on, pressing her face into his shoulder. "Let them do their job. They'll help him."

"I have to see him! He has to know I'm here!" she cried.

"He knows, Tess. He called me when it happened. He expected me to tell you."

"No. He has to hear me, feel me!" She took Dominic's face in her hands. "Please, you have to get me in there."

She knew the instant her brother resigned himself to the fact that she would see Gunnar no matter what.

"You can handle it?" he asked. She blinked tear-drenched eyes. "Wait here."

Dominic kept his gaze on her as he backed away. In the small, blood steeped room where people worked feverishly to save Gunnar, she saw her brother hold out his badge, and pull aside a man in bloody greens. A clear plastic mask concealed most of the doctor's face but she could see the resistance in his eyes, and the insistence in Dominic's. Both men looked at her.

She rushed forward to Gunnar's side and didn't draw back when she saw the tube down his throat or the other tubes and wires protruding from his body. None of it scared her as much as his pallor. It didn't look as though there could be any blood left in him and lying motionless, she would suppose him already dead if not for the beeping of machines.

"Gunnar." Laying a hand on his forehead, she wept. "I'm here."

His eyes moved, rolling around under closed lids before they tried to flicker open. "Please, stay with me," she whispered with a desperation she'd never known before. "Please." She pressed a kiss to his cheek, transferring tears, dampening his skin until a gentle hand pulled her away.

"We have to get him to the O.R. right now," the doctor said, passing her into Dominic's waiting arms.

Dominic held her to his side, walking her into the waiting area.

"I can't lose him, Dom," Tessa said. "I won't lose him."

"Let's pray, baby."

∂∞∞

He'd expected the darkness. But not this complete. He'd expected pain. There wasn't any. Flat on his back and sightless, the only thing Gunnar felt was a detectable Presence all around, a tingling awareness that he wasn't alone. It was peaceful.

He heard a voice, quiet, though full of power. Tessa. She was sobbing, and something wet touched his face. For a second he felt himself rise toward her.

And then there was pain. Raw, searing pain throughout his chest and back. Just as suddenly, it vanished.

Gunnar stood but when he looked down, he saw himself lying on a table draped in bloody sheets as doctors and technicians worked on him. He could see their eyes over the masks, filled with acceptance when blood spurted from a hole in his chest.

"I'm dead?" he asked aloud. The monotone of the machine beside his body gave the only reply. "I can't be," Gunnar insisted. "I'm supposed to be alive for a reason. I'm going back, right?"

33

The waiting room was as comfortable as it could be. There was plenty of light and the cushioned chairs were wide and wrapped in neutral fabrics, suitable for receiving good news or bad. Tessa's stomach was in knots, and the squiggle pattern in the carpet wasn't making her feel any better.

"What's taking so long?" she asked Dominic. "It's been two and a half hours. There should be some word."

Every time she allowed herself to slip from faith to fear, Dominic hugged her to him across the arm rest and patted her shoulder. He did so now.

She sighed. "I'm sorry."

"Don't be sorry, Tess. You're human."

"I can't afford to be human," she snapped, pushing to her feet. "He'll die."

Dominic rose too, taking her firmly by the shoulders. "You are human, and you're going to be afraid and angry and confused."

Tessa's lips trembled. "I'm all of those things. And I can't feel my prayers working. I'm just so…I've never been in this position before. Not at this level."

Dominic pressed her head to his chest and held on, swaying gently. "God hears you, and Gunnar isn't going to die based on whether or not you hold it together. Don't put that kind of weight on yourself."

"I have to believe, Dom. God can do anything. Anything." The tears erupted, harder and faster than before. "And He's going to bring Gunnar back to me."

"Tessa?"

The familiar voice had her head popping up like a cork. "Pastor. What are you doing here?"

"Sister Townsend is in again." He came toward her, concern etching his face as he took in her clothes, stained with blood. "What's happened?"

"It's Gunnar," Dominic answered, sitting Tessa down. "Men broke into his house. He's been shot."

"Oh, no," Bob said. "Well…" He grabbed their hands, forming a circle and lowered his head.

Forty minutes later the doctor from the emergency room walked toward them in slippered feet. He still wore the elastic cap but the cloth mask was around his neck. Tessa, Dominic, and Bob got to their feet.

"We didn't have time for introductions before, I'm Dr. Paxton," he said, shaking hands with them. "He's stabilized, the bleeding's stopped."

The way he let the sentence hang tempted Tessa to worry. He wanted to say more but held back.

"And?" she asked.

"The damage was extensive, but it helps that he's strong and healthy."

No, she would not fixate on his frightening word selection. "He'll be all right," she said, willing her spirit to believe it. And he was saved, Pastor had told her about Gunnar's conversion, so even if he died—she had to stop thinking like that!

The doctor clapped a hand to the back of his neck. "You understand, it's a marvel he isn't dead."

"Doc," Dominic said, with a covert shake of his head.

"What I mean is the first bullet to enter his chest should have—"

"The first?" Tessa darted incredulous eyes to her brother. "You knew?"

Slicing a look to the doctor, Dominic touched her arm and nodded dourly. "You freaked over one bullet, Tess, there was no point telling you about the other."

She would have argued, except he was right. "You were saying?" she asked the doctor.

"A heartbeat saved him, literally. The bullet must have passed through in that split second when the heart is contracted, *juuust* skimming it. Pretty amazing."

"It's a miracle," Bob said.

The doctor gave him a patronizing smirk. "Well he's not out of the woods yet. They're bringing him to I.C.U."

"I have to see him," Tessa said.

Dr. Paxton's mouth dipped down at the corners. "I don't—" He paused when he met with three determined faces. "He won't know you're there."

When Tessa maintained her resolute stance, the doctor cleared his throat. "I'll give you a few minutes. I'll be right back."

What could have been an hour later, Tessa followed the doctor past the speculative glances of the staff at the nurses' station. Directly across from them was a room with a large glass window. Inside, she could see Gunnar hooked to tubes and machines. As she walked in and sat by his bed, she refused to be terrified by the sound of the ventilator breathing for him.

Dr. Paxton spoke quietly from behind her. "I'll be right outside if you have any questions."

Tessa imagined a grateful smile that didn't quite reach her lips. Her hand trembled as she touched Gunnar's face with the backs of her fingers. His color looked no better but he felt warmer. That was good, right?

"Gunnar, it's Tessa," she said, gulping back tears. "I'm here."

The only reply came from the steady up and down of the ventilator. Slowly, she moved her hands over any part of him not hidden beneath white cotton. She touched his arm, stroked his face, held his hand.

"Squeeze my hand if you can hear me." He didn't. She cleared her throat. "I know part of you hears me. I love you, Gunnar, and I need you. Please come back to me. Please."

Bowing, she prayed until a nurse asked her to leave. This time when she parted from Gunnar she was confident they would have another miracle.

❧

In the murky gray sea where he floated, the pain was the worst thing he'd ever known. Almost. It hurt just to think of it and he considered it a blessing that he could hardly think at all.

There was light somewhere on the surface but each time he floated toward it the pain grew worse, and he would have to submerge into the greedy depths of darkness where the pain couldn't follow. This time he fought the urge to seek refuge there.

Tessa waited for him on the other side of the gray.

"Gunnar."

He heard his name, wanted to answer back, but to do so meant rising all the way out of the blackness, through the pain. Somehow not going to her was worse. Grappling with the pain, he climbed.

Tessa looked down on the busy street, watching the traffic light change from green to yellow, yellow to red, and wondered how many times she'd witnessed the sequence in the last five days. Exciting though it may be, Gunnar was missing it as he lay only a few feet away.

He'd be shocked to hear he missed a visit from her parents and equally shocked to learn they were sincerely concerned. She had thrown her arms around her father's neck after overhearing him bluster at Gunnar's doctors, demanding assurance that everything that could be done was being done.

Tessa sat on the edge of Gunnar's bed and took his hand in hers, recalling the night he'd spent in her bed when she'd been so worried. She'd wanted to touch him then but hadn't dared.

That reminded her; she should call Aunt Elaine back and tell her there was no need for her to cut short her Bali vacation to sit with her beside Gunnar's bed. It was sweet but unnecessary. Her parents and brother, and Connie and Mike were already catering to her needs and Krueger's, and Gunnar's sister, Samantha, had been staying with her since the day after the shooting. Sam was such a blessing. From the moment they met, it was as though each had found a long lost companion.

Gunnar's hand twitched.

"Gunnar?" She looked down. Did it move? It could have been her. "Try to squeeze my hand if you hear me. Open your eyes. Give me anything."

In spite of the fact he had been unconscious for almost a week, she knew he was drawing closer, gaining strength to fight his way back.

"Gunnar, can you hear me?"

This time she saw his hand twitch in hers. Her heart stumbled in immediate response and she brought his hand to her cheek.

"You're OK," she murmured against his skin. "I'm here."

His eyes fluttered, as they had in the E.R. the night he'd been shot, but this time she wasn't afraid. Tears of happiness streamed down her cheeks, and she bent to kiss his face.

"What is it? What's wrong?" Dominic stood in the doorway.

Tessa's voice was little more than a hoarse undertone through the clog in her throat. "God is bringing him back to me."

∂∽∾

Gunnar opened his eyes to a room filled with machines. One in particular was making disconcerting rattle, click, whoosh sounds. Even more disturbing, he was attached to it. But he heard a woman's voice humming a pleasant melody.

His mouth opened. "Tess." He wasn't sure a word came out, but she swiveled to look at him, her eyes wide and bright.

"Gunnar!"

He was happy to see her and know he could make her smile. When he tried to speak, she touched his cheek with tender fingers.

"Don't try to talk," she said. "You're on a ventilator."

He was so happy to be with her. He wanted to stay but the gray was pulling him under.

When he woke again, Tessa was gone. A dream? How cruel would that be, to have fought this hard for a dream? Despair pricked him right before Dominic strode into the room.

"Ready to stop lounging around taking up bed space?" Dominic asked.

"Dom." He didn't recognize the voice but knew by the rumble in his throat it was his and that the tube was gone. *Must be breathing on my own.* Inwardly, he smiled.

Dominic sat in the high back burnt orange chair next to the bed. "You really rattled us good."

Gunnar heard the words but the emotion behind them was new for Dominic. Signs of strain were evident in and around his eyes. "Sorry."

Dominic's face broke into a grin erasing the tension. "You are one lucky man. I thought you were gone."

"I was," Gunnar whispered. "I saw...things. Tess?"

"I made her go home to get some rest. She'll be here soon."

"She was just here," Gunnar said.

Dominic looked blank, and then smiled. "You've been in and out, she'll be back. Your sister was here. She's coming tonight."

"Sam." His tongue felt like a sandbag. He wanted to point to the water pitcher but didn't have the strength. He closed his eyes and found he couldn't reopen them.

34

"Where's my chain?" Gunnar asked.

Tessa opened the nightstand drawer. "Right here." She was glad she'd had a mind to bring it back after she'd taken it home to scrub off the blood.

"I want it on."

He was adamant so she promptly complied, slipping the chain around his neck, brushing her knuckles across the smooth skin above his emergent beard.

"Thanks," he said.

"I wanted to be here when you woke up," she said, going for an unaffected tone. "I wanted to be the first person you saw, instead of a nurse or the guy who cleans the bathroom."

"Dom was here. He's not you, but he's pretty enough in his own right."

She let out a choked laugh. Gunnar didn't return the humor.

"You were with me in that place, Tessa. I heard you. I sensed you with me."

Tessa's chest felt too small for her heart, and she took his hand between hers. The heat of his fingers was wonderful as life flowed through him.

But his gaze fixed her with an intensity, strong even for him. "What is it?" she asked.

He licked his parched lips and closed his eyes,

keeping them closed long enough for her to wonder if he'd fallen asleep.

"Did Dom tell you what happened?" he asked, his lids still lowered. "The break-in?"

Oh no, he wanted to talk about the shooting. She didn't think she could handle the details. "Yes," she said, shoring up her courage.

"You know I..." He opened his eyes, fixed them on hers.

"Shh. You don't have to talk."

"...killed another man," he finished.

The hand in her grasp squeezed hard. "You had to."

"Sorry. This time, I didn't want to."

"We all know, the police, too." When he closed his eyes, she took the opportunity to wipe away a stray tear.

"He wanted me dead," Gunnar said, his voice sounding further away as his grip on her hand loosened. "Instead I got saved."

She knew he didn't refer to the man who physically fired the gun, but to the devil. Her spirit rejoiced. There would be more talk of the shooting, the trial of the surviving burglar, whom Gunnar shot in the gut, but for now they had peace. Gunnar was safe and saved. What more could she ask for?

❧

"Where's the nurse with those papers?" Gunnar asked.

"You've been here this long," Dominic answered from his seat beside the bed. "A little while longer won't matter."

Gunnar gave a wry smile. Each day laid-up meant a day further behind schedule. His physical ability would be limited once he was back at the shop, and he could expect his clients to be only so understanding. He adjusted the pillow behind him, gritting his teeth at the pain that zipped through his body. Fortunately, Dom and Bob didn't notice.

Nor did they seem to notice the frown as he admitted to himself that his work, his clients and his business weren't the main reason for his impatience to get out of here. Not even Matt, whom he'd hated to disappoint by missing the bike show.

Intellectually he knew it was stupid, but his ego took a hit every time Tessa walked in and looked on him with concern and pity. It made him feel weak. While he wasn't flat on his back anymore, he needed to get away from here, where he could heal and get strong and leave no doubt in her mind that she was his lone weakness.

Bob moved from the window where he'd been reading get well cards, and sat in the chair they'd borrowed from an empty room. "I hate to ask but I can't stand the suspense any longer. Dom said you hinted about seeing something while..."

"While I was dead—well almost dead?" Bob and Dominic both nodded. Gunnar paused, bringing images into startling focus. "I saw angels. A whole mess of them."

Bob leaned closer. "I need to know, what are they really like?"

"Yeah, do they all look the same?" Dom asked.

Gunnar reached for the fruit cup on the rolling table, lifting his chin briefly in thanks when Dominic pushed it closer. "No. Well yeah, the way a battalion of soldiers looks the same, but when you see them up close, they're all different. Some have long hair, some have longer hair, some to about here," he said, drawing a finger across the middle of his neck. "Most of them have light eyes, some are metallic looking, some dark, a few red, and they all...it's like they're lit from inside."

"Red eyes?" Dom asked.

Gunnar swallowed a spoonful of diced fruit. "Yeah, but they're pretty much all the same height and build, which is huge."

"I hear they're around thirteen feet tall," Bob said.

Gunnar considered. "Yeah."

"No way," Dom said, his eyes sharp and doubtful.

"I'm not about to lie," Gunnar said. Dom shrugged, agreeing. "I wouldn't want to be on the bad side of any one of them." He glanced down at the tattoo on his stomach. It was very nearly funny that he'd once presumed to understand what power was.

"So they look human?" Dom asked.

"The ones I saw. But not *us* human," he replied. "There's no doubt they aren't souls of dead people with wings."

"I could have told you that," Bob said. "They're created beings."

"What did they do?" Dom wanted to know.

"The ones I saw just stood there, arms up, praising God." Like the tattoo on his back, he realized.

"And then there was this other Presence," Gunnar said. "I didn't see or hear it but it was tangible. I knew it was God."

The memory of that Presence filled him with joy. At least how he always expected joy would feel.

35

Tessa glanced up at Gunnar's hospital room window as she walked toward the entrance with one a small suitcase. His duffel was hopelessly stained with blood and had been thrown away, so she'd used one of her bags to carry his belongings. After just two weeks, he was going home.

By all appearances, Gunnar was fine with returning to the scene of the crime, but despite the "clean team" having gone through the room, Tessa felt weird being in there even long enough to grab him a change of clothes. It would be great if he would just accept Dominic's offer to stay with him until Gunnar sufficiently mended, but he refused.

Tessa had a good mind to tell Aunt Elaine. She called Gunnar every day from ports far and wide. They had become close; surely she could make him see reason.

Tessa smiled, crossing the lobby in time to grab the elevator. The support she'd received from her family through this terrible ordeal confounded her. Her parents, the same people who critiqued her life, who drilled her on finding a "proper" career; the same people who once threatened to take her out of the will if she didn't come to her senses and reconcile with Scott, were now a huge source of comfort.

They supported her inn venture, had taken to

keeping company with Gunnar's sister, and showed real concern for the man himself. If Tessa had a suspicious mind, she might be inclined to believe their acceptance was due to his growing popularity and subsequent projected income, thus making him a more suitable match. But she was beginning to see her parents with new eyes and had only God to thank for it.

It was suddenly easy to identify that all these years Anna's primary goal had been to see her children happy. Perhaps she couldn't be blamed for imagining she knew how to accomplish that better than they did. And her father...

A short time ago, Tessa might have lost him to a heart attack. She was ashamed to admit that for the little he was involved in her life, there would have been pain but not devastation. Now the man who hardly made time for a phone conversation, hovered. Tessa loved it.

Gunnar was hanging up the phone when she walked in. "Your escape outfit," she said, setting the suitcase at the foot of the bed.

"I have a question," Gunnar said. "How do I get your friends to stop calling me?"

"Connie?"

"Doesn't she have anything better to do?" He was whiny.

Tessa giggled. "Well, she doesn't have your home number."

For just a moment, he looked troubled, and Tessa realized he must be remembering home and what had happened there. Well if he wouldn't see reason and stay with Dominic, she would just have to use her trump card.

"I was thinking, you're going to have to come home with me," she told him. One black brow rose slowly. "You're going to need looking after."

"Looking after?" Gunnar held out a hand, gently pulling her to his side on the bed. "What'd you have in mind?"

Tessa's body turned liquid when he nuzzled her neck. "Um…"

"Sponge baths?"

His hand came to her throat, his thumb drawing a sensuous line along her jaw. "Yes," she managed. "Sure, of course." She had no idea what she was agreeing to.

"Hmm. I was joking, but that would be great."

"No—I wasn't paying attention." How could she with his warm breath skittering across the sensitive skin just below her ear?

"It's OK," he murmured, his voice low and flavored with rising passion. "I'll pay attention for both of us."

When voices in the hall broke through the seductive haze, Tessa jumped off the bed and did her best to pretend she'd been standing by the window.

"Afraid we'll get grounded if they catch us?" he asked, a glint of mischief in his eyes.

Tessa waited until the voices faded before daring to come near the bed. "It's hospital property."

Gunnar laughed. It sounded full and alive and she was instantly drawn back to his side.

"You get a kick out of teasing me, don't you?" she asked, sitting beside him.

Gunnar made an attempt to straighten his lips. "I'd rather satisfy you."

Before she could think of something to say to that,

he did.

"Marry me."

Each time she'd dreamed of this moment—more times than she could count—she'd been positive of her response, prepared to answer with poise and just the right words. Emotion rushed through her now, sweeping away most brain activity and the closest she could come to words was a wheezed, "Uh huh."

Gunnar stood, pulling her to her feet. "I don't know how good a husband I'll be, but I'll do all kinds of stupid things to keep you happy." He framed her face with his hands. "And I don't know how good a father I'll be, but I want kids."

Tessa gripped his wrists and pressed her cheeks more firmly to his hands. "Oh, Gunnar."

"How does two sound?" He rubbed her nose with his. "To start."

Tessa threw her arms around his neck and held on. "I knew there was a romantic under those tattoos."

He kissed her, hard and long and kept right on kissing her even when two nurses stopped to sigh in the doorway. But Tessa didn't pull away. This was the first kiss shared with her new fiancé and she intended to enjoy every second.

With one last nibble, Gunnar ended the kiss and took her by the shoulders. "You saved me Tessa," he told her. He shook his head right back at her when she tried to argue. "You made me human. You opened my heart and held it open long enough for God to get in."

Tessa slipped her left arm around his waist and rested her right hand on his chest, cheered by the strong, steady beat of his heart. A heart once so hard, abused by others, caged of his own volition, and nearly destroyed. He'd given it to her, but more importantly, he'd given it to Christ.

Holding back a tear, Tessa pressed a kiss above the scar on his chest, the entry point for the bullet that had just about killed him. The other bullet had left a smaller hole and been deemed too dangerous to risk retrieval, so would remain inside him for the rest of his life.

Seconds ticked by in silence. She knew Gunnar must be thinking the same thoughts as her, of all they could have lost, but also of all they would now have—a long life together under the guidance and blessing of the Lord.

"Sure you don't want to elope?" Gunnar asked, finally.

"Not on your life," Tessa replied.

EPILOGUE

Three years later

Tessa looked across the green lawn to where Krueger slept in a hole he'd dug under a shady bush. He was big now, intimidating to look at but retained the temperament of the clumsy puppy she'd had to scold for tearing up a chair cushion three years earlier. It was time for his dinner but he looked so content she hesitated to call him. She knew exactly how he felt.

Absently, Tessa rubbed circles over the swell of her belly, and leaving Krueger to his nap, continued on her way to see how Gunnar and Dominic were progressing on assembling the porch swing at the front of the house.

The sight of her husband working in the August heat, made her catch her breath. He was beautiful. His hair, shimmering in the sun, was a little unkempt and curling around his ears in damp black coils. He'd wanted to shave it off for the summer, as he used to do before they met, but gave in when she pouted. She loved playing with it as they sat on the sofa watching TV, or thrusting her hands through it as he kissed her neck, stroked her bare back...

"Can I help you?" Gunnar asked, his voice matching the teasing twinkle in his eye.

Tessa always marveled at how adept he was at

reading her mind. She reined in her ill-timed longings and shelved them for later. "I wanted to see if you were finished, and ask you guys if you want iced tea."

"Yeah," Gunnar said, setting down the hammer and slipping his arms around Tessa.

Her eyes skimmed his dog tag to his chest, pausing on the fading marks where bullets had blasted through his flesh. For months after the shooting, she had viewed them as glaring reminders of how he had almost been murdered. Then one night, watching him sleep beside her, the lamplight glinting off her wedding ring as she toyed with the ends of his hair, she came to understand they were reminders of a miracle. For both of them. Now whenever her eyes fell upon them her soul filled with gratitude.

"Oh!" Tessa laid a hand on her tummy.

"What?"

The concern in Gunnar's voice and the way Dominic dropped the ratchet he'd been using made her chuckle. "He kicked me, that's all."

Gunnar's relief was evident before bending to place a kiss on her steadily expanding stomach. Tessa's heart went to her throat. The gesture was so uncharacteristic of the Gunnar she had first met. But this man, raising his head to drop a kiss on her mouth, smiling broadly at her, derived as much pleasure from giving affection as he did from receiving it. He was still tough and intense but no one could deny he was changed.

"You mean *she*," he said.

Tessa giggled. He wanted a girl so bad, a little sister for their two-year-old son. "I'll see what I can do."

She went inside to get the iced tea, passing a

framed photo of Gunnar taken in the shop several days after his release from the hospital. The shooting had brought more publicity to Mason Custom than anyone imagined, and with it came customers begging for Gunnar's attention, most of whom were put on a waiting list until the chess set was completed. Nearly dying had set him far behind on that job, but the man who'd commissioned it was more than patient.

He also happened to be the CEO of Zillion Media, a fact that became relevant when he'd insisted on featuring Gunnar in a segment on one of his evening news programs. MC's name and reputation shot from national to global overnight, and with it, Gunnar's testimony.

In one night, a ministry was born and over the next few days he had received literally thousands of letters from teenagers who had given their lives to Christ or just wanted to know more about Jesus. His effect on people, kids in particular, was astounding, and watching him lead a young person to the Lord was the most powerful thing she'd ever witnessed.

In the photo, the bike Gunnar designed for her was proudly displayed in a row of other phenomenal creations. Being stored at the MC shop, she had yet to ride it. Gunnar had second thoughts about teaching her, and every time she'd mentioned it he'd changed the subject by kissing her brainless. Pretty effective.

For Tessa, it was enough to have found her purpose in caring for her husband and children. Family. Content, she took the drinks outside.

∂∘∽

Gunnar watched his wife come toward him with

an innate grace even seven months of pregnancy couldn't lessen. Was it possible she was more beautiful than she'd been just a few moments ago? He was amazed he could think of the word *mother* with happiness, but since deciding Tessa would be the mother of his children and doing all in his power to make it happen, the word held a fascinating beauty and power he willingly succumbed to. The words *wife* and *friend* and *lover* had taken on new meanings as well.

He remembered the first night he'd shared with her as man and wife, the first night he'd touched her in the most intimate of ways, and afterward when they'd fallen asleep wrapped around each other. He'd sworn he would always respect that sense of awe, knowing she loved him enough to give herself to him alone. In every way, he was incredibly blessed to have her. Blessed to have *them*. His spirit rocketed at the sight of his son, racing from the house behind his mother.

He no longer viewed himself as the ogre he once had, and if he were the emotional sort, he would cry tears of joy for all the Lord had done and continued to do in his life, but emotion had little to do with gratitude. He told God daily how thankful he was— but as Gunnar watched his pregnant wife and giggling son, he laughed, and tears fell.